# Simple Pleasures

by

## Kenna White

BELLA
BOOKS

2013

Bella Books, Inc.
P.O. Box 10543
Tallahassee, FL 32302

Printed in the United States of America on acid-free paper.

First Bella Books Edition 2013

Editor: Katherine V. Forrest
Cover Designed by: Judith Fellows

ISBN: 978-159493-370-7

## Other Books by Kenna White

*Beautiful Journey*
*Beneath the Willow*
*Body Language*
*Braggin' Rights*
*Comfortable Distance*
*Romancing the Zone*
*Shared Winds*
*Skin Deep*
*Taken by Surprise*
*Yours for the Asking*

**About the Author**

Award-winning author, Kenna White resides in Southwest Missouri and enjoys traveling, creating dollhouse miniatures, her family, and writing with a good cup of coffee by her side. After living from the Rocky Mountains to New England, she is once again back where bare feet, faded jeans and lazy streams fill her life.

## Acknowledgments

I'd like to send a big hug and thank you to Mary H. for her kindhearted support of my work. To Beth and Craig for accepting mom just as I am and with unconditional love. To Marla for cooking a poached egg to perfection. She is a cook-extraordinaire. And to all my friends here in Joplin who opened their hearts and shared their heart-wrenching stories of survival during and after the tornado. This book could not have happened without you.

## Dedication

This book is dedicated to Joplin, Missouri, my hometown. The tornado of May 2011 may have taken loved ones from us, ripped at our homes and businesses and left us wanting of normality. But with the support of our neighbors, friends and volunteers, we continue to rebuild. We are stronger, wiser and more determined than ever not to let this disaster define us. Joplin is a great place to live, to work, to raise a family and to build dreams. Come visit us sometime and see how a city conquers.

# CHAPTER ONE

Dale stepped out of the batter's box and shielded her eyes as a small dust devil blew across the infield. She couldn't concentrate. It wasn't the bead of sweat running down her back and into her sports bra. It wasn't Janice, who, although she had promised to be there cheering Dale's team to victory, had yet to show up. And it wasn't her sister's relentless hooting and whistling from third base, insisting Dale whack a grounder and bring her home. It was something else that had her insides churning up memories she thought long-healed.

"Batter up," the umpire said, replacing her face mask after sweeping off home plate.

Dale held the bat between her legs as she adjusted the Velcro strap on her batting glove, forcing her attention back to the game. It was only a charity softball game, of little importance in the grand scheme of things. But at this moment forty-six-year-old Dale Kinsel needed something to think about other than the ponytailed woman wandering around right field with a pair of bejeweled sunglasses perched on her smug little nose. Why was she here? She obviously didn't know how to play softball. She looked like a commuter waiting for a bus, wearing her fielder's glove as if afraid it would break a nail.

"Come on, Dale," the umpire whined. "Let's get this thing going."

"What's your hurry? Got a hot date, Phyllis?" Dale stepped into the batter's box and worked her cleats down into the soft dirt.

"Yes, I do. With my recliner. My bunions are killing me. And my left hearing aid is squealing like a mother." She touched her fingertip against it, adjusting the volume.

Phyllis was one of those friends Dale knew by first name only. She assumed she was gay. She had that dashing butch confidence behind a pair of soft blue eyes and a thin albeit muscular body. Somewhere in her fifties, Phyllis had been umpiring softball and Little League games as long as Dale had known her. She occasionally came into Home Depot and seemingly respected Dale's opinion of which do-it-yourself doodads she needed. She never used the word *we*. Dale assumed she was single either by choice or happenstance. They respected each other but that didn't mean they couldn't tease mercilessly on the softball field.

"Bring me home, Dale," Zoe shouted from third, clapping enthusiastically.

Dale crouched over the plate, swirling the bat aloft. She had been a good player in high school and college. She still loved to play. She even considered herself in good shape for her age, better than some of the women who dug out their glove and cleats once in a blue moon. But the best she could do was bounce into a double play, sending her and Zoe back to the bench.

"Okay, Amber," Zoe said as she trotted past the on-deck batter. "Little base hit now." She smacked the batter's fanny then turned to Dale with a scowl. "Why did you swing at that pitch? It was down around your ankles! All we needed was a single up the middle. What's the matter? Did you forget how to bat?"

Zoe was forty with mousy brown hair and wide hips. They shared little sibling resemblance. Shorter and far less athletic than Dale, Zoe had a muffin top while Dale had trim hips and legs. Dale wore nylon hiking shorts. Zoe was poured into a pair of sweatpants. Neither of them had boobs worthy of a centerfold although Dale's were still firm and up where they belonged. They did share their mother's hazel eyes, long fingers and tendency to tan easily. Zoe was the self-appointed team captain. She had a critical set to her jaw and was best described as feisty. Dale called it bossy and chose not to argue with her. Zoe organized the team right down to the color for the T-shirts and who played where.

"What is she doing here?" Dale stood at the chain-link fence in front of the team bench and stared across the field.

"Who?" Zoe was applying sunblock to her face and paid little attention.

"Her," she grumbled, nodding toward the woman in right field.

Zoe took a quick look then went back to the sunblock.

"I wondered how long it would take before you said something. I'd say she's playing charity softball." Zoe was the queen of smug replies, many meant to raise Dale's ire.

"So you knew she'd be here?"

"I saw her name on the sign-up sheet, yes. Hey, it's for charity. She has a right to play. Be glad she isn't on our team." She gave a witchy cackle. "Wouldn't that be hilarious?"

The longer Dale stared at the woman the more her lip curled and the angrier she became. Angry at Zoe for not warning her. Angry at the woman for crossing her path, a path Dale had been certain she would never cross again. And angry at herself for giving the woman that kind of importance. She hadn't seen Taren Dorsey in three years. As far as Dale was concerned it wasn't long enough. The accusations and bitter words had cemented a discontent between them worthy of the Hatfields and McCoys.

"Can't you two just get along? Let bygones be bygones."

"I doubt it," Dale muttered and turned her back.

"Hey, Mom, can I have a hot dog," a girl said from the opening in the fence.

"Hi, Sasha." Dale greeted her with a big smile and a hug.

"Hi, Aunt Dale. Mom, can I?" Sasha was an eleven-year-old who looked like she was experiencing a growth spurt into the gangly stage. She was wearing flip-flops, jean shorts and two layers of tank tops, each a different shade of pink. She hadn't grown nubbins yet but if genetics had anything to do with it, she'd be wearing a training bra by Christmas.

"You've got your allowance. If you want to spend it on a hot dog go right ahead." Zoe gave her a scrutinizing glance. "Where's your retainer?"

"In my pocket. Dentist said I can take it out when I eat."

"Well, you're not eating. Put it in." Zoe pointed menacingly at her mouth.

The girl groaned but obeyed. "Mom, couldn't you buy me a hot dog?" she whined.

"What did you buy with your money?"

"Nothing." She instantly looked guilty. "Just a bracelet." She pulled a wadded cord from her pocket and slipped it on proudly. "It's a friendship bracelet. Amy and I got matching ones. We're going to wear them the last week of school."

"So everyone will know you're best friends, right?" Dale said, examining the braided cord.

"Yeah, isn't that cool?"

"How much did you pay for that?" Zoe tossed her a disapproving smirk.

"Never mind how much, Mom," Dale interrupted. "You can't put a price on friendship, right Sasha?" She wrapped her arm around Sasha's shoulder and stuffed some money in her hand. "Here. Have a hot dog on me."

"Thank you." She headed off before Zoe could stop her.

"See if they have strawberry Twizzlers," Dale called after her.

"I'm trying to teach her fiscal responsibility," Zoe said, watching her child gallop toward the snack bar.

"So teach her tomorrow."

"How much did you give her?"

"You don't need to know." Dale slapped Zoe's cap down over her eyes playfully.

"You'd make a terrible mother. Your kids would be hell on wheels. Brats through and through."

"Probably," Dale agreed with a laugh.

The batter popped up to the pitcher, ending the first inning. Dale couldn't help watch as Taren meandered in from the outfield and took a seat on the bench.

"Look at the bright side. You only have six and a half more innings to look at her." Zoe gave her a cheeky grin then slipped on her sunglasses and headed onto the field. "You're playing shortstop by the way," she said over her shoulder. "You can glare savagely at her if she gets on base."

"I'd like to do more than glare at her," Dale muttered.

She stuffed a piece of gum in her mouth and trotted across the diamond, scooping up a practice ground ball from the first base player. She tossed it back then gave another quick scan of the bleachers. Still no Janice. Dale reminded herself theirs was a new relationship. They were still learning about each other. Maybe she misunderstood Janice's intentions. Or maybe she was just late. Dale would go with that. It was easier to dwell on Janice's tardiness than her ex's ponytailed sister sitting on the opponent's bench.

Dale couldn't escape the cruel irony of it. As if cancer hadn't done enough, taking her beloved Sydney in the prime of her life, now it had brought her and Taren together again for a charity softball game. If she had known Taren would be there would she have stayed away? She'd never know. But she told herself no. She was playing for Sydney and in her memory. Was that why Taren was there? Or was she there to toss one last barb in Dale's direction? She didn't have to say a word to do so. Just the sight of Sydney's sister was enough to resurrect those painful last days of her life. The memory of baby powder and urine, of disinfectant and chicken soup, of Band-Aids and alcohol. Of Sydney's face, her eyes dark and sunken, her cheeks hollow, her once glowing complexion pale, her once voluptuous body little more than skin stretched over bones. Why were those the memories that hovered in her subconscious? Why not the happy ones? Why not the tender ones? Why not the times they shared in each other's arms? Why were Sydney's last gruesome, painful moments the ones that haunted her soul?

"*Dale!*" Zoe screamed, running toward her from centerfield. "Shit! What are you doing? Get the damn ball. She's heading for first."

Dale scrambled for the ball that had bounced into her chest and rolled a few feet away. She scooped it up and fired it to first base but the runner had rounded the base and was well on her way to second.

"Sorry. My bad," Dale called, mad at herself for drifting so far from reality.

"Will you please get your head in the game?" Zoe said caustically, slapping her glove against Dale's arm before returning to centerfield.

"Yeah, yeah." She kicked the dirt on her way back to her position. It's all Taren's fault, she thought. Why doesn't she go home?

As one of only four players on the team with any softball experience she was proud that she was normally able to gobble up anything hit in her direction. In spite of her age, she still had a lethal throwing arm capable of ranging far to her right and throwing out the runner at first. She'd need an ice bag for her arm after the game but it was fun showing off her gun if only for herself.

The batter swung at the next pitch. "I've got it," Dale shouted, waving off her teammates. She settled under the pop-up, catching it easily to end the inning.

"Where's Janet?" Zoe asked on the way back to the bench. "I thought you said she was coming to watch."

"Her name is Janice and I have no idea." She gave a quick scan of the growing spectators. "Maybe she had to work late."

"She's an accountant, for Pete's sake. Why would she be working on Sunday? Tax season is over. It's May."

"Maybe she had a flat or got stuck in traffic. I don't know." Dale glanced toward the parking lot, looking for a black Jeep Cherokee with a roof rack.

"Yeah, right. Joplin doesn't have traffic," Zoe said with a raised eyebrow. "Maybe her elbow is sore from bending it."

"Give it a rest, Zoe." Dale pulled a bottle of water from the cooler, took a swig then fitted it into the mesh fence for later. She was in no mood for her sister's sarcasm. As much as she loved her, Zoe could be a pain in the ass. Their childhood was filled with sisterly catfights to prove it.

"Maybe she doesn't like softball. It's an acquired taste." Zoe ran her finger down the batting roster taped to the fence post. "Jody, you're up."

"Maybe she heard I have a sister who's a be-aach," Dale quipped.

After the fifth inning Dale stopped looking for Janice. She resisted the temptation to text and find out where she was. If she wasn't here, she wasn't here. Dale had something else in the pit of her stomach digging up a fresh helping of disgust with Taren Dorsey's name all over it. Taren had yet to catch a fly ball. She threw like a girl and seemed more interested in the fit of her visor than participating in the game. Since she had struck out each and every time she came to the plate, the chances she would ever pass Dale as she rounded second base were slim.

"Come on, Taren," one of her teammates shouted, clapping enthusiastically as she picked a bat from the pile.

"She's never going to hit the ball," Dale sang quietly as Taren strode to the batter's box.

She took an awkward stance and waited for the first pitch. Just as the pitcher began her windup Dale dropped her glove on the ground and squatted to retie her shoes, taking a long and deliberate time of it.

"Strike one," Phyllis announced as Taren swung, missing badly.

Dale nodded to the pitcher to go ahead and deliver the second pitch as she continued to fiddle with her laces.

"Strike two."

Dale looked up just as Taren stepped out of the batter's box and stared at her over the top of her sunglasses. Taren muttered something through clenched teeth then stepped back in, a determined set to her jaw.

"Not even on a good day, Ms. Dorsey," Dale mumbled then slowly stood up.

Taren wiggled her rear and licked her lips, anxiously waiting for the next pitch. She swung and missed by a foot. Dale smiled to herself as Taren returned to the bench with an angry scowl on her face. Sympathy? Heck no, Dale told herself. Taren Dorsey deserved to strike out. And Dale had a right to revel in it.

"Pick a lighter bat next time," she heard herself yell.

Taren shot a defiant glare at her as she flung the bat on the pile. She took a seat at the far end of bench and began texting on her cell phone as if blocking out the game and Dale's sarcasm.

The score seesawed back and forth for several innings. Dale had driven in five runs and scored three times herself. She did her best to hit the ball into right field, knowing Taren couldn't catch it and relatively sure she could outrun her best throw. The top of the seventh inning, with the score tied with two outs, Dale stepped to the plate. She was tired, hungry and her muscles were beginning to cramp but she wasn't going to lose this game. Charity, sharmity. She wanted to win. She took a couple practice swings but noticed Taren wasn't playing right field. She had been moved to left field. No problem, Dale told herself and adjusted her stance, giving a devilish cackle as she waited for the first pitch. It was right where she wanted it, high and outside. Dale swung, driving the ball into left field where it dropped at Taren's feet. Dale charged around first base and headed for second. When Taren's throw came dribbling in from the outfield she headed for third, sliding in safely to cheers from her teammates and the spectators. Dale stood on the bag, catching her breath and brushing the dirt from her legs.

"Come on, Amber. Base hit now," she shouted. "Eye on the ball. Level swing."

"One damn minute," Taren yelled as she came trotting in from the outfield. She had Dale fixed in her sights and even through the sunglasses was shooting daggers at her.

"Time out." Phyllis raised her hands and stepped away from the plate. "This ought to be good."

"No shit," the catcher said with a chuckle. "Dale's been hitting the ball at Taren all game. You'd think she was doing it on purpose."

Taren threw her glove down, perched her hands on her hips and stood face-to-face with Dale. She ripped off her sunglasses, her nostrils flaring.

"Now look. I don't care if you make fun of my batting. And I don't care if you belittle me just because I can't catch the damn ball. And I don't give a crap if we win or you win." Taren's voice was dripping with venom. "But of all the days you could choose to best me how dare you do it on her day."

Dale saw a glisten in her eyes and like a slap in the face, she instantly knew what Taren meant. *Her day*, Sydney's day, the reason they both were there. A day to honor cancer victims and survivors. Taren was right. It was a day to honor Sydney and put personal differences aside. Dale was several inches taller than Taren but she suddenly felt very small. She couldn't think of a thing to say.

"You're still an ass," Taren said so only Dale could hear. "Honor her memory, Dale. Forget your ever-loving hatred for me and honor Sydney today."

Taren picked up her glove and headed back to the outfield, leaving Dale with a dumbfounded look on her face. A breeze drifted across the infield, swirling dust at Dale's feet as she stood watching Taren's retreat. Somewhere in the midst of the whirlwind Dale swore she smelled Sydney's cologne, so much so that she turned expecting to see Sydney's beaming face.

"I hate to interrupt such an eloquent speech but if you two are finished, could we get on with it?" Phyllis walked a few steps up the third base line. She grinned at Dale as if gloating over her humiliation. "Are you ladies ready to play ball?"

"Yes, thank you," Taren shouted matter-of-factly before Dale could reply.

"Good. PLAY BALL!" she shouted. "Batter up."

Amber grounded out to the first baseman, ending their half of the inning and leaving the score tied.

"Can I say neener neener?" Zoe teased, tossing Dale her glove as she trotted onto the field.

"No. You can't." Dale slipped on her glove then slapped it against her thigh. "She's right. I'm an ass," she muttered under her breath.

The game was tied at the end of regulation, sending it into extra innings. With one out, Taren went to the pile of bats, picked the one closest to her and headed to the batter's box. She was ready to step in when she turned and walked back to the pile. She sifted through the dozen or so bats, holding up several different ones as if testing their weight. Dale was tempted to shout, *Use the green one with the black handle.* To her surprise, that's the one Taren finally selected. Her stance was still awkward and her hands were still apart on the handle but to everyone's amazement she hit the first pitch, sending it just over the first baseman's head. The ball was mishandled and Taren scampered down to second. Dale caught the throw on a bounce and tagged Taren's leg as she stepped on the bag.

"Safe," Phyllis shouted. She had hustled into the middle of the infield for a good view of the play.

Dale knew she tagged her. She heard the glove slap Taren's leg before the sound of her sneaker on the canvas base.

"She's out," Dale chuckled, assuming Phyllis was joking.

"Safe!" She thrust her arms out definitively.

"Are you nuts? I got her leg." Dale touched Taren again to demonstrate but Phyllis was shaking her head.

"Ha ha. I'm safe." Taren swatted Dale's glove away as she began to sing, imitating a rap song. "Oh, yeah. I did it. I hit it. I'm safe," she gloated, circling her fists in the air. The crowd cheered as her teammates joined her victory dance, waving their arms and singing *She did it, she hit it, she did it, she hit it.*

"She's out." Dale continued to argue but Phyllis had turned her back and was walking back to home plate.

"Only in your dreams, Dale," Phyllis yelled.

"I hope your bunions are killing you."

"They are but she's still safe."

Dale flipped the ball back to the pitcher, trying to ignore Taren's dance and the jeering crowd. It's all for charity, she reminded herself. Giving up a base hit wasn't the end of the world.

"Batter up."

Taren stood on the base with her feet together like she was stranded on the last square foot of dry land in a flood. Dale suspected she didn't have a clue about base running strategy. Sure enough she took off running when the next batter popped up to centerfield. She was nearly to third when the ball was caught and the coach began waving her arms and screaming.

"Go back! Go back!"

The throw came to Dale waiting at second. She could have easily tagged Taren out, ending the inning with a double play. It wouldn't have even been close. But as Dale caught the ball that same smell swirled around her, Sydney's smell. Gardenias and jasmine. An innocent whimsical scent like butterflies fluttering around her.

"This one's for you, Sydney," Dale whispered and let the ball fall out of her glove. She scrambled to pick it up but that was enough for Taren to scoot into second base ahead of Dale's tag. As much as Dale knew it was Sunday she knew what was coming next.

"What are you doing?" Zoe screamed, coming toward her like a runaway freight train. "Why didn't you tag her? There was only one out. Double play, Dale. Double play."

Dale couldn't tell her why she did it. She couldn't tell her she was distracted by Sydney's cologne. Zoe already thought Dale had lost her mind.

"Sorry. My fault." Dale pounded her fist into her glove.

"Come on, Dale. If she scores we lose. So get your ass in the game. Focus." Zoe pinched her arm then trotted back to the outfield.

Dale noticed a smug little grin on Taren's face.

*Come on somebody. I don't care who. Just score so I can go home. I've had enough of my sister for one day and enough Taren Dorsey forever.*

Dale's prayer was answered. The next batter hit a long fly ball that bounced over the fence and into the weeds. Taren scored the winning run, raising her hands in victory as she crossed the plate.

As Dale worked her way along the line congratulating the other team she wondered what she would say to Taren. Maybe a perfunctory nod of the head and a robotic "nice game" would be sufficient to keep from being thought an ass anymore.

"Hey, Taren," Zoe said with a smile.

"Hey, Zoe." They exchanged a polite albeit brief hug. "Nice game."

"It would have been a nice game if we had won," Zoe replied then chuckled. "But I forgive you."

Why do they have to visit like they're best buddies, Dale thought. Sure they both worked at the university but just say nice game and move on, Zoe. She couldn't help but overhear their chitchat. And she couldn't help but stare at Taren. She still looked as fresh as she did in the first inning when she headed into the outfield and began her wafting through the clover. Her hair was still pulled tightly into a ponytail. Her sneakers still looked clean. Even her white socks were spotless. Femme-pot, Dale kept herself from saying out loud.

"We would have won if one of our players kept her head in the game and didn't spend all her time pouting over some new girlfriend."

"Zoe!" Dale said sternly. *I can't believe you just said that. Taren doesn't need to know my personal business. And I wasn't pouting.*

"Oh, yeah?" Taren removed her sunglasses and looked over at Dale. "I guess some things never change."

Here it comes, Dale thought. But she didn't have to listen to this woman's smart-aleck comments. Those days were over. And Dale was prepared to say so.

But Taren slipped on her sunglasses, said, "Nice to see you again, Dale," and walked away.

# CHAPTER TWO

Dale had had enough softball. She collected her glove, bat and sneakers and headed for the parking lot. She planned on spending the rest of the day mowing her grass and doing a few chores around the house. And with any luck, not let the ponytailed woman from her past grate on her nerves a minute longer. She tossed her stuff in the back of the pickup and climbed in. Before she started the engine she pulled out her cell phone and checked her messages. She always had messages. One from the store manager, double-checking that she would be in tomorrow. One from her brother asking her price on a three-quarter horsepower submersible pump. And a voice mail from Janice.

*Hey there, peaches. Sorry I missed the game. Got tied up. If I promise to cook dinner next week will you forgive me? Homemade pesto. Mine is to die for. Anyway, sorry. I hope you won. Of course you won. You're fabulous. I really was busy and time just got away from me. I'll make it up to you. I promise. Wink wink. Got to run. Talk to you soon. Hugs and kisses.*

Dale was about to call Janice's number when she saw Taren crossing the parking lot. Dale draped her hand over the steering wheel and watched as she climbed into her car. She still drove the red hatchback Sydney had said was so cute.

*Zippy little car, sis. You look like a giant strawberry coming down the street.*

"She still drives it, Syd," Dale mumbled. "And it still looks like a giant strawberry." She heaved a sigh. "She looks the same too. She hasn't aged like me."

Dale headed home. She drove south on Range Line Road, the heart of Joplin's commercial district. She stopped at the light in front of Home Depot where she had been a department head for nearly five years. The parking lot had surprisingly few cars for a Sunday. Spring was almost over. People were planting and decorating and celebrating the beginning of summer. At least that's what she would have expected. Then she remembered today was Joplin's high school graduation. The gymnasium at Missouri Southern State University north of town was probably packed with several thousand would-be customers with long honey-do lists. That meant next weekend would be mobbed. She contemplated stopping at the store for light bulbs and furnace filters but it was her day off. She knew if she went in someone would corner her with a question and she'd spend the rest of her day off working. She sat at the stoplight, drumming her fingers on the gear shift and watching one of the employees collect shopping carts from the parking lot. She remembered when she was one of the new faces and that was part of her job.

The blue-skied morning had given way to a cloudy afternoon. If the local weatherman was to be believed, evening showers and even thunderstorms were possible. She hoped the rain clouds darkening the western horizon would hold off long enough for her to do a little yard work. She loved to play softball or go canoeing. She'd do anything athletic until she was sweaty and filthy but she hated mowing her grass. It was almost as distasteful as ironing. She enjoyed a lush green lawn to match her neighbors but disliked the monotony of cutting it.

She followed Twentieth Street and turned in to her

neighborhood. The street was lined with middle-class ranch-style homes, most of them built in the 1960s with attached garages, mature shade trees and well-manicured yards. Some were brick. Some were vinyl sided. There were six houses in her short block, three on each side, lined up like soldiers facing each other. Her house was in the middle of the block and faced west. It had two bedrooms, two bathrooms and a single-car garage. It had white windows and trim and sage green siding. Dale had allowed Sydney to pick the color scheme. They'd bought the house together but Sydney was the driving force behind all decorating choices.

"You pick, sweetheart. So long as it's vinyl and I don't have to paint it, whatever you like is fine with me," Dale had said. Now it was a pleasant reminder of Sydney. Many things were a reminder of Sydney, not the least of which was her ponytailed sister.

"Hey, Marvin." Dale waved a greeting to the gray-haired man walking his dog along the curb. He waved and gave the leash a jerk, discouraging the mutt from pooping on Dale's yard. She smiled as if acknowledging his discretion. She knew he wouldn't have bothered if she hadn't been turning into her driveway. Marvin lived on the corner, was single and had the deepest comb-over Dale had ever seen. Rumor was he was too impossible to live with and had scared off two wives. Dale had no problem with him other than the occasional dog droppings.

Milo, the neighbor across the street with a thick accent and a peculiar last name Dale could never remember, was unloading suitcases from the back of an SUV. He and his wife, Amelia, had been on a long-awaited trip back home to Prague. They were nice people, always smiling and waving hello. The other house on that side of the street was empty and had been for sale for months. Dale had always admired that house. It was brick. It had a basement, three bedrooms, a fenced yard and a stone fireplace, all things she didn't have. She and Sydney couldn't afford it when it was for sale five years ago. But what would Dale do now with three bedrooms? And a fireplace wasn't energy efficient. Her house was just fine. It was comfortable and affordable. She didn't need to heat or pay taxes on two thousand square feet, but it was fun to dream.

She climbed out of the truck, her cleats slung over her shoulder. Her next-door neighbor, Patty, a newly widowed woman in her seventies, was being dropped off after her weekly Sunday bridge and brunch with friends. Patty waved as she scurried inside, carrying a white foam container of leftovers. She was a pleasant woman. She had lived under the oppressive rule of her husband for nearly fifty years. He wasn't a mean man. But he was, as she admitted to Dale the day after his funeral, tighter with his money than Scrooge. She had been systematically spending it ever since. Her first purchase was a newer car, trading in her twenty-year-old Honda for a "pretty blue one." Her second purchase was a new kitchen, from cabinets to flooring and everything in between.

"Ed would be turning over in his grave if he knew what I was doing," she had told Dale with a giggle. Patty had been a concerned and caring neighbor during Sydney's last few months. She would drop off a casserole or a dessert with little notes of inspiration tucked in the box. She was a Bible-carrying church-goer but never seemed to mind she was living next door to a lesbian couple. Or maybe she didn't know.

The neighbors on the other side of Dale were an unknown. They were new to the neighborhood and seldom socialized. They both drove new cars and dressed professionally. The wife was a handsome woman in her fifties. He was tall, gaunt and always seemed to be in a hurry. They had one son who attended the University of Oklahoma. At least Dale assumed he did from the bumper stickers. Dale promised herself someday she would go over and introduce herself. Someday.

"Hey, Butterscotch, you little mooch." Dale scratched the cat sprawled across her front steps. It wasn't her cat. It belonged somewhere in the next block. She had no idea what the owner named it but she called it Butterscotch because of its long-haired orange coat. Dale didn't want to own a cat but she didn't mind rewarding it with a few kitty treats whenever it showed up and meowed plaintively. "I suppose you want something," she said, stroking the cat's silky fur. "Which flavor is your pleasure? Chicken or tuna?" Butterscotch meowed sleepily. "Okay. Hang on a minute."

Dale fed the cat several kitty treats then turned her attention to chores. She peeled off her dirty T-shirt as she headed down the hall to change into her lawn-mowing clothes. She kept a pair of jeans, shirt and sneakers for just this purpose. Grass stains and snags from the scrubs couldn't hurt them.

As busy as Dale tried to keep herself, the confrontation with Taren was still gnawing at her. That had to be the reason she opened the top dresser drawer and stared down at the neatly folded purple T-shirt, the one Dale had bought Sydney when they visited Colorado on their last vacation together. It was Sydney's favorite shirt. It formed nicely over her small breasts, revealing her perpetually erect nipples even through her bra. It was also the one she wore the day the ambulance transported her to the hospice unit. Dale touched the shirt then closed the drawer. Why couldn't the memories stop at the good times? Why did they always go to the painful conclusion?

Dale leaned against the kitchen counter, peeling and eating an orange one segment at a time, one of those things she enjoyed doing while planning the tasks ahead of her. Laundry and mowing the grass were simple enough. Ignoring the confrontation with Taren, not so much. She finished the last wedge and ran the peel down the disposal then went to start a load of laundry. She pulled the mower out of the garage and filled the gas tank. Before she pulled the cord to start it she pressed the buttons on her cell phone to call Janice. Even though she hadn't found time for the softball game, maybe she'd be free for a phone visit.

Introduced by friends and with only a few dates behind them, Dale had made it clear from the beginning she wasn't looking for an instant roommate. Things had gone a little faster than Dale had liked but Janice was a hot babe. She had a great body. Toned, tanned and energetic. And she knew how to use it. She could whisper things that turned Dale on faster than a speeding bullet. They were still working out the glitches but sex was good for the most part—Dale sometimes felt like she was giving more than receiving. But they'd discuss that in due time.

"Hey there, jock," Janice answered with a giggle. She sounded out of breath.

"Hey there yourself." Dale smiled and leaned against the side of her truck.

"I'm so sorry I couldn't make the game, baby. I really wanted to be there but you know how it is when you get busy. Time gets away from you."

"No problem. The game was a bust anyway. We lost." It hadn't been a bust as much as an inadvertent walk down memory lane, something Dale was trying to ignore.

"Aw, I'm sorry, baby. You'd have won if I had been there cheering for your team. You know I was a cheerleader in high school. Go, team, go!"

"With pompons and everything?" Dale teased.

"You know it. BIG pompons," she said in a seductively husky voice. "You want to see my pompons?"

"I'd love to see your pompons but I've got a lawn to mow before it rains."

"Awww," she whined.

"I know it isn't as much fun as fondling the pompons but I've got no choice. Should I call you later?"

"Absolutely. Call me and I'll talk dirty to you."

"Okay." Dale chuckled then scanned the sky. "I better go before I run out of time."

"Hey, Dale, do you forgive me for not being at the game?"

"Sure. I told you, it's no big deal. I gotta go. Later, okay?"

Janice's repeated apologies seemed excessive but Dale didn't have time to think about it. The wind had picked up and the smell of rain was in the air.

"Come on," she grunted, repeatedly pulling the stubborn mower cord. She adjusted the choke and tried again but it still wouldn't start. "Not today." She scanned the sky. The gray clouds had moved ever closer. "I bet it's raining in Kansas," she said to Butterscotch who had come to the corner of the garage to watch. The cat meowed. "No, I'm not getting you anything else to eat. I've got work to do. Go pester someone else."

Dale was ready to pull the cord again when she heard the warning sirens begin to squeal. But it wasn't even raining and like so many other times when the sirens sounded over Joplin, it seemed unnecessarily premature. She and her neighbors had become desensitized to it. Like crying wolf, whatever urgency was implied had lost all credibility. Dale pulled the cord and started the mower. Beginning tomorrow she would be working fourteen days straight. If she didn't mow today it would be too tall to get the mower through it by her next day off. She hurried back and forth across the front yard, circling her large shade trees like it was a NASCAR race. She took another look at the sky before heading to the backyard. She circled the weeping willow tree Sydney planted, mad at herself for accidentally scuffing the bark. She was nearly finished when she felt the first drops of rain against her cheek. Just a few minutes more, that's all she needed. Three more swipes across the yard and it would be done.

"Not yet," she grumbled and pushed faster. She *was* going to finish. But the mower became bogged down in the damp grass and stalled. She bounced the mower to free the clog then yanked the cord. "Come on, come on." She gritted her teeth and pulled again as the rain and wind increased. "I swear to all that is holy, I'm going to leave you on the side of the road for vultures if you don't start." She pulled the cord again. The mower started, belching smoke as she throttled up for the last pass. The rain was stinging her face and soaking her clothes as she pushed the mower into the garage.

Normally she didn't care if her truck sat out in the rain. But if it was going to hail, something the greenish-black clouds told her was possible, she wanted it inside. She had just pulled it in when she heard a crack and a limb dropped across the driveway where the truck had been sitting. The trees up and down the street were swaying back and forth, their leaves being sucked from the branches. Dale scanned the blackened wall of rain as it moved ever closer, now just a few blocks away. She put the garage door down and headed inside. She grabbed a bath towel to dry off and went to the living room window to watch what she knew would be a downpour.

Dale had seen dark clouds before. But what she saw was much more than a band of rain. This was evil. Pure and simple evil that stretched for blocks. It was rotating across the sky, spinning, collecting and flinging debris. Through the whistling wind she heard the warning sirens begin to blare again. A tree branch blew across the yard. It smacked the window, cracking it. The massive shade tree in her front yard heaved to the side then tipped over. She could feel the ground shake as it landed with a thud, exposing a giant root ball. She stood frozen as she stared into the jaws of a giant tornado. There was no time to think. It was too late to warn Zoe. Too late to check on her neighbors or on Butterscotch. Too late to do anything but run for cover. She rounded the corner into the bathroom as the living room window exploded in a shower of glass. She had always heard the safest place to ride out a tornado was in a bathtub. Whether it was instinct or divine intervention that's where she headed.

She climbed in and slid down as the lights flashed then went out, plunging her into darkness. The roar of the wind grew louder. But it wasn't loud enough to smother the sounds of breaking glass and the thud of objects hitting the side of her house. A musty stench filled the air and her nostrils. She covered her head with the towel as her ears popped. She cringed as the walls creaked and wood snapped. Dale knew she was listening to her house breaking apart around her.

She cupped her hands over her ears as the wind became even more painfully loud. She wanted to look. She wanted to know what was happening. But there was nothing to see. It was only five thirty in the evening but it was black as night. She heard a ripping noise then a loud whoosh. For a moment she could smell fresh air then rain began to soak her clothes. Pieces of debris slapped and whipped at her as she slid deeper into the tub. Something pulled at the towel in her hands. She tightened her grip but couldn't hold it. It gave a snap then disappeared upward. The noise became louder, so loud she wasn't sure she could survive it.

*Please don't let them find me dead in this bathtub. Don't let Zoe find me. Protect her from that.*

Dale wedged herself as far down in the tub as she could manage. She braced her feet and grabbed the faucet. Driving rain and bits of debris pelted her so hard it was like being squirted with a fire hose. She closed her eyes and winced as sting after sting struck her body. The wind hovered overhead, chewing and grinding at the house as if it were searching for her. The bathroom walls began to crumble, pieces of it falling in on her. She struggled to catch her breath through the wind, the rain and the flying debris.

"NO," she screamed as something grazed her forehead. "I'm not ready. Please Sydney. I'm not ready."

Dale screamed long and loud, hoping to block out the inevitable. If she was going to die she wasn't going quietly. The bathtub lifted up then came crashing down, tossing her onto the floor. Dale lay huddled in a ball with her arms cradled over her head, waiting for the next gust of wind to take her.

But miraculously the wind subsided. Slowly the darkness gave way to gray skies and rain. And to an eerie silence.

Dale climbed to her feet, barely able to find her balance. She stood in the pounding rain, surrounded by the shattered remnants of her house. The roof was gone. Her bathroom walls were gone. So were her living room and bedroom walls. Everything was broken. Nothing was where it belonged. The security and privacy that had been her home were little more than splintered wood and broken furniture. So was every other house on her street and for as far as she could see. Nothing but unrecognizable piles of debris. Cars overturned. Trees uprooted or snapped off like toothpicks. Was this what hell looked like? How did she begin to process this? Why was a hot water tank in her front yard? Where was her front door? Why were bricks in her living room?

She mindlessly stumbled through the rubble, climbing over sections of rafters, doors and corrugated aluminum. Splintered two-by-fours with exposed nails, shards of glass stabbed into pieces of Sheetrock, asphalt shingles and tree branches created an obstacle course everywhere she turned. Her living room carpeting had been ripped up and was draped over a tree stump. A pink toilet lay in her front yard. She didn't have a pink toilet. Rain-soaked bits of insulation littered the ground like snowflakes. One of her kitchen cabinets was in the hall. A section of wall with flowered wallpaper was wedged under one of her downed trees. She didn't have flowered wallpaper. She didn't have white bedroom doors either but one was speared with a length of guttering against her foundation. Her sofa was upside down in the street. Her refrigerator lay on its side in the kitchen. Her stainless steel kitchen sink with the new faucet she had installed only last week lay beside it. She could see the side of her pickup truck, still in the garage, the walls fallen in on it. Sections of the end walls stood like bookends to the demolished center of her house. Clothes still hung on hangers in her bedroom closet even though the door and ceiling had been ripped away. Her mattress was gone. The box spring was standing on end, a board stabbed through the center.

She pushed through the debris into her bedroom, looking for something to put on. She was cold and wet and operating on instinct. She pulled on a hoodie over her wet T-shirt and zipped it. It was damp but it didn't matter. Her whole world was now damp. The sound of gushing water meant water pipes had been broken deep within the rubble. But it was the smell of natural gas that sent a fresh wave of terror through her. She knew the entire neighborhood could explode at any moment.

"Don't light a match," she yelled. "There's a gas leak." There was no one around. For all she knew she was alone in this wasteland. She dug in her pocket for her cell phone. She desperately punched in Zoe's number, frantic to hear her voice and know she and Sasha were all right. She redialed, refusing to accept she had no service. She needed to hear a voice, any voice to reassure her she hadn't died and gone to hell.

"HELLO?" A man stood in the street. A trickle of blood ran down his forehead and onto his rain-soaked shirt. He began walking toward her, stumbling over tree branches in his path. It was Marvin. He had a dazed look on his face.

"Are you all right, Marvin?" she called.

"My house," he said, his eyes focusing on nothing in particular.

"I know, Marvin. We had a tornado," she said, the words catching in her throat.

"A tornado?" He stared at her as if he didn't understand.

"Help," Dale heard someone call. But from where? Her ears were still ringing from the wind. She wasn't sure which way to look.

"Why don't you sit down, Marvin?" She pointed to a downed tree trunk. "I'll be back in a minute."

"Is anyone out there?" the voice called again.

"Yes," she shouted. "Where are you?" She couldn't help Marvin but she could help free whoever was trapped.

"Here. We're here." It was Milo. "We're in the bathroom. The wall is down over us. Help us, please."

Dale followed the voice through the debris. Marvin followed, as if he had no place else to go. With his help they lifted a section of collapsed wall enough for Milo and Amelia to crawl out, both of them shaken and stunned but seemingly unharmed.

"Are you hurt?" Dale asked, helping Amelia to her feet. "Can you stand up?"

She nodded then looked past Dale at the remnants of their home. She screamed then began to cry, her hands trembling as she held them to her face.

"Our house. Where is it?" She looked at Milo with desperation in her eyes.

Milo didn't answer. He seemed on the verge of tears himself as he comforted his wife. Like Dale, they stood for a moment, staring in disbelief at the wreckage that had been their home. Dale headed across the street to Patty's house, following the sound of a voice.

"Help me. Please," someone called.

"Patty? This is Dale. I'm coming. Hang on. Let me know where you are."

Marvin continued to follow, waiting for Dale to tell him what to do.

"Look under that door, Marvin. But be careful. There are nails everywhere. Where are you, Patty?" Dale called. She frantically peeled back chunks of Sheetrock and splintered two-by-fours. The voice stopped but she kept digging. "Patty!"

"Here. I'm here," a fragile voice finally said.

Dale turned and saw a shirtless woman cowering in the hole left by the root ball of an overturned tree. Milo had heard her cries and also came to help. They gently lifted her out of the hole and seated her on an overturned plastic tub. Patty was dressed in slacks and a bra and didn't seem to realize she wasn't wearing a shirt. Dale took off her hoodie and slipped it around Patty's shoulders, guiding her arms through the sleeves.

"Is this mine?" Patty seemed stunned and confused.

"It is now, sweetheart. It is now," Dale said, zipping it for her. Patty was as white as a ghost. She had a few scrapes and cuts but didn't seem to be seriously injured. "Will you be okay for a few minutes?" she asked, squatting in front of Patty and holding her hands. "I'll be back, okay?"

"My wife will sit with her," Milo said, motioning to Amelia.

The rain had become little more than a drizzle. Dale checked her cell phone again, praying for a signal. There wasn't one but she pushed the buttons and held it to her ear anyway.

"No cell?" Milo asked, fishing in his pocket for his.

"No. The towers are probably down." Dale did a slow scan, listening for cries for help. "Did you hear that?"

"Over there." He pointed to the house behind Patty's. Dale, Milo and Marvin headed through the debris-strewn backyard and over the smashed chain-link fence. The houses on the next street fared no better. All had sustained massive damage. A few residents had climbed out of the rubble and were digging for survivors.

"Help us," a woman screamed from the corner of the house. "I smell gas. It's going to explode. Get us out. Get us out." She beat frantically on the wall.

Dale didn't know the family who lived there. She knew they had two kids and drove a brown minivan. That van was upside down in the street on top of a white car too crushed to recognized its make.

"We're coming. We're coming. Hold on," Dale shouted.

Milo dug like a man possessed, flinging boards and wreckage out of the way. They finally uncovered a woman on the floor in what had been a bedroom closet, an arm hugging each of her children to her chest. They all looked horrified. The woman climbed to her feet, her children clinging to her side.

"Where's Isaac?" she demanded as if Dale should know. "Where's my husband?" She pulled the children closer, panic gripping her face.

"Was he with you in the closet?" Milo asked, looking around.

"He went to put the car in the garage. He said he'd be right back." She looked toward the street and the overturned van and screamed.

Dale was the first one to get to the driver's side door. All the windows were broken out. It didn't occur to her not to look. It was instinct. She wanted to help. But she wished she hadn't. Isaac was lying on the headliner, blood-covered. Dale carefully reached in and felt his wrist for a pulse. She half expected not to find one.

"Please, please, please be alive," she whispered.

"Do you feel anything?" someone asked.

"I can't tell."

"Let's get him out of there," a man said, looking in from the other side. He had a calm, self-assured voice. "We'll have to take him out through the windshield."

It was Dale's unknown neighbor, the one she hadn't met yet. He was dressed in slacks, a dress shirt and tie, all of them soaked from the rain. Dale wanted to introduce herself and ask if he and his wife were okay. But this wasn't the time for that. Their eyes met through the van as if in silent acknowledgment of being neighbors then they went to work pulling Isaac from the van. Three men came to help ease him out, being careful not to do any further damage. Dale held his wrist, again feeling for a pulse.

"Take it here," the man in the tie said calmly, pressing his fingers to Isaac's neck. "He's alive. He's lost a lot of blood but he's alive. He needs medical attention."

The sound of sirens could be heard in the distance but Dale knew nothing could navigate the streets with all the downed trees and power lines. Using a door as a litter, the group of men decided to carry Isaac the five blocks to Twentieth Street where they could surely find help for him. Dale tried to help but found she couldn't lift her share. That was strange. She considered herself a strong woman, strong enough to share the load. "We've got it, ma'am," one of the men said, taking her place.

As if sprouting from the ruins, several more residents began to appear, joining the search and rescue. Most of them Dale had never seen before. That didn't matter. Everyone was a friend, someone to lean on and share the grief.

On her way back to check on Patty, Dale stopped in the street and stared down at the rain-soaked remnants of a shirt. It was snagged under a broken piece of a utility pole. The sleeve was bloodstained. For a moment Dale's mind refused to accept what she saw. It couldn't be real. It was just a sleeve. That's all. But it was real. The shirtsleeve still contained an arm, the fingers curled into a ball. She had to look away or vomit.

This day was now more than just about demolished houses and wounded neighbors. It was now about death, something Dale wasn't ready to accept. She took a deep breath then slowly looked at it again. She squinted, trying to soften the reality of it but there was no way to soften it. This was someone's arm. It had been ripped from their body perhaps while they were still alive. In spite of the chill in the air Dale felt perspiration forming on her upper lip. She felt faint. She sat down in the street with her back to the arm, taking several deep breaths. She was not going to pass out. She was not.

It was a grisly task but she couldn't leave the arm in the street. It belonged to someone. And whoever that was, they deserved respect. She pulled a sheet from the wreckage and wrapped the arm in it. She cradled it in her arms as she walked the five blocks to Twentieth Street and turned it over to the first emergency vehicle she flagged to a stop. In her wildest imagination she could never have conceived that she would carry someone's bloodied arm wrapped in a rain-soaked sheet in search of a police officer. But she had already seen and done many things that day she never thought possible.

"How much of Joplin is damaged?" she asked the officer after he scribbled a report, seemingly impatient to leave.

"Everything south of Fifteenth Street," he said, shaking his head in amazement. "It's bad. Do you need anything else, ma'am?" He was in a hurry and Dale couldn't blame him.

"No." She stepped back onto the curb.

"Take care of yourself, ma'am." He pulled away with his lights flashing.

Dale headed back, relieved that Zoe's side of town wasn't involved. And if Taren still lived in north Joplin, she wasn't involved either. Why had Taren crossed her mind? She didn't have time to pursue it. Her home had been destroyed. Her world had been turned upside down. And she was still fighting nausea.

As she passed block after block of damaged homes and overturned cars she had time to think. She had always been an independent woman who could support herself. She never asked for a handout. But where would she live now? How would she get to work? What was left in her home that she could use? She had homeowner's insurance but how soon could she rebuild? She began making a mental list of the bare essentials she would need to merely exist. The more she thought about it the more desperate she felt. She knew how much was in her wallet and she knew it would last for a vanishingly small amount of time.

"How do I start from scratch?" she mumbled as she rounded the corner onto her street. At least she thought it was her street but she couldn't really tell. The street sign was gone and all the houses looked the same, lot after lot of devastation. The only way she could surmise where she was were the house numbers stenciled onto the curb. It was amazing how much one crushed house looked like the next. She had walked two blocks too far and had to backtrack. While she was gone several people she didn't recognize had brought chain saws into the neighborhood. They were cutting and clearing the trees that had fallen into the street. A man with a backhoe was plowing the debris to the curb.

Dale heard someone squealing in the distance. She looked up to see Zoe running down the middle of the street. Tears streamed down her face as she ran into Dale's arms.

"Oh, my God. I was so scared, Dale."

Even Zoe's high-pitched squeal was a comforting sound. Dale felt her shaking in her arms as she sobbed.

"I'm all right, Zoe. Are you and Sasha okay?"

"I couldn't get through. There's no cell service. I've been trying and trying," she said frantically. "I didn't know what to think."

"Zoe, I'm fine." Dale was relieved Zoe was unharmed but she refused to cry. If she started she was afraid she couldn't stop. That wouldn't solve anything. "Where's Sasha?"

"She's at Haley's in Carl Junction. I'll pick her up later. I didn't know what I would find so I didn't want to bring her. You're sure you're all right?" Zoe brushed Dale's bangs back as she did a cursory inspection.

"Yes, I'm sure." Zoe didn't need to know her insides were still in knots and her shoulder felt like it had been hit with a baseball bat.

"You're soaking wet."

"Yeah, well, it rained." Zoe's comment struck her as funny. Being wet was the least of her concerns and she couldn't help but laugh. She led the way across the yard, pointing out the dangers as they climbed over and around debris. "Have you heard from Bryant and Kim? Are they all right?" She assumed forty miles was far enough away for her brother not to have had any damage.

"I sent them a text. When they couldn't get through to you they were going to drive up here. I told them to wait. It's a good thing I did. The streets are impassable. I had to park and walk from Main Street." Zoe pulled out her cell phone and checked for messages. "I told them I'd text once I got here. How am I supposed to text when there's no cell service?" She stabbed at the buttons in frustration.

"Compose the text and send it. It'll go through when it finds a cell."

"No, it won't. It'll just sit there." She did it anyway. "I'm telling them Joplin looks like a bomb went off. They definitely shouldn't come up. It's a mess." Zoe took a picture of Dale's house and included it in the text. "You're lucky. At least you have partial walls still standing. I saw some streets where there's nothing left. Houses wiped right off the foundation. The only way you can tell where they were is the dip in the curb for the driveway." She scanned Dale's house, a pained look on her face. "I can't believe this. It's surreal." She stood in the former living room as if she didn't know where to start or what to do.

"Zoe, I need your help."

"Of course. You're coming home with me. You'll sleep on the couch until we figure out what to do." Chattering away seemed to be Zoe's defense mechanism.

"I meant I need your help moving some stuff off my truck. I want to see if it's drivable."

"Why don't we leave that for another day? Let's see if we can find any of your clothes and maybe a toothbrush."

"Later. I need my truck."

"Is this yours?" Zoe picked up a vacuum sweeper hose with two fingers as if it were contaminated.

"No. Are you coming?"

"Yes, I'm coming but that's not safe. The whole thing is going to fall in on you. And what is that smell? Is that gas?"

"Yes. I shut off mine at the meter but the gas company will have to shut off the main. Don't light a match."

"The whole freaking neighborhood is going to blow up," Zoe argued.

"Look around, Zoe. It already did. Now, are you coming?"

"Yes," she grumbled, carefully climbing through the debris. "But I don't know what good I'll be. I can't lift a wall."

Zoe was right. She was little help. With Milo's help they were able to fold the collapsed wall back enough for Dale to climb in the driver's door.

"It looks like someone took a hammer to your truck," Zoe said. "The tailgate is smashed. The back window is broken out."

"I don't care about the back. I just want to know if it'll start." She held her breath and turned the key. It started right up. "All right!" Dale pumped her fist. It wasn't the answer to all her problems but it was a small victory, enough to bring tears to her eyes.

"Are you okay?" Zoe stared through the window at her.

"Yep." Dale wiped away the tear.

"I'm here for you, sis. You know that," she said, reaching in and squeezing Dale's hand.

Dale nodded as another tear trailed down her cheek.

Zoe left Dale to her pickup truck and the garage while she went in search of salvageable clothing.

As the evening wore on, the chain saw crews made a sizable dent in the downed tree and broken power poles that blocked the street. But that didn't take care of the jungle of toppled trees in Dale's yard and across her driveway.

"Did that text to Bryant go through yet?" Dale asked.

"Yes," she said, checking her phone. "Twelve minutes ago. No reply yet. Hey, I've got two bars." She held it up proudly.

"Quick. Send another text. Ask him if I can borrow his chain saw. I can't get my truck out of the garage until I clear away these trees."

Zoe sent it then went back to picking through Dale's bedroom. They started a pile of anything not broken and usable. It was an eclectic mix of linens, clothes, dishes and toiletries.

"Oh, look," Zoe declared loudly. "Your underwear drawer survived."

"Good," Dale replied with a groan as she dragged a tree branch out of the way.

"I don't know how good it is. These are some ug-ly underwear."

Even with flashlights Dale found in her truck it was getting too dark to search. They finally gave up and walked the seven blocks to Zoe's car, each carrying a trash bag of Dale's clothes. She felt a twinge of guilt as she left her home and her neighbors. But she had no choice. She couldn't sleep there. She couldn't even use the bathroom. That didn't make it easier. A lump rose in her throat as she looked back down the street. That was her home. And it was gone.

# CHAPTER THREE

"Ham and Swiss?" Zoe said from the kitchen.

"No, thanks." Dale stood in the hall towel-drying her hair and wearing one of Zoe's clean T-shirts and shorts. "It's almost ten o'clock. I'm not hungry."

"Sasha, Dale's out of the bathroom. Come take your bath. It's ten o'clock," she called. "I wasn't asking if you wanted a sandwich. I was asking if you preferred Swiss or American cheese. You have to eat. Mustard or mayo?"

"You're not my mother," Dale said, although it was a common complaint about Zoe.

"I know you. When you're stressed you don't eat. You just shut down and fester. Like today at the game when you saw Taren."

"I wasn't stressed over seeing Taren. And I don't fester."

Zoe gave her a long I-don't-believe-you look. "Mustard or mayo?"

"Mustard. And how did Taren's name creep into this conversation?"

"Just for the fun of it," she giggled.

"Isn't it awesome, Mom?" Sasha said, coming into the kitchen. "No school."

"Yes, very awesome. Go take your bath."

"Did they cancel school tomorrow?" Dale asked, tickling Sasha as she passed.

"Yeah."

Zoe waited until the bathroom door closed then said quietly, "It was on the news while you were in the shower. Five of the Joplin schools were hit by the tornado. They had to cancel the whole last week of school. I wonder what they would have done if this happened in the middle of the school year."

"I knew the high school took a direct hit but five? How big was this thing?"

"Big," she said in a whisper and nodded toward the muted television.

Zoe's apartment was small. Two bedrooms. One bathroom. A living room attached to a kitchen with a counter that doubled as a dining room. It was in a good location, came with all the appliances and best of all, was within her limited budget. Zoe's ex had left her with substantial credit card debt. He also felt little responsibility for his daughter and was frequently behind on his child support. He had moved six hundred miles away to avoid occasional babysitting, leaving Zoe to raise her daughter alone. Dale shared her sister's hatred for the man but they didn't talk about it.

"Saint John's Hospital took a direct hit. Look at that. All the windows are blown out," Zoe said, joining Dale on the couch as they ate their sandwiches and watched the news reports. "I'm sorry none of my phone chargers fit your phone."

"That's okay. I'll look again tomorrow. If I can't find any of mine I'll buy one. I can do without a phone for one day." Dale suddenly stopped chewing and pointed at the screen. "What?" she gasped.

"That's Home Depot. That's your store."

"Shh," Dale demanded, turning up the volume. As if the day couldn't possibly get any worse, there it was. The Home Depot store at Twentieth and Range Line lay in ruins. The roof had been ripped off and the front wall had collapsed. The cars in the parking lot were tossed together like Matchbox cars in the bottom of a toy box. Emergency vehicles surrounded the building. Rescue crews used floodlights in the darkness as they swarmed over the wreckage. "People are in there," she said desperately, her heart pounding.

"And there's Walmart. Pizza Hut. IHOP. Walgreens," Zoe said, her voice cracking. "All those stores are just gone."

"Zoe, it was dinner time on a Sunday. People were in those stores. People were in Home Depot."

Dale felt a desperate pain in her chest. Who was in her store? Were any of them hurt? She hadn't told Zoe about the arm she found but it was now clear many more lives could be lost. They watched in silence. This wasn't like the winter ice storm that had taken out several hundred trees and left the city without power for a week. This was heartbreaking devastation that had ripped a six-mile-long scar across Joplin. Lives as well as livelihoods were gone. And her own livelihood was one of them. She had no home and possibly no job. How did she make sense of this? How did she reconcile herself to losing everything? She looked over at her sister as a feeling of desperation washed over her.

"Please, please, tell me you have insurance." Zoe placed a hand on Dale's knee.

"Yes. I'm calling tomorrow."

Zoe's cell phone chimed on the counter.

"Thank God," she said, rushing to answer it. "That news report is making me crazy. I don't know how you can stand watching it."

Dale muted the TV. She didn't need to hear the details. The pictures spoke for themselves.

"I got a reply from Bryant about the chain saw. He said he'll bring it up tomorrow. He needs to sharpen the chain and get some oil. Is that okay?"

"Tell him yes, thanks."

Zoe started to compose the text then hesitated, a crease growing across her forehead.

"What's wrong?" Dale asked.

"You're going to think I'm a terrible sister but would it be okay if I ask him to pick you up here?"

"Why does that make you a terrible sister? I just thought you could drop me off at the house on your way to work. I've got some things to do before he gets here."

"It's stupid but I don't know if I can do that." Zoe swallowed hard.

"Do what?"

"Go back there tomorrow." She looked away as her chin began to quiver. "It's just so awful. I don't know if I can face it. You probably think I'm a chickenshit?"

"Zoe, I understand. And no, I don't think you're a chickenshit." She smiled and wiped the lone tear trailing down Zoe's cheek. "Don't feel guilty if you can't face it. Sometimes I'm not sure I can."

"I just need some time."

"Take all the time you need." She patted Zoe's leg. "Ask Bryant if he can be here by eight."

"Sasha, you'll be turn-key Tessa tomorrow, okay?" Zoe called through the bathroom door. "Remember the rules."

"I know," Sasha replied. "Don't answer the door except if it's you or Aunt Dale. And don't answer the phone unless I recognize the caller ID."

"And no Facebook. Be sure you rinse that glittery body wash off really well. It makes a mess on your sheets." Zoe went back to the counter to read another incoming text. "Well, well. Speak of the devil." Zoe cackled wickedly.

"Did he say eight o'clock was okay?" Dale asked, flipping through the stations for a fresh perspective on the storm.

"It's not from Bryant. It's from Taren Dorsey."

"You're kidding. I didn't know you two were friends."

"I'm a secretary. She's a teacher. That doesn't make us friends." Zoe read the text then quickly tapped out a reply.

Dale's curiosity waited only so long before she said, "What did she want? Is she still mad about the softball game?"

"I wondered when you'd ask." Zoe brought the phone for Dale to read.

*Is Dale ok? Wrrd!*

"What is w-r-r-d?" Dale asked, squinting at the screen.

"Worried. I told her you were, but not your house."

"Don't tell her my business."

"She texted me. Not you. I can tell her anything I want." The phone chimed another incoming text.

"She probably wants to know if I'm dead yet. Tell her I got picked up and deposited in Oz where I'm following the yellow brick road."

"Tell her yourself." Zoe dropped the phone in Dale's lap and went to check on Sasha. "Why don't you tell her you're sorry for being an ass at the game." She chuckled.

"Here. I'm not texting her," she said, waving the phone.

"Send something. Just be nice."

Dale read Taren's reply.

*So sorry. Heartbreaking. At least she's ok.*

Dale tried several versions of a reply but wasn't happy with any of them. She left Zoe's phone on the coffee table and went out onto the front steps to get away from the storm coverage. She had seen more than enough. The chilly night air was filled with an acrid smoky stench. The sound of sirens crisscrossing the city wailed in the distance. She was lost in thought when she heard the rattle of the doorknob. She looked up to see Sasha, freshly scrubbed and in her pajamas but with a frightened look on her face.

"Hey, Sasha," Dale said and held out an arm to welcome her. "How are you doing, sweetheart?" She pulled her close and kissed the top of her head.

"I'm scared," she said softly as she snuggled against Dale's side.

"Of what, sweetie?"

"Is the tornado coming back? Is it going to hit my house, too?"

"No." Dale wrapped her in a bear hug. "You don't have to worry. It's long gone. I promise you're safe."

"But they said on TV Joplin was destroyed."

"I know what they said on TV but they exaggerated. Joplin was not destroyed. Some of it has damage. But it can be rebuilt.

You'll see." Dale rocked Sasha in her arms, trying to reassure her own fear as much as the child's.

"Bedtime, Sasha," Zoe said, stepping onto the porch. "Go brush your teeth and I'll be there in a minute to tuck you in."

"Good night, babycakes," Dale said. "You sleep tight." She waited for her to go inside then said, "She's scared, Zoe."

"I'm not surprised. The storm damage is all you see on television." Zoe snorted. "I'll talk with her." She turned for the door then stopped, hesitating as if she had something else to say. "By the way, Bryant and Kim want to know if it's okay to go ahead with the wedding."

"Why ask me? I'm not performing the ceremony."

"Your brother's worried you'd think they were insensitive if they planned a big party right after the tornado."

"I don't care." Dale shrugged. She had completely forgotten her niece's wedding. It was no surprise Judy was marrying her high school sweetheart. They had dated since she was a freshman and he was a junior.

"Judy's dress is gorgeous. They found it online. It's kind of a soft creamy beige color with lace and sequins. She looks like a princess in it. Are you listening to me?"

"Yeah, creamy beige." Dale had been distracted, remembering the arm in the street and the gruesome news of the bodies found amid the rubble.

"I'm handling the guest book and making sure the caterer gets set up. The buffet is going to be delicious." Zoe gave the details of the meal as if she were planning battle tactics. Even on a good day Dale didn't care if they served meatballs or fried chicken. Today it was just so much white noise. "And just so you don't jump down my throat later, I'm letting you know now. Taren was invited." Zoe looked back for Dale's reaction. "And her RSVP said yes, she is coming."

"Oh yippee skippee." Dale didn't need to ask why she was invited. She knew why. Taren had tutored Judy when she was having trouble in high school. Without Taren's endless hours of online help she might have given up and dropped out. To them, Taren was part of one big happy family.

"You don't have to sit next to her. Just be nice. This is Judy and Lucas's day."

"I'm always nice."

"Are you still bringing Janice?"

"I don't know. I mentioned it a few weeks ago."

"What do you see in her anyway?"

"Zoe, don't." Dale gave her a hard stare. "You pick who you date. I'll pick who I date."

"Okay, but I feel an eventual I-told-you-so coming."

"Resist the urge."

"I left sheets and a blanket on the couch. I'm going to bed. Do you need anything?" Zoe said through a yawn.

Dale followed Zoe inside. "Wake me when you get up. Good night, sis. And thanks."

"I wish I could do more, honey." She gave Dale a hug then went to bed.

Dale tossed the sheet over the couch and turned out the lights. She couldn't tell if she was tired or mentally exhausted. She pulled the blanket over her legs and lay staring at the streetlight's reflection on the ceiling. As hard as Dale tried to ignore it, her OCD kept returning to Taren's text and the reply she didn't send.

"Dammit," she muttered. She opened Zoe's phone and hastily composed one. *I hope you weren't affected by the storm.*

She stared at the text on the screen, fighting with herself over the wording. Was it the polite thing to say? Would she think it sarcasm? Exasperated with her indecision, she took a deep breath and sent it. She'll think it's from Zoe anyway, she thought and placed the phone on the table.

Dale tossed and turned, blaming her insomnia on the couch. She spent the wee hours making mental lists of things she needed to do and people she needed to contact. The list that seemed unending was the possessions she had lost. The one thing she kept coming back to was the insurance. Sydney had set it up when they bought the house. She handled the bills and business part of the relationship. It wasn't that Dale couldn't but Sydney seemed to enjoy it, telling Dale her obsession to detail was driving her crazy. Dale wasn't sure what kind of coverage she had. The premium was all part of her mortgage payment and held in escrow. Other than the dwelling, how much of the contents were covered? Would it pay for temporary housing? Would it pay to clear away the rubble so she could start over? She assumed Home Depot would rebuild. But when? How many months would she be out of work? Could she find a job that paid enough for her to live and pay her mortgage in the meantime? She was still wrestling with her options when at dawn she heard Zoe's bedroom door open.

"Dale?" Zoe said, leaning over the back of the couch.

"I'm awake," Dale said, her arms folded behind her head.

"Don't say anything, okay? But if you'll get up and get dressed I'll drop you off at your house." Zoe had a guilty frown on her face. "I sent Bryant a text already."

Whatever had caused Zoe's epiphany, Dale wasn't going to challenge it. She appreciated her decision and hurriedly dressed before she could change her mind.

The southern half of Joplin was without power. Traffic signals had either been destroyed or were nonfunctioning. Even at this early hour intersections were snarled with traffic. Gas stations, ATMs, convenience stores, fast-food restaurants, even those that survived the tornado had no power. Volunteers did their best to direct cars and rescue vehicles through the crowded streets.

"I can't tell where we are. The street signs are gone," Zoe said, slowing at each intersection. "I can't tell where to turn. It's just one demolished street after another."

"This is Grand. It looks like someone spray-painted the street names on the pavement. Three more blocks."

Dale's neighborhood was already clogged with activity as they turned the corner and stopped in front of her house. It took a moment for her to adjust to the reality of it and climb out of the car.

"Thanks," Dale started to say but Zoe held up her hand, her eyes closed tight.

"You and Bryant be careful."

Dale watched as she pulled away. It must have been hard for Zoe to change her mind. But it was comforting to know she had done it, whatever the reason.

Dale was picking through the kitchen, searching for the phone charger she kept plugged in next to the microwave, when she heard the rhythmic honk of a horn. Without looking, she knew it was Bryant. He waved then held a pair of work gloves out the driver's side window. Dale circled the truck and leaned her elbows on the window frame, smiling in at her brother. He sat for a moment, looking up and down the street with a deep-set frown on his face. Like Zoe, Dale knew he needed some time to absorb this catastrophe. He wasn't an overly emotional man but she could see he was stunned by what he saw. She touched her fingertips to her lips as she said thank you. She then signed *I appreciate your help.*

Bryant had been deaf since he was a child, the result of chicken pox. He was several years older than Dale so communicating with him by sign language was all she had ever known. Even though he spent much of his childhood at an out-of-town school for the deaf, he had always been Dale's big brother and her hero.

Bryant signed *you're welcome.* He took another look at what was left of her house. He sat shaking his head and signed, *This breaks my heart, sis.* He climbed out. *Show me where to start.* They walked the yard, deciding what to cut first and how much they could accomplish in a day. *We'll get it done. At least we can get it cut up today.*

*Are you sure you want to do this?* she asked, speaking the words as she signed, the way she had learned to do it as a child.

Bryant gave a firm nod then went to the truck for his chain saw. He handed Dale a pair of earplugs and insisted she wear them, making a silly face about it. He had admitted once he could hear a faint hum when he ran the chain saw, making it one of his favorite things to do. As a mechanic, and a good one, he had learned to tell if an engine was running correctly by the vibration and the instrument readings. He didn't consider himself handicapped and asked for no special treatment. He was a simple hard-working man who loved his family and always tried to do the right thing. He was like Dale, preferring to keep his emotions private.

They took turns running the chain saw and dragging branches to the curb. Dale explained she wanted the driveway cleared first so she could get her truck out of the garage. Finally, covered with wood chips and sawdust, Bryant shut off the chain saw and set it on a stump. He stretched his back then signaled time for lunch. Kim had packed a cooler with bottled water and cans of soda. She also packed cold fried chicken and bags of chips. Dale picked a piece of chicken from the container and sat down on the tailgate to eat.

*Kim's a good cook*, she said, speaking as she signed.

*Don't sign with your mouth full*, he signed, struggling not to drop his drumstick.

*Don't sign with your hands full*, she replied, giving him a playful bump.

Bryant tossed his chicken bones in a trash sack then wiped his hands on his jeans.

*Are you going to live with Zoe until you rebuild?* He used the sign for Indian Chief, a joke that had stuck since Zoe's domineering childhood days.

Dale shrugged then asked how long he thought it would take to rebuild it. He studied the lot and what was left of her house.

*Couple months if you keep it simple. Nothing special order. If you can reuse the foundation you can save time and money. Is it damaged?*

*I can't tell*, she replied.

*Did you see what happened to Home Depot?* His expression was pained.

She nodded. *I haven't driven by to see but it looks bad on TV.*

Bryant reached for his wallet and pulled out several bills but Dale shook her head adamantly.

*Thanks, but no. I've got insurance. It'll cover everything.* She had no idea if it would but she knew Bryant couldn't afford to do that. He pressed a twenty-dollar bill in her pocket with an insistent nod. He was being the protective big brother and she let him.

Before they went back to cutting he helped her clear away the rubble so she could back her truck out of the garage. He circled the truck, studying the damage.

*You need a taillight on the driver's side or you'll get a ticket.* He tried the passenger door handle but it didn't open.

*I know it looks pretty bad but at least it runs.* She picked the broken glass off the seat.

*You've got a crack in the windshield but it doesn't cross your field of vision so you should be okay.*

*I think the cops have more important things to worry about than cracked windshields.* Dale tapped her knuckles on the glass, testing to see if the crack grew.

*Is this yours?* Bryant pulled a white cell phone auto charger from the front grill of the truck.

*Yes! I've been looking for that.* She started the engine and plugged in her phone then placed a call to her insurance agent. Not surprisingly, the call went to voice mail. She left her information, repeating her phone number twice. Hopefully she'd hear from them soon but she had a feeling this was going to be a long slow process.

The weather forecast warned of more afternoon thunderstorms and sure enough, darkening clouds began to brew northwest of Joplin. The chances another tornado would rip through Joplin were slim. Dale logically knew that. But it wasn't logic that tied her stomach in knots and threatened a panic attack. Where would they seek shelter? How bad would this one be? Dale stood staring at the boiling clouds, unable to calm her nerves or ignore the memories of yesterday. Bryant continued to rev the saw, rocking it through the trunk of a large walnut tree. She wanted him to stop cutting and see the danger she saw. She waved to get his attention just as the saw belched smoke and died.

*The chain's dull. But I got most of it cut. You just have to drag it to the front.* He brushed the sawdust from his shirt. *Looks like rain.*

*It's a good time to quit. Thanks for your help, Bryant. You need to head home.*

Dale had never been afraid of thunderstorms. Even as a child she loved to count the Mississippis between the lightning and the thunder then giggle if the concussion was loud enough to make her flinch. But yesterday's storm had changed all that. She wanted to run and hide. The clouds were dark but nothing like yesterday. She clung to that.

They loaded Bryant's truck, exchanged hugs and she stood in the street waving as he pulled away. But her smile was cut short by the wail of the storm sirens. She scanned the sky for a funnel cloud. It wasn't raining yet but she could smell it coming. She could also hear the faint rumble of thunder in the distance.

"We don't need that," Milo called from his driveway. He, too, was studying the clouds.

"It's probably just a precaution," she said, feeling a shiver run up her back.

"Come on, Milo," Amelia called from the car, panic in her voice. "We need to leave. I don't want anything to happen to Eve's car." He gave a last look then climbed in and drove away.

The first drops of rain splattered against the windshield as Dale sat deciding what to do. She didn't want to leave her house and what was left of her possessions but she didn't want to ride out another tornado in her pickup truck either. The jingle of incoming messages on her cell phone captured her attention. There was a voice mail from Home Depot's regional office. She opened it first.

*Dale, this is Betty McKuhn. I'm calling for David, your store manager. We are trying to contact all our employees and make sure they are all right. Please let us know. David and Home Depot send their blessings and prayers during this terrible time.*

It sounded like a prepared statement but it was considerate nonetheless. Dale returned a text saying she was okay and hoped everyone in the store was safe, although she feared that wasn't the case. She opened Zoe's voice mail from yesterday, knowing it would be hysteric.

*Dale, this is Zoe. Oh my God. Dale. Are you there? Are you all right, honey? Call me. Call me. I'm so worried. Oh God, oh God.*

Dale tapped out a text.

*Charging my phone but service is intermittent still. See you later.*
Zoe quickly replied. *B careful.*

Dale opened Janice's text, looking forward to hearing from her.

*Sweet Jesus. Dale, ARE YOU OK? I heard about the tornado. Are you hurt? I tried to call but nothing goes through. They're telling everyone to text instead of call because the towers are down. I can come up if you need me. Tell me what I can bring. Call me when you get a chance. Hugs and kisses.*

Dale appreciated Janice's concern but she didn't want or need her to come to Joplin. She knew it sounded selfish but she wasn't sure she could deal with anything else right now.

*Hi babe. Yes, I'm okay. The house took a hit but I'm okay. This isn't a good time to come up. The town's a mess. Electricity is out. No water. No gas. We're running on instinct. I wouldn't be good company. I've got tons to do. I'll let you know when I'm ready but thanks, sweetie. Talk with you soon.*

Dale flipped to the next text. It was from Kim and sent yesterday evening expressing their concern. Dale sent a reply, telling her Bryant was on his way home.

*He'll be tired and hungry. I really appreciate his help. I couldn't have done it without him.*

There were more than a dozen messages from friends and co-workers, all of them worried about her and her house. She sent polite though short replies. There was one more text message. It had been sent before dawn and surprisingly from Taren.

*No, I had no damage. Couple branches down. Thx for asking. So sorry for ur loss.*

Last night's message had been sent from Zoe's phone. Why did she think it came from Dale? This had to be a mistake. She must have meant it for Zoe.

The rain became an unimpressive drizzle that lasted thirty minutes then moved on, thankfully. Dale headed across town. She wanted to see the Home Depot damage for herself. Zoe hadn't wanted to drive through the disaster zone. She said it was too upsetting. But Dale wanted to see what happened to her town. Was it as bad as the TV reporters said? Was the swath of devastation as wide and as long as she had heard? She couldn't imagine it being that bad. She drove down Twentieth Street, following the route the storm took. It was much worse than she thought. The TV videos were bad but seeing it in person was shocking. Block after block of complete devastation. Whole apartment complexes reduced to rubble. Hundred-year-old trees snapped off like twigs. Wadded lumps of metal that had once been cars. Joplin was a war zone. Twice Dale pulled to the curb to wait for the tears to stop.

The Home Depot parking lot was closed to traffic, blocked by emergency vehicles. Dozens of rescue workers and heavy equipment sifted through the wreckage. Dale drove over the curb and pulled into a vacant spot at the corner of the parking lot.

"Sorry, lady. You can't park there," a burly man declared gruffly. His orange reflector vest seemed to give him a sense of authority.

"I'm an assistant manager. I have a right to be here," she said. It was a small fib. Department head and assistant manager sounded similar and if it got her access to the site, so much the better. She climbed out and looked past his smug posture. "Where's David?"

"I don't know who that is. All I know is no one is allowed in the parking lot unless they're emergency personnel."

"Dale? Is that you?" a man stepped out of a truck cab and waved. "It's okay. She's an employee."

"I'm not supposed to let anyone in," the man in the safety vest argued.

"Then go find your boss and tell him." He walked past the man and extended a handshake to Dale. "What are you doing here, Dale? I heard your house got hit."

"Yes but I wanted to see how things are going here. How bad is it, David?" she asked, bracing herself for bad news. She could tell he had been crying.

"It's not good." He frowned painfully. "They've found four bodies so far. I can't tell you who they are but it's bad, Dale. At least a dozen injured."

"Anyone I know?"

The look in his eyes told Dale yes.

"Employee?" she asked as a knot rose into her throat.

He swallowed hard then gave a slight nod. "I'm not supposed to say. They want time to notify next of kin."

"Who the hell am I going to tell, David?"

He nodded toward a demolished silver pickup truck, part of a pile bulldozed to the side of the parking lot. Dale followed his gaze, squinting at the vehicle.

"B.J.?" she gasped, barely able to speak.

Dale felt as if a knife had been stabbed through her heart. She walked away a few feet, folding her arms over her head then stared back at the demolished truck. "Not B.J." She leaned over and braced her hands on her knees as tears rolled down her cheeks. B.J. was a gentle soul. Tireless. Dependable. A family man with grandkids he adored. He had been working Dale's shift while she took a day off to play softball.

David placed a hand on Dale's back and said quietly, "His wife doesn't know yet. You can't say anything, okay? You won't, will you?"

Dale shook her head then wiped the tears from her cheeks. This wasn't the first death she had experienced in this disaster. But this one was different. She knew this one personally. She almost wished she hadn't stopped.

"Is there anyone else in there?" she asked.

"I don't know. Maybe." He stared at the blinking lights on one of the ambulances as if in a trance.

"What can I do, David?"

"Nothing. Go home. Take care of your house. We've got this. The Atlanta office is sending a disaster team to assess."

"David, was your house hit?"

"No." He tossed a nod toward the pile of vehicles. "That's my car. Looks like a boat anchor now."

"Where were you here when it happened?"

"In the back of the store. It happened so fast." David's eyes drifted away as if he were reliving that terrible moment. "It's just like they say. It sounded like a train. It was really loud then the roof flew off and the front wall came down."

"What happened to your hand?" Dale pointed to the bandage wrapped around his palm.

"I don't know. It was just bleeding." He picked at the bandage then smoothed it down again.

David had always been confident and decisive, the perfect store manager. But now he seemed preoccupied. Lucid one minute. Traumatized the next. Dale couldn't blame him. He was in shock. Maybe so was she.

"You should go home and get some rest," Dale offered, suspecting he had been there all night.

"I can't. I have to stay until everyone is out of there. You go on. I'll call you if I need you." He wandered back toward the building, lost in his thoughts.

Dale felt helpless. She knew if she stayed she'd just cry and she didn't want to do any more of that. She needed food, a shower and clean clothes. She also needed this nightmare to end. Staring at a demolished building wasn't accomplishing any of that. Zoe's apartment might not be the answer to her problems but she needed family, someone to understand her pain.

"Please don't be your usual bitchy self tonight, Zoe. Please." Dale slammed the door to the truck and headed across town.

# CHAPTER FOUR

"Don't do that," Dale mumbled, rolling her shoulder. She opened her eyes to the smell of brewing coffee and expected to see Zoe pinching her shoulder. No one was there. She groaned and turned over to check the time on her cell phone. She was tired when she went to bed last night. This morning she could hardly move. She wondered if Bryant was as stiff and sore as she was. The sooner she got up and dressed the better she'd feel. That had always been her answer to overworking the day before. But it was all she could do to sit up. She stumbled into the bathroom, hoping a hot shower would soothe her sore muscles.

"Don't use all the hot water," Zoe called from the hall.

"All three gallons of it?" Dale opened the door, showered and dressed in clean underwear and bra.

"That's one gallon each," she teased, pushing her way in the bathroom but stopped with a gasp. "Oh my God, Dale! What happened to your back? You've got bruises all over it." Zoe looked in the waistband of Dale's panties. "There's even some on your butt."

Dale stood sideways to the mirror trying to see. She flinched as she ran her hand over herself.

"Was that from the tornado?" Zoe's face bore a pained expression as if Dale had the plague.

"Probably. There was a lot of stuff blowing around."

"What should we put on it?" Zoe opened the medicine cabinet.

"Nothing. You don't treat bruises." Dale went to dress.

"How about ice on it?" Zoe followed her into the living room.

"It's just bruises. I'll be okay. Go take your shower or you'll be late for work." Dale struggled her legs into her jeans, wincing at the pain.

"At least take some ibuprofen," Zoe said, helping her on with her shirt. "The bottle is in the cabinet with the glasses. By the way, the Red Cross is setting up disaster relief tents. There's a temporary shelter at the college too. They're serving meals to anyone who needs—"

Dale interrupted her. "I don't need disaster relief. I have insurance."

"I know but this is for meals and emergency supplies. You qualify. Your house was destroyed."

"I don't need it."

"Fine. Suit yourself." Zoe raised her hands in surrender. "Do I need to drop you off this morning?"

"No. I have my truck outside. Remember?"

"You are actually going to drive that? It's all bashed. The back window is broken out. You can't even open the passenger door. You said so."

"But I can open the driver's door and it is drivable. And in case you haven't noticed, people all over town are driving damaged cars and trucks."

"I'm not going to argue with you." Zoe headed for the shower.

\* \* \*

"Hey you! What are you doing?" Dale shouted at the young man rummaging through Patty's belongings amid the ruin of her house. The evening of the storm her family had whisked her away to Tulsa to care for her injuries. They'd taken a few hastily collected possessions and said they'd be back in a few days to finish sifting through the remnants. Dale had met Patty's family and this young man was not one of them. He looked up in surprise then dropped the jewelry box in his hand and ran. Dale chased him for two blocks but he seemed adrenaline-energized and she couldn't catch him. She stopped at the corner, out of breath, and watched as he disappeared down the street.

"You son of a bitch," she yelled. "Keep your looting ass out of our neighborhood!"

Just what Joplin needed, she thought. Vultures picking the last morsels of flesh from the tornado victims.

"Joplin police. What is your emergency?" a female voice asked.

"How do I report a looter?" she said angrily.

"Is the looter still on the property?"

"No. He's running north. Baggy jeans and black T-shirt with a skull on the front. He's maybe twenty, twenty-two. It looked like he had tattoos up both arms, the little creep," she added. "I chased him a couple blocks but I couldn't catch him."

"Ma'am, please don't do that. You're putting yourself in danger when you pursue a looter. We've got extra patrol cars out covering the tornado-affected areas."

"Well, I'm not going to stand by and just watch him take whatever he wants," Dale replied bitterly. She knew this operator was just doing her job but that didn't make it any easier to accept.

"I'll report this for you. We are advising those with tornado damage to remove your valuables as soon as possible. And try and have a presence in the neighborhood. Lights on, if possible. People on the ground. High visibility. This can discourage looting. But please report looters. Don't chase them."

The operator took Dale's report but it was little solace. Now she had something else to worry about.

"What was that all about?" Milo asked as Dale walked back up the street. He had been stacking branches along the curb. "Who was that?"

"That little creep was going through Patty's stuff." She looked back in the direction he had run.

"A looter? I wonder if he's the same guy who took my chain saw."

"You had a looter?"

"Yes. First night. They took my saw, extra chains, sharpener, everything. They got my new cordless drill, too. Next time I'm not calling the cops. I'm taking care of it myself." Milo patted his cargo pants pocket, revealing the outline of a small pistol. "If I catch the bastard he's going to wish he never set foot on my property. If I had a tent I'd camp out right here in my yard." He went back to stacking branches.

Normally Dale didn't like guns. But Milo's calm defiance sounded almost heroic. She had no doubt he would shoot a prowler. The threat of looting was more real at night. In a darkened neighborhood, lit only by the moon, it was a criminal's playground. Dale checked the pile of possessions she and Zoe had rescued from her home and hidden under a plastic tarp. Sure enough, she too had been the victim of looting. The few tools she had found were gone. So was the suitcase she had filled with salvageable towels and sheets.

"Shit!" She dropped a sweater back in the box. What else would they take? Her refrigerator, microwave, the few pieces of furniture that survived? Milo was right. Maybe staying on her property was the only way to protect what was hers. And the only way she knew to do that involved going where she hoped she'd never have to go.

An hour later Dale circled the block in north Joplin, miles from the tornado devastation. The homes were mostly older, stately brick structures from the early 1900s where Joplin's once business-rich lived. A few were smaller more modest versions but all were well-maintained. Except for a few branches bundled in neat piles awaiting trash removal this part of town showed no evidence of a tornado. She circled the block twice, looking between houses. A part of her wished Taren didn't still have it, but there it was. The sixteen-foot travel trailer Sydney had given her sister when they no longer needed it was parked in the corner of the backyard like an abandoned swing set. A wheelbarrow was overturned onto the hitch. It was covered with leaves and tree sap. But there it sat, right where Dale had parked it four years ago.

Dale rang the doorbell then braced herself. She disliked asking anyone for charity. Even as a teenager she did odd jobs for pocket money. Now she had to ask and not just anyone, but Taren Dorsey, the last person in the world she ever wanted to ask for anything.

"Hello." Taren looked surprised then smiled pleasantly. "Did you need something?"

"Did I come at a bad time? If you're getting ready for work I can come back." Dale knew she was going to have to grovel. Their past dictated it. The last time she was in Taren's house they had had a shouting match that rattled pictures on the wall.

"Classes are over for the semester. Come in." Taren held the screen door and watched suspiciously as Dale entered. "What did you need?"

"I wanted to ask if you would consider renting me the trailer." Dale couldn't help scanning the room for what had changed. It looked the same and so did Taren. She wore slacks that fit just right over her hips and a top that revealed just a hint of cleavage. She wore her hair in a ponytail during the softball game. Today it was down, longer than Dale remembered and not as blond.

"What trailer?" She looked as if she had no idea what Dale was talking about.

"The one in your backyard. The one Sydney gave you." Dale refrained from saying the one she had carefully backed into the yard so as not to disturb her precious rose bushes.

"That old thing? You can't stay in that." She scowled.

Dale had her answer. Taren wouldn't let her use it. The trip out here was wasted. And again, Taren had the upper hand.

"All right," Dale said and stepped out on the porch.

"Wait a minute. You didn't give me a chance to explain. I use it as a garden shed. It's filthy."

"I understand. I'm sorry to bother you."

"I'm not doing this to be a bitch. Let me show you something." Taren snatched a ring of keys from the table by the door and waved Dale to follow her around the house. She unlocked the trailer door and swung it open for Dale to enter. "I keep my gardening tools and flower pots in it. There's a leak in the roof somewhere and I wouldn't be surprised if mice have found their way inside. I'd let you use it but it's not fit to live in."

"Where's the leak?" Dale asked, looking inside from the top step.

"In the bathroom, I think."

"So, not over the bed?"

"No, I don't think so."

Dale stepped inside. The air smelled like potting soil but it didn't reek like she expected.

"See what I mean?" Taren said from outside. "It's nasty. It works as a tool shed but as a travel trailer, not so much." She started for the front yard as if Dale would follow.

"Do the lights and water work?" Dale tried the faucet but she didn't expect anything to come out.

"I have no idea. I haven't tried them."

Dale flipped the switch to check the battery system. It was dead. "Probably needs a charge." She opened the closet and bathroom. They looked okay though dirty. The mattress still had the plastic cover she and Sydney had put on it.

"I gave my neighbor's daughter the dishes and pans when she went off to college. I wasn't going to use them. And I think one of the cushions in the kitchen booth is missing."

"How much do you want for it?" Dale asked, testing the crank on the roof vent.

"You can't still want to use this." Taren gave a patronizing laugh. "It's disgusting."

"Do you want to rent it or sell it outright? I can do either." Dale was undeterred, in spite of Taren's condescending smirk. "Look, I need a temporary place to live. I'd pitch a tent but some asshole would probably steal it. This has a bed and a bathroom. That's all I need."

"Can't you stay with Zoe or Bryant?"

"Zoe doesn't have room and Bryant is too far away. I'll pay whatever you think is fair." She hoped she didn't end up in a bidding war over this old thing.

"If you want it that bad you can have it. It's yours anyway. Sydney said you paid for it. I don't know why she thought I wanted a trailer."

"She said you liked nature so she thought you'd go camping."

"I do. I like trees and mountains and all that but you and Sydney were the camp lovers. Not me. And what was I supposed to tow it with? My car wouldn't even get it out of the backyard."

"How much?" Dale pulled her wallet from her back pocket, hoping she had enough to cover whatever Taren decided it was worth. Or at least enough to make a down payment.

"Nothing." Taren peeled the trailer key off her key ring and held it out for Dale.

"I won't take it unless I can pay for it."

"Okay." Taren thought a moment. "Forty dollars. That's how much it will cost to have this part of the yard reseeded and fertilized."

Dale counted out fifty dollars, folded it and handed it to Taren.

"I said forty," she said, pushing it back.

"Use the extra ten to plant a lilac bush in this corner. Sydney loved lilacs."

Taren seemed momentarily taken aback at the sentiment. She nodded, slipping the money into her pocket.

Dale looked down at the license plate. She knew she was looking for trouble if she towed a trailer across town with an out-of-date plate but she didn't have a choice. There wasn't time to find the title, file taxes and license it. Still, Joplin had far more pressing problems than one unlicensed travel trailer. Taren seemed to realize Dale's dilemma. She stared at the license plate but said nothing. That surprised Dale. She expected to get a lecture or at least a warning.

"By the way, the propane tanks are full," Taren said, carrying her gardening tools out of the trailer. "I had them filled when we had that ice storm last winter. I thought I could use the stove in the trailer if the power was out but I never needed it."

"I'll be glad to pay for the propane."

"No, no. I just wanted you to know they should be full."

"Thanks." Dale was now officially in Taren Dorsey's debt. With only sixteen dollars in her wallet and the power still out at her bank, she couldn't access the funds in her account. She was embarrassed she couldn't insist on paying for the propane. Sixteen dollars wasn't enough to cover one of the tanks, let alone two.

Dale backed her truck into the yard while Taren guided her around trees and flowerbeds.

"Little more. Little more." Taren waved her back. "Right there! Stop!" She watched as Dale dropped the trailer hitch onto the ball and attached the safety chain. "That's all you have to do?" She seemed amazed at how easy it was.

"Yep." She yanked up on the tongue to make sure the hitch was secure. "Lock it down and you're good to go."

Taren's eyes drifted over Dale's truck, discreetly moving from one dent to the next.

"It looks worse than it is," Dale said.

"I didn't say anything."

"Zoe thinks I shouldn't drive it."

"If it gets you where you're going, why not? This is a special time. What we thought was normal has all been changed." Taren seemed suddenly lost in a memory.

"What?" Dale asked, wondering what she had done now.

"Oh, nothing. I was just remembering Sydney told me once that you'd teach me how to drive a stick shift. She said all I had to do was ask."

"I don't remember her saying that."

"Sydney had a strange sense of humor."

"I better get going." Dale wasn't in the mood to reminisce. She had a trailer to set up. Taren watched as she eased the trailer out of the backyard and over the curb into the street.

"Hey, Dale," Taren called, waving Dale to a stop.

"Yeah?" Dale said, putting the window down.

"I didn't tell you but I should have. I'm really sorry about your house. It's a terrible tragedy. You had lovely memories of Sydney there."

"Thanks."

"I mean it. You and I haven't had the best relationship but I want you to know I'm sincerely sorry for your loss. I can't imagine going through something like that. It must have been terrible. Are you okay?" Taren asked curiously. "You don't look very good."

"Yeah, I'm okay. I'm one of the lucky ones. I was able to walk away. By the way, did you know you sent me a text that was meant for Zoe?"

"If you mean the one yesterday, it was meant for you. I knew it was you who sent me that text from her phone." She pulled a wry smile. "Zoe always uses acronyms like I do. You didn't. It couldn't have been from her."

Dale felt her face flush. She hadn't fooled anybody and there was no need to lie. "Thanks again for letting me use the trailer." she said, hoping to hide whatever mindless look she had on her face.

"You're welcome." Taren gave a last look in the driver's window then stepped back. "Drive carefully."

Dale made a beeline to her neighborhood, hoping police didn't notice the trailer plate. She cleared a spot near the sewer cleanout in the backyard and backed the trailer into place.

"Are you going to live in that?" Milo came to watch.

"You bet." Dale opened the windows and door to air it out. "A little soap and water is all it needs."

"By the way, did you hear the water isn't safe? The city said not to use it for anything but flushing." He laughed. "We don't have anything that flushes."

"Are you ready, Milo?" Amelia called from the curb. She looked tired. "Ask Dale if she wants to go with us."

"Yes. Do you want some lunch?" Milo seemed excited to offer the invitation. "Come with us."

"Where are you going?" Dale remembered the limited funds in her wallet. It wouldn't buy much when she still had a list of supplies she needed.

"The high school parking lot. They're serving lunch to storm victims and volunteers. Come." He waved her on.

"Are you sure anyone can just show up?"

"Absolutely. I work with one of the volunteers. They're cooking hamburgers and hot dogs."

Dale was hungry and just the mention of food made her mouth water. As much as she didn't want to take charity she wasn't sure how long she could stretch sixteen dollars. She agreed and walked with them the five blocks to the high school.

The destroyed two-story brick building was a gruesome reminder of what had happened. Large tents had been set up in the parking lot as feeding stations and emergency distribution sites. Tractor-trailers were being unloaded with cases of bottled water, cleaning supplies, plastic tarps, canned goods, baby formula, diapers and boxes of donated clothing. Volunteers in reflective vests ranged in age from teenagers to senior citizens. Some in aprons stood at the row of barbecue grills. Some manned the food lines, handing out whatever was ready. Teenagers cleared and cleaned the tables, did fetch-and-carry duty and helped unload incoming supplies. As if they had been coached, every one of the volunteers was smiling and friendly, willing to listen or offer a hug.

Dale moved down the line, accepting a hamburger, scoop of baked beans and a bag of chips. She picked a bottle of water from one of the coolers filled with ice then found a seat. Milo and Amelia had drifted off to visit with friends. Dale was just as glad. She wasn't in the mood to visit. She ate in silence, occasionally overhearing someone's survival story or heartbreaking loss. She didn't want to share her story or relive how she found someone's arm in the street. That was for her to know. The long tables of weary people, many of them with stunned looks on their faces, were a reminder she was not alone in this tragedy. She didn't know these people but she felt a kinship for them.

She dropped her trash in a barrel. She didn't have time to sit and chat. She had a trailer to clean. She was ready to head back when she noticed a bin with bottles of hand sanitizer, hundreds of them. Next to it were tables of paper towels, work gloves, spray cleaner, toilet paper, batteries, flashlights and trash bags, all the things she needed and would have to buy.

"Do you need a box or a bag?" a cheery woman asked, holding out an empty cardboard box. Dale didn't want to take anything. These supplies were for those in real need. "They're still unloading so if there's something you need and don't see, let someone know and we'll see if we can find it." She stroked Dale's arm sympathetically. "If you need someone to help carry, we've got some strong young people."

Dale had said no thanks, but she must have looked pathetic and needy. The woman dropped a bottle of sanitizer in the box and handed it to Dale then steered her down the aisle of tables.

"These work gloves are only cotton but they're better than nothing." She dropped a pair in the box as well. When Dale admitted she had a trailer to clean so she could live in it to discourage looting the woman went to work filling the box until Dale needed both hands to hold it.

"This is very generous of you. I feel guilty taking all this when so many families were affected."

"This has all been donated for people just like you. We've got more coming, lots more. It's the least we can do. Here, take these, too." She placed a package of pudding cups on top. "You know, I heard Tyson is donating a truckload of chicken so tomorrow is barbecue chicken." She grinned knowingly.

"I know it's none of my business but did you lose your house in the tornado?" Dale thought her very kind for a storm victim.

"No. I'm from Iowa. A bunch of us came down to help. It's such a tragedy. I heard they found another body in Home Depot and one in the apartments up the street."

"Thanks again for your help and for the supplies."

Dale had heard the mention of Home Depot with a sinking feeling. Another body in Home Depot. Was it anyone she knew? Was it an employee? She fought the urge to set the box down and call David. She wanted to know who was found but then again she didn't.

By the time she returned to the trailer her shoulder was screaming for an Advil, something she needed to put on her shopping list. She spent the afternoon cleaning the spilled potting soil and cobwebs from her new home. She also removed the trailer hitch coupler so no one could hook up the trailer and drag it away.

She again called her insurance company. "This is Dale Kinsel. I've left several messages but I haven't heard back from you yet. I don't have my policy number but I'm sure you have that in your files. Please call me so we can set up a meeting. I have both vehicle and home damage." It was hard not to sound exasperated. "I know you're probably busy but I need to hear from you. Even a text message would be appreciated."

Dale locked the trailer and headed to Zoe's to finish her laundry. Tonight she would sleep in her new home, thanks to Taren's ability to overlook their differences...for now.

# CHAPTER FIVE

Dale came out of the bathroom, towel-drying her hair. With no potable water in the trailer yet she knew a hot shower would become a luxury. Zoe's offer to use her laundry facilities would also come in handy.

"You get your couch back," Dale said, pulling laundry out of the dryer and stuffing it in trash bags.

"Oh? Where are you going?" Zoe leaned her elbows on the counter, seeming more interested in the text she was composing.

"I put a trailer on my property. We've had looters in the neighborhood and the cops said we need greater presence to discourage theft."

"Looters?" Zoe looked up from her phone with a scowl. "What the hell is there to steal? That whole part of town is trashed. They ought to shoot the little creeps on sight." She went back to texting. "What kind of trailer are you going to use? Some of those RV motor homes are really nice. Flat screen TV, sunken bathtub, slide-out living room. Nicer than my apartment. Bigger too." Zoe grinned in Dale's direction. "You can have us over for a slumber party."

"It's just a sixteen-foot travel trailer."

"You can't live in a dinky little travel trailer," Zoe said disgustedly.

"I'd live in my house but it's a wee bit drafty just now. And what's wrong with a trailer? It has a generator and I can hook up to the sewer. You and I stayed in one that summer we spent in Galveston."

"That was twenty years ago. We were camping out."

"So, I'll be camping out in my own backyard."

Zoe hesitated then squinted suspiciously. "Don't tell me you're getting that trailer back from Taren, the one you and Sydney had. You can't stay in that."

"There's nothing wrong with it. Everything works just fine," Dale argued, although she hadn't really checked everything.

"It smelled like garlic." Zoe wrinkled her nose.

"It smelled like oregano. And that was years ago. It doesn't smell anymore. I checked."

"You went over to Taren's house?" Zoe chuckled. "That must have been something for the record books. Did you two claw and scratch at each other like cats fighting over a mouse?"

"No! She had the trailer and didn't use it. So I asked if I could."

"And she said yes?"

"Yes. I needed a place to stay, Zoe. I can't live here forever. By the way, do you still have that sleeping bag I gave you?"

"Talk about camping out," Zoe snickered. "What? Taren didn't give you the sheets for the bed?"

"I don't think there were any. And the sleeping bag will work fine for now."

Zoe pulled a sleeping bag from the hall closet. "Do you have a pillow?"

"I'll get one."

"Here. You can have this one."

Dale carried a load to the truck. When she returned for another armful Zoe was back to texting. "I just thought of something," she said, texting as she talked. "You can't live in that trailer. You won't have TV. All the wires are down."

"I can live without television for a while."

"No, you can't. You're always watching sports. Tennis, basketball, volleyball. If it has a ball, you watch it. You're addicted. You'll go crazy in that dinky little trailer without a TV."

"I'm not addicted and I won't go crazy. I've got a lot to do to keep me busy."

"I know you. You'll be knocking on my door every time there's some big game on." Zoe cackled. "Well, I'm not watching baseball. I hate it. It's boring. All those guys do is spit and play with themselves." She frowned at the trash bags. "Do you need some help?" A surprising offer.

"Thanks, but I can do it. I'll call you later if I can get a cell." She gave her sister a hug and carried her laundry out to the truck.

Dale opened a text from Janice as she sat at the corner.

*How's it going? I saw pics on the news. It's terrible. All those people killed. I cried and cried when I saw it. I'm worried about you. Call me, honey. I need to hear your voice.*

Dale leaned her head back against the headrest and heaved a desperate sigh. She wasn't sure she was up to a conversation with anyone. Not tonight. She tapped out a text and sent it, hoping Janice would understand.

*Hey there, stranger. It's like pulling teeth to get a cell. Don't worry about me, honey. I'm doing okay. Really. By the way, remember I mentioned my niece's wedding two weeks from Saturday? We'll talk about it, okay? I hope you can go. Take care.*

Dale took a deep breath as she neared the disaster zone. Each time she entered the blast zone of demolished homes and businesses she felt a twinge of pain. Or was it a flush of anxiety? Whatever it was, she couldn't explain it but it was real. She pulled into her driveway, steering around the growing mountain of debris and tree branches she had piled along the curb, now tall enough that she couldn't see over it.

She spent her evening picking through the debris until it was too dark to see. It seemed like an endless job of sorting through what was worth keeping and what was trash. She piled the rafters and floorboards to one side. She'd probably toss them on the pile to be hauled away later but for now throwing away hundreds of board feet of seasoned lumber seemed a waste.

Dale wasn't afraid of the dark. At least she didn't think she was. She was athletic, quietly confident and independent. She drove a truck and carried her wallet in her back pocket. But the silence and pitch-black darkness outside her trailer window had her staring at the ceiling, too afraid to sleep. It wasn't until sometime after midnight that she was able to close her eyes for a few hours' sleep. She occasionally awoke and for those first few groggy moments she lived in blissful oblivion until the pain in her shoulder and the fact she was living in an oregano-perfumed trailer kicked in. She turned on the flashlight and scanned the inside of the trailer, shining the light into every crack and corner. Satisfied she was alone and safe, she went back to sleep.

She woke at six fifteen, something her body did automatically. The morning was quiet but she knew it wouldn't last. Sooner or later the roar of chain saws and traffic would fill the neighborhood. But for now it was quiet. No tell-tale sounds of barking dogs and chirping birds. And sadly, no plaintive meow of Butterscotch looking for a treat. She missed that. She wouldn't have thought she would but she had grown accustomed to her sweet face and saucy independence. She couldn't help wonder how many pets were lost across the disaster zone, sucked up by the deadly swirling winds. And that tugged at her heartstrings.

She dressed and walked to the relief center. The smell of coffee filled the tent along with fresh volunteers and their smiling faces. Breakfast was crates of donated fruit, granola bars and Krispy Kreme doughnuts until they ran out.

As she rounded the corner on her way back she noticed Taren's red hatchback in the driveway. Taren climbed out, carrying a folder. Dale couldn't help wonder what she had done now.

"Hello." Taren scanned the pile of trash growing along the street, a wounded look on her face.

She looked dressed for a picnic, Dale thought. And she had on those damn sequined sunglasses. At least she was wearing sensible shoes for tromping around a disaster zone.

"Be careful where you walk," Dale warned her. "There are nails everywhere."

"Yes, I see that." She looked down at a board with protruding nails. "I thought you'd want this." She handed Dale the folder.

"What is it?" *Oh, boy. Here it comes. She wants something.*

"It's the trailer title and registration renewal." She opened the envelope and took out the sticker. "This goes on the license plate."

"Where did that come from?"

"I didn't want you to have trouble with an unlicensed trailer. Sydney left it to me so technically I'm responsible. I was worried it was going to cost a fortune to get it current but Joplin is waiving late fees. Something to do with the state of emergency we're under. Lots of people are registering old trailers and campers to use until they find someplace to live."

"With the supply and demand I bet you could sell it for a tidy profit." Dale wondered if Taren was having second thoughts about how cheaply she sold it.

"Well, if you want to sell it, go ahead. It's in your name now. It's your responsibility."

"If I sold it I'd be literally living in the street." Dale looked over at the paint-faded trailer and gave a sarcastic grin. "It's not much but its home."

"Maybe you can use these." She pulled two solar powered yard lights from a store sack and held them up. "You could leave them outside during the day to charge then take them inside at night. They could be like nightlights. Maybe one in the bathroom and one by the bed." She shrugged indifferently. "You don't have to take them if you don't want them."

"Actually that's a great idea. Yes, I want them. Thank you. How much do I owe you for the license and the lights?"

"Nothing. You'll have enough to replace. Consider it my contribution to rebuilding Joplin."

The list of indebtedness to Taren was growing and Dale didn't like it. She appreciated it but that didn't make it any easier to accept. "Taren, this is very nice of you but I can't have you doing that. I can't live in your debt."

"Sure you can. Besides, I'm not doing it for you. I'm doing it for Sydney." Taren opened the sack. "I've got one more thing I thought you might want." She carefully pulled out a small picture frame. She blew off the dust then handed it to Dale. "With all the things you lost, I thought you might not have one of these."

It was a picture of Sydney and Dale sitting on the end of Bryant's boat dock watching the sunset. Their toes touched the surface of the water, ripples of amber fire radiating outward.

"Where did you get this?" Dale studied Sydney's silhouette. "I don't remember this."

"I took it. It was Kim's birthday. Remember? She had that cake with green frosting." Taren gave a reflective sigh. "Syd looked so peaceful that day. She didn't feel good but she wanted to see the sunset."

"Yeah." Dale ran her finger over Sydney's image. Did she want the picture? Of course she did. But she'd thought the grief-stricken days were all behind her. The tornado had crushed her emotional defenses, leaving her perilously brittle. She wasn't sure this was the right time to accept it. "Here, you better keep it."

"Were you able to salvage your pictures of Sydney?"

"Some of them." Dale looked away for fear Taren would see her eyes and know she was lying. She had lost them all. All the snapshots of their vacations and family gatherings. Even the silly ones they'd taken of each other. And the hundreds of digital shots were trapped in an inaccessible hard drive on her waterlogged laptop that didn't survive the tornado.

Taren studied Dale a moment, almost critically. She then headed for the trailer, carrying the frame. "If it's okay, I'll leave it here for now. I'll put it on the table."

Dale didn't argue with her. When Taren returned she had a worried look, as if she needed to say something but didn't know how to begin.

"What?" Dale asked.

"I have some news but it isn't good. I wasn't sure if I should tell you."

"Well, this is the week for it. Shoot."

"It's Phyllis. The umpire from the softball game." She crossed her arms and took a deep preparatory breath.

"Oh, Phil?" Dale chuckled. "She's probably going to be calling for me to get her a generator or something. I think her neighborhood had tornado damage. Get me good deal, Ms. Dale, she'll say."

Taren slowly shook her head.

"What? Her neighborhood didn't get hit?"

"Yes, it was hit. They found Phyllis's hearing aids on the counter in the bathroom. She must have left them there. She didn't hear the sirens."

"What are you saying?" Dale held her breath, afraid to breathe or it would be true.

"I know you and she were friends. That's why I wanted to tell you. I didn't want you to hear about it in the newspaper or on TV. Phyllis didn't make it. Her roof collapsed. She died in her living room." Taren's eyes went soft. "I'm really sorry. She was a nice person. Very generous. Always volunteering. A truly kind soul. I'm sure if she were here she'd be right in the middle, helping whoever needed it."

"Yeah, I'm sure." Dale scanned the sky, trying to make sense of it. Phyllis wasn't supposed to be a victim of the tornado. No one Dale knew was supposed to be a victim. It wasn't supposed to hit that close to home, but this was the second friend she had lost. She sat down on the steps of the trailer. Her knees felt weak. Her muscles began to twitch involuntarily. She held her head in her hands and breathed deep, hoping to clear her mind. This was the second time she felt faint. The other was when she found the arm.

*Come on, Dale. Snap out of it. Grow up. Sure it's bad. Phyllis was a friend but this isn't the way to reconcile it. And what will Taren think. She already thinks I'm tidal scum.*

"Are you okay?" Taren's hand touched her shoulder.

Dale couldn't speak. She just nodded.

"I'm really sorry. I didn't mean to upset you." Taren knelt in front of her, folding her hands over Dale's.

"It's not you. I just didn't expect it." Dale took several deep breaths to regain her composure.

"Maybe I should have just mailed the title and registration."

Dale looked up with surprise.

"Mail! I forgot all about my mail. Saturday was my last delivery. I don't even have a mailbox anymore."

"According to the newspaper you're supposed to go to the main post office downtown to pick up your mail. There will be no mail service in the tornado zone for the foreseeable future. And just so you know, there's a crowd out the door and down the street. I drove past there on my way here."

Dale groaned, knowing she'd have another wasted day waiting in line.

"May I make a suggestion? Why don't you have your mail forwarded to Zoe's address? You can do that online. You don't even have to go in."

"I don't have a computer or Internet access anymore."

Taren went to her car and returned with her cell phone. She opened the post office website and handed the phone to Dale. "Do it on here."

"Are you sure?" Dale squinted at the tiny screen, trying to read the instructions.

"I'm sure. Touch the bar at the top."

"Oops, what did I do?" The screen changed to a weather forecast.

"Well, it looks like rain and temperatures in the seventies in North Carolina," she said with a chuckle. "May I?"

"Sure." Dale handed the phone back and waited.

"What's Zoe's address?"

Taren tapped it in then showed Dale the screen. "I had them email the confirmation to me. I'll print it off and bring it to you. Is that okay?"

"Yes, that's fine." Dale's cell phone rang in her pocket. "Finally, my insurance agent. I need to take this."

"I've got an appointment anyway. I'm really sorry about Phyllis," she said then headed to her car.

"Taren," Dale called, muffling the phone to her chest. "Thank you."

She nodded but said nothing.

"Hello, this is Dale Kinsel," she said, watching as Taren drove away, her little red strawberry zooming up the street. "I'm sorry. Would you repeat that?" Whatever the woman on the phone said had gone in one ear and out the other. Dale didn't know why. She had been waiting for this call for two days and here she was, staring at a car's taillights as it drove down the street. An adjuster was scheduled to be out on Thursday.

The rest of the week was one frustration and delay after another. City water wasn't safe to use until Saturday. Permits were required to be in the disaster zone and the lines to get them were long and confusing. For many, proving ownership was nearly impossible. A curfew was instituted to combat looting with only marginal success. The loss of three of Joplin's largest grocery stores meant the ones that remained had long lines and shortages. Generators and chain saws were hot items and hard to find. Flat tires were commonplace. Dale had had two in three days. Occasional fires broke out in damaged and destroyed homes, sending a plume of smoke over the devastation like the remnants of a bombed-out city. The insurance adjuster had been pushed back to Friday—hopefully.

A spark of good news came in the form of a text from David, the store manager. Home Depot was committed to rebuild with six months as the target date. A temporary structure was going up in the parking lot and would be ready within two weeks. It would provide the essentials Joplin residents would need as they repaired and rebuilt. Dale knew it was more than just a devotion to Joplin. It was financial. Home Depot didn't want to miss out on the millions of dollars in sales the tornado created. It also meant Dale could go back to work. Home Depot had guaranteed her a job, a place to go to take her mind off what she had been through.

It was Saturday morning when a man in a pickup truck with ladder racks pulled up at the curb. He sat writing on a clipboard and talking on a cell phone for several minutes before climbing out and introducing himself as the insurance adjuster. He measured, took pictures and asked a few questions with an almost robotic indifference. When Dale pressed him on how much and when she would receive her settlement he admitted that wasn't his job. He submitted a report of damages but the check would come from the central office in St. Louis. All he could promise was she'd hear something in the mail within a week or two. Since Dale's auto insurance was with the same company she hoped he would handle the damage to her truck as well.

"Sorry, ma'am. I don't handle vehicle claims. You'll have to contact your agent for that."

He drove away, leaving Dale with no more information than before he arrived. Zoe had told her to keep calling and eventually the insurance company would tell her something. But Dale knew that wouldn't ingratiate herself to anyone. And probably wouldn't get her an answer.

Dale was on her way back from lunch at the relief center when she noticed Marvin in his backyard. He was picking at the ground with a shovel with a broken handle.

"Hey there, Marvin. How's it going?"

He didn't look up. He seemed tired, as if the job was too much for him.

"Can I help with something?" Dale asked, climbing over the rubble to where he was digging.

"My damn shovel's broke." He scratched the point of it across the ground. A large shoebox sealed with masking tape was perched on a nearby downed tree. Marvin's long gray comb-over had fallen over his eyes but he didn't seem to care. He continued to work, feebly scraping at a would-be hole. Dale assumed he was burying some papers or broken mementoes he didn't want put out with the trash. As eccentric as he was, she still felt sorry for him. Like everyone else on the street, he had lost his home.

"Can I help?" She reached for the shovel. He stepped back and watched as she dug a hole large enough for the box. Once it was buried and the dirt patted into place, he stood quietly, staring at the mound of dirt, muttering something Dale couldn't hear.

"Amen," he said then pulled a handkerchief from his back pocket and blew his nose. "I called her to come out but she was scared."

"Who?"

"She was under the bed. I couldn't reach her." He looked up, tears glistening in his eyes. "I had to leave her. She wouldn't come out."

Dale suddenly knew who they had buried. "Your dog?"

"My Jenny. Goddamn tornado took my Jenny."

"Oh, Marvin. I'm so sorry. She was a sweet dog." No wonder he'd wandered the neighborhood after the storm with a dazed look on his face. He stood at the grave, mumbling something about going for a walk. Dale left him to his grief as tears welled up in her own eyes. She hoped whoever found Butterscotch gave her a dignified burial as well. Someplace in the shade where flowers bloom.

# CHAPTER SIX

Zoe pulled into her driveway behind Dale's truck. She was home early from work, carrying a pizza box.

"What are you doing sitting out here in your truck?" she said, looking in the driver's side window. "Aren't you going to start your laundry?"

Dale tossed the packet of papers she had been reading on the dashboard. She had stared at them long enough. The numbers weren't going to change.

"What's wrong?" Zoe slung her purse strap over her shoulder impatiently.

"I got a statement from the insurance company today," Dale said flatly, wondering if her sister really cared.

"Okay," she said, reading Dale's face. "But why isn't this good news?"

Dale handed her the paper. Zoe studied it a moment then asked, "Why will the check be made out to you and the bank?"

"Because they hold the mortgage. They dispense the funds to me as the house is rebuilt."

"What is this amount?"

"That's it. That's my coverage. That's the maximum amount that will be sent to me."

"WHAT?" Zoe said it loud enough for the neighbors to hear.

"That's the coverage on my house the way the policy was written. That includes contents."

"Contents? You mean your furniture and things inside is part of this?" Zoe's eyes widened.

"Yep. I'm supposed to rebuild my house with that." She flipped her fingernail against the paper.

"What the hell? Your house was worth way more than this."

"No kidding."

"What happened? Did your agent screw up your policy? If he did, they should fix it. It's not your fault if he's an asshole."

"That's what I thought. But it wasn't my agent who wrote the policy like this." Dale took an exasperated breath. "It was Sydney. She had the policy written to cover the market value at the time we bought the house. That's all. There was no cost of living adjustment. No increase for actual replacement cost. The policy was written to just cover the mortgage. She didn't allow for the equity we already had in the property from the down payment either. The agent tried to talk her out of it but she wouldn't listen."

"Why did you let her do something so stupid?" Zoe glared at her.

"Zoe." Dale lowered her eyes. She didn't want to see Zoe's contempt for Sydney's decision. Sydney couldn't have known a tornado would rip the house apart. She certainly didn't mean to hurt Dale.

"Can't you say she did it without your permission?"

"She was my partner. I gave her permission to handle our financial affairs. I'm responsible for what she did. I have to live with it."

"But how are you going to rebuild your house with this?" She sailed the paper onto Dale's lap.

"I don't know."

"Well, you can't live in that dinky trailer forever. It doesn't even have air conditioning. It's already in the eighties. What are you going to do when it's a hundred and ten?"

"I don't know, Zoe." She pushed the paper back into the envelope and climbed out. "Sweat, I guess."

Dale hurried through her laundry, stuffing still damp clothes back into the pillowcase. She'd hang them around the trailer to dry. She'd heard all she wanted to hear from Zoe for one evening.

Dale pulled into the church parking lot, still undecided if she would go inside. She had a dozen reasons not to. She was frustrated with the insurance company and with Zoe's pompous attitude. She was tired. She was fighting a PMS headache. And she was frustrated over how she should deal with Taren. It was easier when their paths didn't cross. She sat in the truck, checking email and texts on her phone to delay her decision. They weren't important messages but it helped ease the apprehension. She took a deep breath then tapped in Janice's phone number. She had been selfish when she told her not to come to Joplin. She knew that. Janice had wanted to be supportive and comforting and she turned her away. It was time to remedy that. She wasn't sure how much she had to offer but she could at least try.

"Hi there," Janice said softly. "How are you doing, peaches?"

"I'm okay. Tired but okay. How about you? How's work?"

"I'm worried about you. I don't know what to do to help. Tell me something you need. How about a few days at my house away from Joplin? I'll cook for you and we can just chill. What do you say? How about a little R & R and a good fuck?"

"Sounds wonderful but I can't. I'm trying to get my insurance settlement squared away and I start back to work in a couple days." Dale could always use a good fuck but somehow that seemed unimportant compared to her list of to-do's.

"I know you're preoccupied with your house and all but promise me you'll tell me if there is anything I can do."

"There is."

"Tell me, baby. Tell me what you need."

"My niece's wedding. It's next Saturday. Church ceremony then a dinner reception afterward at the VFW. Go with me.

What do you say? I'll pick you up at two. I need a day with family and friends."

"I agree. You absolutely do need a day of fun. And I'd love to go with you," Janice replied willingly. "We'll have an awesome time."

"Great. I'm looking forward to it and to you."

Dale didn't know how to tell Janice how much she needed this time away. Just to hear her enthusiasm was comforting enough. She finally powered off her cell phone and wiped her sweaty palms on her pants. She was late but headed inside. The small group of six or seven were in mid-prayer as she quietly took a seat and bowed her head.

"Amen," a woman said then smiled at Dale. "Hello stranger. We missed you."

"Hi, Kay. I missed you, too."

Kay Timbers was a thin woman with big teeth behind a wide smile. She had a weathered face and gravelly voice. She sat with her legs crossed over her lap yoga style, cradling a foam cup of black coffee. She was the only person Dale recognized but that didn't surprise her. It had been over a year since she attended. It would have been nice to see a few old faces but that wasn't why Dale had stopped by.

"We're going to do things a little differently this time," Kay announced, then reached over and patted Dale on the knee. "It's good to see you, Dale. Why don't you go ahead and start us out?"

"Okay." Dale took a deep breath and waited while a flood of memories washed over her. Memories full of guilt and regret. It wasn't until she felt a peaceful calm take hold that she began. "My name is Dale. I'm an alcoholic. It's been a little over three years since my last drink."

"Hello, Dale," the group said in unison. Each stranger instantly became an understanding, non-judgmental fellow warrior. Dale needed that. She needed to be grounded in her past. She had come a long way from the hapless drunk she had once been. She had acknowledged her addiction and worked the steps. Now she needed to remember how much she had to be grateful for and how much she had to lose. If she let it, the tornado could steal more than just her home. She wasn't about to let that happen.

They went around the circle, each person proclaiming their own truth. Some proudly. Some humbly. A man in his forties with a cigarette behind his ear seemed eager to share his story of newfound sobriety. He rambled on for ten minutes, his eyes darting back and forth nervously. Dale recognized that look. His profanity-laced rhetoric couldn't hide his fear and anxiety. He had been sober five days. Dale bet he wouldn't make six. He hadn't yet humbled himself before his addiction. He professed control over it and that would be his downfall. Accept you are powerless over alcohol or it will conquer you, she wanted to tell him. But Dale knew he had to face this battle for himself. No one could do it for him.

"Is anyone here for their first meeting?" Kay asked, her eyes falling gently on a woman who looked scared to death. She encouraged her to share whatever she wanted to say. She wasn't ready. Dale knew that would come with time.

Kay Timbers was Dale's sponsor. They had shared hours of conversations, many of them filled with tears as Dale fought her battle for sobriety. Dale hadn't spoken to Kay in months. She hadn't forgotten Kay's calming voice and understanding smile. She hadn't forgotten how Kay had challenged her to seek her own truth.

Dale was glad she came. After the meeting she climbed back in her truck satisfied she had done the right thing. She had a lot to be thankful for in spite of what she had lost. She didn't want to give that up. One day at a time, she reminded herself. One day at a time. She took a deep cleansing breath and headed home. She would spend the night in a trailer but, like she had done for three years, she would do it sober. And for that she was most thankful.

# CHAPTER SEVEN

"That store they're putting up in the Home Depot parking lot looks like a circus tent. Did you see it?" Zoe said.

"Yes, I saw it. It's not a circus tent. It's a semi-rigid retail store. And it's temporary until the store is rebuilt." Dale reached in the dryer to see if her jeans were dry.

"Someone said the floor is just the parking lot pavement."

"It's temporary, Zoe. So long as it's flat and safe, what difference does it make?"

"When do you start back to work?"

"The crew from Atlanta is finishing up stocking the shelves this weekend. We're having a meeting to go over the inventory tomorrow morning."

"Saturday? That's the wedding? Aren't you going down with me after breakfast? I promised I'd help set up the table decorations."

"I can't, Zoe. But I'll be there for the wedding. Why are you so giddy about this thing? I thought you hated weddings."

"I don't hate weddings. I hate marriage. At least the asshole I married." She made a gruesome face. "But you should see Judy in her wedding gown. She looks like one of those dolls with a big skirt on top of a birthday cake. Did you hear Kim and Bryant are giving them a front loading washer and dryer as a wedding gift?"

"Yes. I got them a discount at the store last month."

"Taren asked me what they needed. I told her I didn't know. Did she ask you?"

"Heck no. Why would she ask me?"

"What is Janice giving them?"

"I have no idea. She doesn't have to give them anything."

"Sure she does. She's invited to a wedding. You bring something." Zoe scowled. "She's still coming, right?"

"Yes, she's coming. I'm picking her up in Neosho after the store meeting."

"I wonder who Taren's bringing." Zoe slipped a curious look at Dale.

"Maybe she's coming alone."

"No, she's bringing someone. Her RSVP card said she was bringing a guest. I bet it's that coach from school. She's a little older but a nice-looking woman. One of those energetic types, like Taren. I saw them walking across campus together."

"A coach?" Dale couldn't help but chuckle. Why was Taren Dorsey dating a coach? Better yet, why was a coach dating someone with athletic skills that would fit in a thimble? It was hard for Dale to imagine Taren dating anyone at all.

"What are you wearing?" Zoe asked in a critical tone. "This is a wedding. Not a riverside picnic."

"Don't get all freaked out on me. I went shopping. I got a pair of beige slacks and a vest. I'm wearing a lavender silk shirt with it." She waited to see Zoe's reaction then added, "And sneakers." She couldn't keep from laughing.

"You better not." Zoe wrinkled her nose. "I'm glad to see you've put some color in your wardrobe."

"It was on the mannequin when I walked in the store. Easy choice." Dale carried a load of laundry to the truck. It was getting late and she wasn't in the mood to argue fashion with her sister. She also didn't want to hear anymore about Taren and her date.

Dale headed to Home Depot bright and early Saturday morning. Her first tour of the temporary store was a little unsettling. She felt a strange sense of guilt as she walked the makeshift aisles. The tornado wasn't her fault. But the image of B.J. in his orange work apron seemed to follow her, roosting on top of the shelves. She knew he was gone. She had attended his memorial service, hard as it was. But she still couldn't keep from looking over her shoulder as if he were somehow shadowing her every move. The employees shared hugs and stories, several of the women clinging to each other as they roamed the store, familiarizing themselves with the inventory and learning how the new store would function.

"It's only half as big," one cashier said as they gathered around David and the other assistant managers. "How will you decide who gets to work and when? I can't survive on part-time hours."

"Don't worry, Glenda. Everyone will have their same hours. I know it'll be a little confusing at first and we may trip over each other." The crowd chuckled softly. "But we'll make it work. Home Depot is pledged to help all its employees and with your cooperation, we'll get through this. As you've seen, our stock has been reduced for now. We're going to carry the things people will need to repair and rebuild. If a customer wants to match something or special order an item not in stock, you'll direct them to the online counter where we'll have people to help them place the order. They can have it delivered right here to the store within a couple days. The Springfield and Pittsburg stores will be working with us. We want to keep our Home Depot customers coming back. We don't want them going down the street to the competition."

"How will we handle the Sunday sale flyer items?" Dale asked. "Will we have that inventory on hand?" She had already discussed it with David but asked so the other employees could hear.

He nodded to her. "Good question. We are going to try like hell to have everything in stock but we may have some shortages. We'll issue rain checks or possibly substitute a similar item. Look people, we know there are going to be glitches but we'll do our best to keep our customers happy. If they take their dollars down the street it's hard to get them back through our doors." David paused, took a deep breath then said with a catch in his throat. "Our Home Depot family has suffered a terrible loss. B.J. was one of us. He was a friend, a co-worker and an amazingly brave individual. I can't tell you how proud I am to have known him. He will be missed. His wife, Bonnie, is having a pretty rough time but she sent me a message to read to you and all his friends." He unfolded a letter, cleared his throat and began to read. Dale didn't want to listen. She drifted down an aisle, ignoring such words as sacrificed and unselfish. She didn't know why but she was mad at B.J. Sure, he was doing the heroic thing, helping to protect store customers. But he wasn't supposed to become one of the tornado victims.

"I encourage anyone who needs to talk about what they've been through to make an appointment," David continued. "A counselor will be available to all employees and their families. It's free. It's confidential. And I guarantee you won't be the only one."

It took another hour to finalize the work schedule before Dale was free to leave. She had a wedding to attend and she needed the distraction. She was more than ready for a day with her family away from stress and heartache.

By the time she changed into her dress clothes and made it to Janice's, she was thirty minutes late.

"Hi," she said with a smile as Janice opened the door. She was dressed but barefoot. They shared a kiss, a hug, then another passionate kiss as Dale stepped through the door. She enjoyed the kiss and the feel of a woman in her arms. "Are you ready?"

"Almost. I need to put on my makeup and do my hair. I'm running a little late."

"How long will it take you?" Janice was a femme. Dale guessed her prep time something approaching an hour. Which they didn't have.

"When is this wedding?"

"Not until four but it'll take hour to get there."

"We've got lots of time. Those things never start on time anyway. Why don't you watch TV or something?" She gave Dale a quick kiss then headed to the bathroom.

Dale wanted to ask why she wasn't ready but that would only delay things more. She paced nervously, repeatedly checking the time on her phone. They were going to be late.

"How are you doing?" she finally called, forcing a cheery tone.

"Almost ready." Janice stepped out, hooking an earring through her ear. "Have you seen my Bay-Blings?"

"Your what?"

"Bay-Blings. They're white sling-back sandals with rhinestones on the strap." She came into the living room and began searching the floor around the coffee table. "I think they're under there. Can you look while I change my top?"

Dale was willing to do anything to hurry things along. She lay on the floor, searching for the lost shoes.

"Found one," she announced. She moved her search under the couch then the recliner. "Found two. And I like that top. You don't need to change it."

Janice came out of the bedroom, smoothing a short sleeve cashmere sweater into the waist of her white slacks. She handed Dale a necklace then stood in front of her for assistance.

"You look very nice," Dale said, fumbling the delicate clasp into place. She placed a little kiss on the nape of her neck. "Shall we go?"

"Maybe I should change back into the other top. Do you like it better?" She stopped at the mirror by the front door, frowning at the fit of the sweater. "Does this sweater say wedding to you?"

"It says you look fine. Let's go." Dale put her hands on Janice's rear and steered her out the door.

The weekend traffic heading to Grove, Oklahoma and the Grand Lake of the Cherokees made the forty-mile trip seem like a hundred. They were definitely going to be late.

"Have you gone shopping for a new truck yet?" Janice asked.

Dale wasn't surprised. She knew this subject was on Janice's mind from the moment she saw Dale's battle-scarred pickup and had to slide across the driver's seat.

"They had a really nice-looking stepside at the dealership here in town," Janice continued. "Two-tone green. Chrome wheels. I think it's a Chevy. Do you want me to check the price for you? The window sticker says low mileage."

"Are you saying my truck isn't cherry anymore?" Dale teased, hoping to divert the conversation.

"Not hardly." Janice frowned at the plastic sheeting taped across the back window.

"It's not that bad. And it's all superficial damage. The tailgate and passenger door are the worst of it. It drives just fine. In fact, I'm getting better gas mileage than before the storm. It's streamlined now."

Janice didn't appreciate the joke. She pursed her lips then said, "Aren't you embarrassed to drive it? You've got a good job. You could get a decent vehicle, something without little dents all over it. Don't you have insurance?"

"Yes, I have insurance but with a high deductible." Dale wasn't sure this was any of Janice's business. They weren't at the point in their relationship where she needed to know the intimate details of Dale's finances. "Come on, buddy. I'm sure you can pull that boat faster than fifteen miles an hour," Dale said, pulling out to pass a flatbed truck. She darted around the line of traffic and headed into town, hoping Janice would drop the subject.

Dale circled the block searching for a parking spot. By the time she found a place to park and trotted up the church steps the ceremony was already underway. They slipped in the side entrance and found a seat in the last pew.

"By the power vested in me by the state of Oklahoma and before God and those assembled here, I now pronounce you husband and wife," the minister said. "You may now kiss the bride."

"We missed it," Dale said, swallowing back her anger. "They're done."

The crowd stood, everyone smiling as the organist began the recessional. Judy and Lucas started up the aisle, both of them grinning from ear to ear.

Dale stood on her toes to see the front pew where Kim was dabbing a tissue at her nose. Zoe was next to her, looking like a wedding professional with a day planner under her arm. They looked nice, dressed simply but stylishly. Taren was in the third row. She looked nice too, the collar of her pink blouse folded over the lapels of her jacket. Her blond hair hung to her shoulders, softly curled and gleaming. Her makeup was flawless. So was her smile as she watched Judy and Lucas. Taren's eyes drifted past the happy couple and fell softly on Dale. She acknowledged her with a polite nod. She seemed to notice Janice as well and tilted her head as if studying her.

"Who's the blonde?" Janice said, obviously seeing the exchange.

"Friend of the family," Dale said. She was still angry with Janice for making them miss the ceremony. She wasn't in the mood to explain her relationship with the woman. Dale looked past Taren to the woman standing next to her. She wondered if this was the coach-slash-date. She looked the part. Trim build, athletic and tanned, short hair, polo shirt with standup collar. She was positioned just inside Taren's interpersonal space. Of course she was in her *space*, Dale chided herself. They were in a church pew at a wedding. Why wouldn't she be? And why was she fueling Dale's curiosity? Dale saw Zoe through the crowd, scowling back at her, probably for being late.

"The one in the front row in the pink dress is my sister, Zoe," Dale said.

"The one who looks like she just sucked a lemon?"

"That's the one."

Dale and Janice filed out, following the receiving line through the crowded lobby to greet the newlyweds. Dale exchanged hugs with relatives and friends, most of whom she hadn't seen since the last family event. She hadn't prepared herself for the barrage of questions about the tornado but she knew she would have to answer them here or later at the reception.

"Whew," Janice groaned, sliding across the seat of the truck. She slipped out of her sandals and ruffled her hair. "That was crazy."

"Why crazy?" Dale pulled out to go to the reception, weaving her way through the back streets of Grove to avoid the traffic on the highway.

"Oh, nothing. Can we stop somewhere? I'm thirsty."

"There's a drive-through up here. What do you want?"

"Oh, no, never mind."

"No problem. I can run in the convenience store and get you a pop or something."

"I'll wait. There'll be a bar at the reception, right?"

"I think so."

Dale hadn't been able to handle alcohol in moderation but if Janice wanted a celebratory drink at the reception she wasn't going to stop her.

The reception was already a buzz of excitement when Dale and Janice entered the banquet room. Dale added her gift, a card containing a generous gift certificate, to the table scattered with yellow rose petals and glitter. She had added Janice's name to the card. After all, she didn't know anyone and Dale didn't mind sharing the gift. There was already a crowd forming at the bar. A few years ago Dale would have been one of those but that was a different Dale. She didn't need that.

Zoe was attending to details like the little general she tried to be. A DJ tested the microphone. Waitresses carried serving pans to the buffet table and lit the burners to keep them warm.

"I'll be right back," Janice said, squeezing Dale's hand then heading to the bar. Dale watched as Janice crossed the room, her wiggle a thing of beauty. Dale had admired it from the first moment they met. She gave a throaty moan and slipped her hands in her pants pockets, envisioning what she might be having for dessert later.

"Hello," a voice called.

Dale turned to see Taren and her date.

"Dale, this is Lee," Taren said, smiling at the woman. "She's our women's assistant athletic director and track coach. Lee, this is Dale Kinsel. The one I was telling you about."

"Hello, Dale," Lee said cheerfully, extending a hand for a hearty handshake.

"Hello." She couldn't help but wonder what exactly Taren had told her. Did the twinkle in Lee's eye mean she knew some deep secret Dale wished Taren hadn't shared?

"I hear you play softball," Lee said.

"I used to play. But that was years ago."

"That's not what Taren tells me." Lee wrapped her arm around Taren's waist, as if claiming her date.

"If you mean the charity softball tournament, I'm a one-trick pony. I play once a year. That's it." They shared a chuckle.

"Hey, peaches," Janice said, carrying two beer bottles. "It's open bar for the first hour." She grinned as if she'd just found a winning lottery ticket. She held one of the bottles out to Dale.

"No, thanks." Dale saw the look on Taren's face as she eyed the beer bottle.

"Ah, come on. Just one."

"No, thanks. I don't want one." Dale was positive she had told Janice she didn't drink. She may not have gone into detail but she had told her alcohol wasn't something she did. How could she have misunderstood? "Here, Lee. Have a longneck on us." She guided Janice's hand toward Lee.

"Thanks." She took a sip then clinked the bottle against Janice's. "Salut." She turned to Taren and asked, "Can I get you one?"

"Nothing for me, thank you."

"Hi. I'm Janice," she said to Lee before Dale could introduce her.

"Hi, Janice," Lee said, her eyes roaming the woman's figure.

A squeal from the microphone then Zoe announced, "Come on in everyone. Find your table. I hope I spelled everyone's name correctly on the place cards. If I didn't, my bad. Get yourself something to drink while the wedding party is having their pictures taken. We'll start the buffet in a few minutes."

"Shall we find our table?" Dale said, taking Janice's hand and leading her through the maze of round banquet tables.

"I think you two are over here, Dale," Taren called, pointing to place cards. "Next to us."

If this was Zoe's idea of a joke, Dale wasn't amused.

"Dale, you sit here." Janice hurried over and switched the cards. "Lee can sit next to me then Taren down there."

Dale held the chair for Janice. When Lee didn't do the same for Taren, Dale offered.

"Thank you," Taren said, seemingly surprised at the gesture.

"Dale, come with me. Quick," Zoe said, rushing up to her. She was out of breath and panic-stricken. "Will you excuse us?" she said to the women at the table then hooked her arm through Dale's insistently. "Hurry."

"I'll be back in a minute," Dale said as she was dragged away. "What is it, Zoe?"

"Come with me," she said through gritted teeth and a forced smile. She ushered her out into the lobby and down the hall. She looked both ways then opened the door to the men's restroom.

"I'm not going in there!"

"Bryant needs your help." Zoe pushed her through the door then followed.

"What did he do? Zip himself in his fly?"

"Worse."

As soon as the door closed behind them Dale heard the sound of violent retching coming from the stall.

"Is that Bryant?" Dale wrinkled her nose.

"Yes," Zoe whispered. "He's been in there throwing up for fifteen minutes. Do something. Help him." She scowled desperately.

"First of all, why are you whispering? Second of all, where is his wife? Why isn't she in here doing this?"

"I don't know. She's out there crying because her baby got married. She said he's just nervous but we can't get the pictures taken without him. He's the father of the bride. The photographer is waiting and we're paying him by the hour." The toilet flushed followed by another expulsion.

"Zoe, will you stop whispering? Bryant can't hear you. And let the damn photographer wait. Bryant is paying for it. If he wants to barf up his socks he has a right to stay in here as long as he wants." Dale peeled off several paper towels, wet them and handed them under the stall. Bryant took them then extended his hand for more. Dale obliged.

"Ask him if he needs Pepto or something."

"He's busy, Zoe."

"Just ask him. Open the door and ask him," she demanded.

"It's locked."

Zoe scowled angrily as she slipped her fingernail through the space and released the lever. The door opened, bumping Bryant in the rear. He wiped a ribbon of drool from his chin then turned a pale face to Dale.

*What can I get you*, she signed.

"Ask him if he needs Pepto-Bismol." Zoe used Dale to block her view.

"You ask him." Dale knew Zoe couldn't or wouldn't. She had never shown an interest in learning sign language. Even as a child she found it tiresome. It was easier to rely on Dale or someone else to sign for her. Dale didn't mind usually. But there were times Zoe's indifference seemed disrespectful. And this was one of them.

The restroom door opened. A man stood in the doorway with his hand on his zipper and a surprised look on his face.

"Can you give us a minute?" Zoe said sternly.

"Sure," he said apologetically and backed out. "Sorry."

Bryant didn't have to hear what was said to find it funny. He looked at Dale and burst out laughing.

*Zoe has a new job title*, he signed. *Bathroom Bitch.*

"What did he say?" Zoe asked.

"He said," Dale started but couldn't keep from laughing as well.

"What?" Zoe demanded.

Bryant touched Zoe's arm to get her attention and signed again, slowly and deliberately. He motioned for Dale to translate, grinning wickedly.

"If he's saying disgusting stuff, I don't want to know." Zoe stiffened. "Now, can we get out of here? The photographer is waiting."

Dale translated for Bryant. He looked at Zoe, bit his teeth together then pointed to his rear.

"Do you want me to translate that?" Dale chuckled.

"Oh, shut up." Zoe stormed out to Dale and Bryant's laughter.

Bryant stepped to the sink to wash his face.

*Are you okay?* Dale signed.

He nodded. *Thanks for your help, sis.*

*Anytime.*

Dale adjusted his tie and followed him out, both of them chuckling at the family rendezvous in the men's room. When she got back to the table Taren and Janice were huddled together with Lee, looking at her cell phone.

"Oh, my God," Janice gasped, her breast pressed against Lee's arm as she stared at the image of a mattress in a tree. "Dale, look at this. Show her the other one, Lee. The one with the two-by-four through the curb."

"I've seen it." Between the well-meaning questions at the wedding and Lee's pictures at the reception, Dale's hopes of ignoring the tornado for one day seemed nonexistent.

Janice seemed mesmerized by the images of destruction and chaos. Taren didn't show the same interest. She looked but turned away from the gruesome images.

"I bet Dale has seen all the storm damage she'll ever want to see," Taren offered sympathetically.

Taren was right. She didn't need to see Lee's trophy pictures of rowboats and trampolines on roofs and baby clothes snagged on telephone poles.

"Look at this one." Janice grabbed Dale's arm. "No wonder you didn't want me to come to up there. Did your house look like that?"

"Uh-huh." Dale didn't look.

She scanned the crowd, looking for someone, anyone, to change the topic of conversation.

"Did you see what they're setting up on the dessert table?" Taren leaned forward and looked across at Dale with raised eyebrows. "A chocolate fountain. How did they know?"

"Know what?" Dale asked, willing to go along with the diversion.

"A chocolate fountain at a wedding reception contains absolutely no calories or fat."

"Really?"

"Yes. It's a documented fact. And if there's dancing involved, the chocolate is actually beneficial."

"I'll remember that." Dale gave an acknowledging chuckle.

"Aren't you going to look at this?" Janice rubbed her hand up and down Dale's arm.

"No, I'm not. You look at it." Dale felt her blood pressure and frustration rising. "I saw it firsthand and that was enough. I saw the blood and the destruction. I felt the wind and heard the screaming. I don't need to see any of that crap," she snapped, unable to stop herself.

Taren covered Lee's phone with her hand and whispered something in her ear. Lee nodded and slipped the phone back in her pocket. Janice scowled contentiously at Taren but the squeal from the microphone stopped her from saying anything.

"I'm glad to report the pictures have been taken and we are ready for dinner," Zoe announced triumphantly. The crowd applauded. "But first, it's time for us to put our hands together and welcome Judy and Lucas, Mr. and Mrs. Bower."

The double doors opened and Judy and Lucas entered the reception hall hand in hand to raucous applause, both of them blushing brightly. Dale whistled and cheered. She was thankful for the interruption. Would Janice have said something caustic about Taren's interference? Perhaps. But Dale knew Taren could take care of herself.

"Shall we get in line?" Dale took Janice's hand and led her to the food line. Taren and Lee tactically chose to move up the other side of the table.

"What's this?" Janice asked, stirring a serving spoon through a pan of deep fried nuggets.

"Catfish. My brother insisted." Dale covered Janice's hand on the spoon and put some on both their plates. A tuxedo-sleeved arm and hand holding a plate appeared between them. Dale looked back at Bryant. *Speak of the devil. Do you want some of this?* she signed.

He nodded. Dale put a helping on his plate. He touched his fingertips to his mouth in thanks. He smiled at Janice and signed, *Hello there, young lady.*

Janice looked at Dale as if expecting clarification.

*This is my brother, Bryant. He's the father of the bride.* Dale signed as she spoke. *Bryant, this is Janice. She's with me so behave yourself.* She grinned at him.

*Nice to meet you.* He looked across at Taren and Lee coming up the other side of the food line and waved. Taren smiled and signed a reply. Dale had forgotten Taren had learned sign language when she was tutoring Judy. She watched proudly as they had a quick conversation before Bryant drifted back to his seat at the head table.

"Is he deaf or something?" Janice asked.

"Yes. That's why there was a translator up on the altar at the church." Dale plopped a spoon of tartar sauce on her fish.

"Can't he just read lips?"

"No, not very well. Not everyone can do that." Dale led the way back to their table. "I'll teach you to sign if you want to learn."

"Why do I need to learn? You already know how." Janice shrugged it off.

"Sounds like Zoe," Dale muttered under her breath.

They talked about plans to meet for dinner and a movie next weekend while they ate. Janice teased about making out in the balcony, bringing a blush to Dale's face.

"Dance with me," Janice said as Dale returned to the table with seconds.

"We haven't finished dinner yet."

Janice had picked at her dinner, leaving most of it pushed around on the plate.

"But they're playing music and there's a dance floor. So dance with me." She leaned into Dale with a seductive gleam in her eye. "I love the way you move."

"Could we wait until after dessert?"

"I'll dance with you." Lee wiped her mouth with her napkin then stood up. "Come on, dancing queen." She took Janice's hand and led her to the dance floor, leaving Dale and Taren at the table.

"She's a good dancer," Taren said as an ice breaker. "You don't mind, do you?"

"I don't care. It's a free country." Dale watched as Lee held Janice in her arms and swayed to the slow song.

"But she's your date. They should have asked if you minded."

"And Lee is your date. She should have asked you, too."

Taren's cell phone chimed. She pulled it from her purse and checked the screen. "Excuse me, I need to take this." she said, covering her other ear with her hand.

Dale didn't want to sit and watch Lee fondle her girlfriend's ass as they swayed back and forth on the dance floor. She didn't want to eavesdrop on Taren's conversation either. She headed to the ladies' room to wash the catfish grease off her hands. Even before she came out she could hear Taren in the hallway outside the door.

"Couldn't you put it in storage somewhere for a few months? I thought you had storage lockers in the basement. Mr. Holburn, I can't come put that stuff in storage myself. I'm not there. And if I were there, I wouldn't need to put it in storage. I'd simply take it home with me."

Dale took her time washing her hands. After a long silence, she stepped out, expecting Taren to be gone.

"But you just said her rent was paid until the end of the month," Taren said angrily. She noticed Dale and stepped into an alcove as if seeking privacy. "I'd like to know why you didn't tell me this sooner. Why did you wait two weeks?" Taren looked back as if to see if Dale was listening. "Yes, I know it needs a thorough cleaning. Okay, yes, painting too. But her contract isn't up until the end of the month." Taren took a deep exasperated breath and pursed her lips. "I know she isn't living there anymore but it's paid for. Mr. Holburn, I'll call you back in a few minutes. No, don't do anything with my aunt's things. I'll call you right back." She ended the call, her eyes on Dale. "Did you need something?"

"No, I'm sorry." Dale headed back up the hall, mad at herself for listening to Taren's private conservation.

"What were you going to say?" Taren asked, following her into the reception.

"I wasn't going to say anything."

"But you wanted to. I could see it in your eyes."

"Nope."

"That was the housing director of the Concord, the senior living center where my aunt lived. She passed away two weeks ago."

"The one in Chicago Sydney said was…"

"Nuts? Yes," Taren replied when Dale hesitated.

"I'm sorry for your loss."

Taren shrugged and said, "Thank you but I barely knew her. Even when I lived there she didn't want me to visit her. She was a hermit. She didn't even want a funeral. She wanted to be cremated and her ashes scattered in the vacant lot behind the apartment building. Since I'm her only family she left everything to me."

"And they want you to get her stuff out so they can rent it."

"Yes. He said they need the rest of the month to clean, repaint and carpet for the next tenant." Taren stared at her curiously. "What was that look about?"

"What look?" Dale didn't want to interfere. This was Taren's business.

"If you have something to say, please say it."

"Okay. But this is just my opinion. If your aunt's rent is paid, you should have the entire month to clean out her things. Painting and repairs should be done on their time. And they don't need two weeks. They can put a crew in there to paint and clean in a day. Two, tops. I bet every room in the building is the same color. Off white. They probably keep five-gallon buckets of it. They can mask, tape and spray an empty apartment in an afternoon. And putting down new carpeting in a small apartment can be done in a few hours. They use cheap foam-backed carpeting that doesn't need padding or special installation. Rip out the old. Tack down the new and voilà. Just like new."

"He said it was standard to vacate immediately after someone passes away."

"I'd want to see that in writing. Another question. My aunt and uncle had a house full of stuff when they passed away. It was mostly out-of-date clothes, mismatched dishes and furniture that smelled like tobacco and cats. But nothing worth a ten-hour drive. Why not just let them donate the stuff to charity? He could send you a box of any photographs and important papers they find. Save yourself a trip."

"I didn't say anything to him but my aunt had an antique dresser, a mirror and a few things that belonged to my great-grandmother. I'd like to have them. I'd rather not ask him to ship them."

"I can certainly understand that."

"So you don't think they need two weeks?"

"For painting and carpeting, no."

"Thanks," Taren said, turning back into the hallway as she redialed her phone.

Dale headed back through the tables where Janice and Lee were sipping from fresh beers. Dale wasn't counting necessarily but that was at least their fourth and the evening wasn't over.

"May I have your attention, please," the groom's father said, stepping to the microphone. He had removed his suit jacket and loosened his tie. "Please join me in welcoming my son and his beautiful new bride, Lucas and Judy Bower." He raised his glass in salute. The crowd stood and applauded as the bride and groom came onto the dance floor. Judy hung her wrists over Lucas's shoulders and stared lovingly into his eyes as they began to dance.

"They look so young," Taren said, coming to the table.

Dale nodded, cupped her hands to her mouth and shouted above the music, "Give her a kiss." The guests cheered encouragement. Lucas finally gave in and placed a quick peck on the lips. "That's not a kiss. Show him how it's done, Judy," Dale shouted even louder. Judy grinned as she wrapped her arms around his neck and pulled him into a big open-mouth lip-lock. The crowd hooted and gave catcalls as she held him for a long kiss.

"Atta girl," Taren cheered. "Show them how it's done."

"Did you and Mr. Holburn reach a compromise?" Dale asked.

"Yes, we did. I have another week to decide what to do with my aunt's things. Thank you for your help."

"You're welcome."

The music changed to a country-western song, attracting a group to join the couple in a line dance. Dale stood up and held out her hand to Janice as she tapped her foot to the rhythm. This was something Dale loved to do. It had been a long time since she'd danced with a pretty woman.

"Shall we join them?" she asked. She expected Janice to agree eagerly.

"A line dance?" she rolled her lip contentiously. "I'm not very good at it but okay." She took Dale's hand but showed little enthusiasm.

"Come on, Lee," Taren said as she rose to her feet. "I need to work off the chocolate fountain." She headed to the dance floor without waiting for an answer.

Taren found a spot at the end of front row and waved for the three women to join her. They stomped and turned in time with the music, laughing when they missed a step or bumped into each other. When the song changed to a slow dance Dale pulled Janice into her arms and twirled her, bringing a giggle as they swayed. Lee and Taren moved around the floor, gracefully weaving their way between the couples. And like she had done with Janice, Lee had a hand on Taren's rear.

*That's not a basketball, lady. Stop fondling your date.*

Dale turned her partner so Lee and her roving hand wasn't in her line of sight When the dance ended Janice headed for the table, Lee right behind her. Before Dale could follow Taren took her hand and gave her a pleading smile as another slow song began.

"Don't you want to do this with Lee?" Dale asked as Taren stepped into her arms like she belonged there.

"We will eventually. But I wanted to ask you something and I can't do it at the table."

"I told you I really don't mind if Lee dances with Janice. I'm not the jealous type." Dale wished it were true. But somehow the thought of Lee dancing with Janice didn't seem as intrusive as Lee dancing with Taren and groping her.

"It's not about dancing." Taren moved closer, her body pressed against Dale's and her face just inches from Dale's ear. "It's none of my business but why her?"

"I beg your pardon?"

"Janice. She's not exactly your type. Don't get me wrong. You can date whoever you want, and I can certainly see the physical attraction, but with your history, is she really the best choice? What is she? Twenty-five? Twenty-six?"

"She's thirty and since when does age have anything to do with it?" Dale couldn't believe she was having this conversation. Taren was right. This was none of her business.

"You know what I mean."

"No, I'm not sure I do. What should I date? A humpback moose?"

"If she was sober, yes," Taren said matter-of-factly.

Dale stopped dancing and released her hold on Taren. She had crossed the line. Dale was not going to defend who she dated. She didn't tolerate it from Zoe and she certainly wasn't going to tolerate it from Taren Dorsey.

"I appreciate the use of your trailer but who I date and why is my business." Dale turned and strode off the dance floor.

"How's it going?" Zoe asked, intercepting Dale between tables.

"Whose brainchild was it to put the four of us at the same table? If it's your idea of a joke, it's a bad one, Zoe," Dale said sharply, still angry at Taren's prying questions.

"You'll survive one evening. If Taren doesn't mind, why should you?"

"You asked her?"

"I might have mentioned it. We were trying to seat like people together."

"But we are not like people."

"Grow up, Dale. For Pete's sake, you're living in her trailer."

Zoe walked on, leaving Dale with the memory of Taren's body against her own and a sour taste in her mouth over their argument. She went to the ladies' room to give her anger a chance to ease. When she returned to the table Taren and Lee had left, telling Janice they had an evening meeting at the college they couldn't miss.

"Can we go?" Janice asked after swigging the last of her beer. "I just want to be with you, honey."

"You bet." Dale took Janice by the hand and led her through the tables and into the sultry evening air. They would miss the bouquet and garter toss. They would also miss throwing birdseed on the departing couple but she didn't mind. She had all the happiness she could take for one day. And if she was lucky, Janice would sober up during the hour ride back to Neosho and they could have a pleasant night together. At least they could try.

# CHAPTER EIGHT

Dale had just climbed the ladder to retrieve a box of PVC joints from the top shelf when she heard Taren's voice.

"Hello, Dale." She stood at the bottom of the ladder, fiddling with the strap on her purse and looking up apprehensively. She wore a yellow and white summer dress that gave her a fresh-as-a-daisy look.

"Hello. Can I help you find something?" Dale pulled a box from the shelf and climbed down. "Let me take care of this first."

"I don't need anything," she said, following Dale around the end of the aisle. "But if you have a minute I need to talk to you. I want to apologize for my reprehensible behavior at the wedding. I'm sorry. It won't happen again."

"No problem. Let's just say it was a stressful time for both of us."

"So you forgive me for sticking my nose into your dating business?"

"If you put it that way, yes."

"Thank you." Taren paused then cleared her throat as if there was more. "Do you remember at the wedding we talked about my aunt's things I need to remove from her apartment?"

"Yes. Chicago. Antique dresser." Dale carried the box to the service desk and added it to a cart. "Did you get it taken care of?" She checked the list taped to the cart handle then headed back down the aisle for the next item, Taren by her side.

"No. That's the other reason I'm here. I understand Home Depot has trucks for rent."

"Yeah, for local delivery."

"What do you consider local? Could I rent one over a weekend and how much do they charge for mileage?" Taren raised her eyebrows expectantly.

Dale knew immediately what she meant. She needed a truck to haul her aunt's possessions from Chicago and she hoped one of the Home Depot's would do the job.

"That's not my department but I heard both of our trucks are out right now. Normally it's first come, first served but because of the tornado, our customers who've already bought merchandise are being given priority."

Taren's expression changed from hopeful to disappointed in a heartbeat. "How long is the wait list?"

"I heard it was several weeks. And our trucks are flatbeds. No sides or cover. They're meant for hauling lumber and building materials. You need a box truck."

"I checked that too. The only one available is way too big and will cost me a fortune in mileage and gas. The tornado's been a boom to the rental business, cars and trucks."

"Have you checked moving companies? Maybe they could pack up what you want and ship it to you without you having to go up there."

"That was plan B. But again, way expensive. Do you know how big a U-Haul box trailer I could pull with my car? I may have to go with plan C."

"You're kidding, right? You can't pull a trailer with your car."

Taren bristled. "Yes, I can. They have hitches that hook right on the back bumper. I've seen them online."

"You could pull a hitch just fine. But if you attach a trailer to it you'd kill your car and maybe yourself. You've got a four-cylinder engine. If you try pulling a trailer to Chicago and back with furniture in it, your transmission will overheat. Plus, the weight on the back of your car will cause the front to pitch up, making steering nearly impossible. You'll have that trailer whipping all over the road."

"I wasn't going to take all my aunt's stuff. How much could a few pieces of furniture and boxes of dishes weigh? I could go slow."

"That won't help. The towing weight is the same regardless of speed. Look in your owner's manual for towing capacity. I bet the maximum recommended towable weight is less than an empty trailer."

Taren scrunched her face disgustedly. "You really are a party pooper, you know."

"Sorry. I wish I could be more helpful. Haven't you got a friend with a van or truck to haul it for you? You need a plan D."

Taren looked up at Dale, her forehead furrowed as she said, "I could do that. I know someone with a truck."

"Good. Problem solved." Dale went back to searching for flexible water lines.

"Well, maybe. How much would you charge?"

"Me? Oh, no. I meant someone else. Not me."

"I'll pay all your travel expenses. Gas, meals, hotel. Everything. I'll even pay for your time if you'll drive me up there."

"Damn, you are desperate, aren't you?" Dale chuckled.

"Yes."

"I can't. I don't have any vacation time left."

"Not even a few days? I told Mr. Holburn I'd be there Saturday morning. I didn't know I was going to have such a problem finding a truck that didn't cost a fortune to rent."

"I thought you reached a compromise with him."

"That's the compromise. He faxed me a copy of my aunt's rental agreement. He's within his legal right to have it cleaned out if I don't take care of it by Monday morning." Taren heaved a resolute sigh. "That's okay. I'll figure something out." She turned and headed up the aisle, her shoulders slumped in defeat.

"Sorry," Dale called after her. She pulled several flexible hoses from a box but stopped in midcount, unable to put Taren out of her mind. "Dammit." She dropped them back in the box with a disgusted sigh and trotted out into the parking lot. Taren had just started her car and began to roll away as Dale slapped at the driver's window.

"What?" Taren said, lowering the window a few inches. Dale could tell she was still frustrated.

"What were you going to do with the rest of your aunt's stuff? The stuff you don't want?"

She shrugged. "Donate it somewhere I guess. I don't need it."

"Would you be willing to work a trade? A truck ride to Chicago to pick up your aunt's dresser and whatever else you want in exchange for giving me first refusal on what's left?"

"There may not be much. She didn't have a lot of furniture. And I thought you didn't have any vacation time."

"I don't. But I'm off this weekend. We could leave after work Friday. I'll just need to be back for work Monday morning."

"That's a twelve-hour drive one way."

"If we drive straight through and don't stop, we could do it."

"But I won't be able to help with the driving. I can't drive a stick shift. How are you going to work all day then drive all night?" Taren asked.

"Coffee and Twizzlers." Dale extended her hand through the open window. "So, it's a deal?"

"Deal." Taren placed her hand in Dale's and smiled appreciatively. "What time can you leave Friday?"

"I'll pick you up a little after seven. I need to get back to work. I'll see you Friday." Dale stepped back from the car, sinking her hands in her apron pocket.

"Thank you," Taren said then pulled away.

Dale could see Taren watching her in her rearview mirror as she left the parking lot.

*I'll be in a closed vehicle with Taren Dorsey for a whole weekend. Who'd have thought I'd ever agree to that?*

She didn't have time to think about it.

She worked overtime the rest of the week. Even with competition down the street, the store struggled to keep up with sales and orders for generators, shingles and plywood. Residents whose homes survived and were livable needed tools and supplies to repair minor damage.

Dale strode down the aisle to where Zoe was searching the bottom shelf. "Hey, sis. What are you doing prowling the plumbing aisle?"

"Looking for one of these." Zoe held up a sticky note with a sketch of a sink sprayer on it. "I'm tired of waiting for the maintenance man to fix it. It's been a week and all he keeps saying is I'll get right on that." She thrust the paper at Dale.

"What's it doing? Leaking down the hose? Spraying sideways? Not spraying at all?"

"Water only comes out of a few of the holes. I cleaned it with vinegar but that didn't help. I thought if I bought a new one and handed it to him he wouldn't have an excuse. He'd have to fix it. Do I have to buy the whole thing? Hose and all?"

"You probably just need the sprayer head. Sounds like calcium deposits clogging the holes. It's an easy fix. You can do it yourself. All you need is needle nose pliers. You unscrew the old sprayer head, remove the clip—"

"Stop right there. I wouldn't know where to start. If I buy it would you come do it this weekend?" she begged woefully. "Please. I'll feed you dinner."

"I'm busy this weekend but you can do it, Zoe. It's easy. I'll walk you through it." She handed Zoe the sprayer she needed.

"And what are you doing this weekend? Another date with Janice, the flirt?"

"No. I'm going to Chicago." She wasn't going to dignify Zoe's remark with a reply.

"Why are you going to Chicago? You don't know anybody there."

"I'm taking Taren up there to pick up some furniture. She needed a truck to haul it."

"And she asked you?" Zoe chuckled wickedly.

"It's more of a trade. She's letting me have some of what's left in her aunt's apartment in exchange for using my truck."

"Okay, why in the world do you want someone's hand-me-down junk? You don't even have a house yet."

"I know but if there is anything I can use it will save me money. The less I spend on furniture, the more I can use on construction costs."

"Why don't you just build a smaller house? Build whatever your insurance allows." Zoe dismissed it with a wave of her hand.

"I can't. The building permit requires I rebuild at least the same square footage and the same number of bedrooms and bathrooms."

"Why?"

"The city planning and zoning department doesn't want developers slapping up a bunch of tiny houses where larger ones once stood. I can build bigger than I had but I can't build smaller."

"Can't you go to the bank and get a loan for the difference?"

"I already have a loan, a big one. It's called a mortgage. And since the check from the insurance settlement will be made out to them as well as me, I have to keep up my payments or they won't release the money for the rebuild." Dale realized they had attracted attention from passing customers. "Here, buy this. The instructions are on the back. If you can't figure it out I'll take care of it next week." She steered Zoe toward the front of the store. "Call me later. I've got work to do."

By the time Dale clocked out Friday evening she had worked a fifty-six-hour week, and her nights had been occasionally interrupted by suspicious sounds that sent her, flashlight in hand, roaming the neighborhood in search of looters. She had originally planned to spend the weekend hauling debris to the curb but trading service for furniture with Taren seemed like a better idea. She hoped she didn't live to regret it.

She stopped by the trailer and changed into jeans and a T-shirt for the trip. She stuffed a change of clothes and a few toiletries in a small gym bag and headed to town to pick up Taren. She was almost there when she remembered she and

Janice made tentative plans for dinner and a movie. She'd left it up to Janice to finalize the details and had expected a call from her. They hadn't talked all week so nothing was definite but Dale felt guilty she had forgotten. She pulled out her cell phone and punched in Janice's number. It rang to her voice mail.

"Hi, Janice. Sorry I haven't called but it's been crazy busy at work. I guess that's a good thing. I hope it's okay if we postpone our plans for the weekend. I have an unexpected trip to Chicago. I'm helping a friend move some furniture. It's kind of a last-minute thing. Hope you don't mind. I'll talk with you soon. Take care."

A small cooler and a tote bag were waiting on the front porch when Dale pulled in Taren's driveway.

"Hello," Taren said, opening the door before Dale could knock. She wore jeans cuffed above the calf and a top that hugged her figure perfectly. Her bejeweled sunglasses were perched on top of her head. Dale couldn't be sure but she looked like she was wearing a push-up bra. When Taren came bouncing down the steps with the cooler and bag, Dale was sure. Definitely a push-up bra. She couldn't believe she was paying attention to Taren's bounce. Janice's was the only one she should be watching. Dale opened the driver's door and waited while Taren loaded her bag behind the seat. "Sorry the passenger's door doesn't open."

"That's okay. I don't mind. Do you want me to drive the first leg?"

"I thought you didn't know how to drive a stick shift."

"I don't. But I watched four videos on YouTube about it. I get the idea. You release the clutch a little bit at a time until you reach the friction point while depressing the gas to increase RPMs."

Dale fought the urge to laugh out loud. "You can do a lot of things on the Internet but I'm not sure learning how to drive a manual transmission is one of them. Besides, sounds like they're teaching you to be a clutch jockey."

"A what?"

"Nothing. I'll drive. You can practice driving some other time." Dale climbed in and started the truck. "Want to take a pillow? That side window isn't very comfortable."

"I won't need one. I'm not going to sleep while you do all the driving. As co-pilot, it's my job to navigate and keep the driver awake."

Dale chuckled to herself. She knew Taren meant well but she'd be snoring by St. Louis, her heading bobbing against the headrest. No doubt about it.

"What's all that stuff in the back?" Taren buckled her seat belt.

"Plastic tarps, rope, bungee cords and a few empty boxes to pack the dishes you want."

"Oh, good idea. I hadn't thought of supplies we'd need." Taren leaned over and examined the fuel gauge.

"Yes, I already filled it," Dale said and pulled out. "And just so you know, this is going to be a shared venture. I pay half. You pay half. You get your furniture moved and I get first choice on what's left. You're not paying for everything. I'll pay my own way."

"But this is my trip," Taren started but Dale quickly pulled to the curb.

"If you can't agree, we're not going. Your choice, lady," she said defiantly.

"You really are a stubborn cuss, aren't you?" Taren wrinkled her nose then nodded. "Okay. Agreed."

They headed east on the interstate toward St. Louis. Dale hoped to cross the Mississippi River into Illinois shortly after midnight.

"Could I turn the radio on for a little music?" Taren asked, reaching for the knob.

"I doubt you'll get anything. The storm snapped off the antenna." Dale tapped her knuckle against the side window at the empty antenna socket on the fender. "I haven't had it fixed yet."

Taren pressed the scan bottom but Dale was right. Nothing but static.

"I should have brought my iPod," Taren mumbled under her breath and took out her cell phone.

They rode in silence while Taren replied to messages and placed a call to her department chairman to discuss summer classes. Dale couldn't help but listen to Taren's side of the conversation. Taren was scheduled to teach two classes, an upper division course in linear algebra and a freshman calculus class, both to start the week after they returned from Chicago. Dale knew Taren was a college math instructor but had never heard her talk about it. Her own degree was in business administration but she had always been a little intimidated by Taren's master's in mathematics.

"Sounds like you're going to be busy," Dale said after Taren ended the call.

"Yes. I was going to only teach one class but Professor Gardener isn't renewing his contract. He lost his house in the tornado and has decided to move."

"I can understand that." Dale eased back in her seat as her mind went to that place and time she'd rather forget.

"How was your day?" Taren asked as she flipped through more messages on her phone. Dale appreciated her offer to change the subject. She didn't want to relive the tornado with every bump of the pavement.

"Busy." She took a deep breath then said, "I think I should apologize for the softball game. You're right. I was being an ass."

"Accepted." She didn't look up.

"It was a tough day."

"Yes, it was."

"It's just that the last time we spoke was at Sydney's funeral."

"I remember."

"Those last few days in hospice are one big gray blur. If someone asked what I said or did I'd have no idea."

"You miss her, huh?" Taren looked over at Dale, her eyes full of compassion.

"Yes." Dale felt a lump rise in her throat.

"Me, too." Taren was silent for a moment then began to hum softly. She looked over again with a twinkle in her eye and sang, "We all live in a yellow submarine, yellow submarine. Yellow submarine."

Dale laughed and joined in. "We all live in a yellow submarine. Yellow submarine. Yellow submarine."

"I hadn't thought of that in years," Taren said, smiling happily. "Why did Sydney like that song?"

"I have no idea but she was always singing it." Dale laughed out loud. "Sydney had the worst singing voice. Yours is much better."

"Thank you." She went back to humming quietly, a smile on her face as they rode along.

They pulled into a rest stop to stretch their legs just before dark.

"How are you doing? Getting tired?" Taren asked as she slid back across the seat.

"Nope. Between the coffee and the potty stops I'm good. How about you?"

"I'm fine. All I'm doing is sitting."

"Seat cover."

"I beg your pardon."

"Truckers call an attractive woman on the passenger side a seat cover."

Taren chuckled as she buckled herself in and slipped out of her shoes. "And thank you for the compliment."

"You're welcome." Dale's cell phone rang. It was Janice. "Hi, Janice."

"Hi, peaches. I miss you. And I'm so sorry about the other night after the wedding. I was just so tired I couldn't keep my eyes open. Forgive me?"

"That's okay. Don't worry about it. I was tired too." Dale knew Taren was listening to every word she said.

"What's this about a trip to Chicago? I thought we were going to Red Lobster tomorrow."

"I know. I'm sorry. This trip just sort of came up at the last minute. You know how things like that happen." Dale didn't feel like explaining the details, not with Taren sitting two feet away. "Tell you what. You decide what you want to do next weekend. Anywhere. My treat. We can go to Springfield or Tulsa. You name it."

"I'm busy next weekend. I thought we agreed on this weekend," Janice whined. "Why couldn't you take your trip next weekend instead?"

"Because she needed to do it this weekend. And you and I really didn't have definite plans. You said you'd call and let me know."

"Who is this friend you're taking to Chicago?" she asked with a suspicious undertone.

"Just a friend who needed help hauling some furniture she inherited." Dale didn't want to hear Janice's opinion of Taren. Not over the phone, anyway. "Is it okay if I call you tomorrow? We'll talk about it then."

"Sure. Whatever." Janice hung up.

"Oops. Was that my fault?" Taren cringed.

"Nope." Dale heaved an exasperated sigh. "That's my fault."

"I'm sorry if I created a problem for you."

"You didn't. Not at all. It was just missed communication. We'll survive." She hung her hand over the steering wheel and headed down the road. It was twenty miles before Taren said anything.

"Do you mind if I ask you a personal question?" Taren stared at the darkness alongside the highway.

"Depends on the question, I guess."

"Do you blame Sydney for what happened with your insurance?"

"How did you know about that? Oh, Zoe," Dale realized as soon as she said it.

"I passed her on campus and she sort of blurted it out. I swear I didn't ask. She's really worried about you. So, do you?"

Dale shifted in her seat. Taren's question was indeed personal and out of left field. She wasn't going to speak ill of her beloved. Sydney hadn't done anything evil. At least not intentionally. She was simply doing what she thought was right at the time. And how could Dale blame her. She'd given Sydney full control over household matters. She didn't question her choices.

"Do I blame Sydney? No."

Taren was quiet for several miles, her eyes fixed on some distant obsession. She finally said, "You should. She should have known better." She pointed at an exit sign. "Can we stop at that gas station? I need some coffee."

"Sure." Dale steered for it.

"This is for gas." Taren tucked some money under Dale's visor. "My turn."

Dale didn't argue with her. She filled the tank then went inside. Taren was roaming the snack aisle carrying two foam cups.

"How do you take your coffee? Still cream, no sugar?" She handed Dale a cup.

"Yes, thanks. I'll get them."

"Already paid for." She continued to search the shelves. "I can't find Twizzlers. Is there something else you'd rather have? Snickers? Doritos?"

"Coffee is good. I think we need to get going. We've got a long way to go."

Dale held the driver's door and waited while Taren slid across and buckled her seat belt, pulling the shoulder strap tight across her cleavage. Dale gave an involuntary groan as she climbed in, her eyes lingering on Taren's figure.

Once they cleared St. Louis and crossed the Mississippi River the interstate north across Illinois became a four-lane ribbon of monotony. But for a few tractor-trailers and midnight travelers, they were alone. Taren occasionally volunteered benign conversation but Dale knew she was fighting sleep. She made a gallant effort but lost the fight just south of Springfield, right after she said, "What would you like to talk about?"

It was an easy drive. Flat, straight and decent surface. Dale occupied herself with mind games, estimating building costs, designing an efficient floor plan and choosing items she could reuse to save expenses. When she felt her eyes growing heavy she shifted in her seat, cracked a window and reached for another stick of gum. Taren slept through a gas and bathroom stop at a crossroads convenience store where Dale bought two cups of coffee in case she awoke, but she didn't stir. Dale draped her jacket over Taren's shoulders then lowered her window a few inches to let a breeze blow through the cab. Taren rustled, tucking the jacket under her chin but didn't open her eyes. She sighed and went back to sleep, her head wedged between the headrest and the door frame.

She was a beautiful woman. Unmistakably beautiful. Dale had always thought so. From that first time Sydney introduced her, Dale thought Taren was the gorgeous one. Sydney had a Scandinavian blonde wholesome look. Round-faced. Ample bosom. Hearty laugh. The kind of woman the Vikings sailed home to find waiting on the shore. Taren, on the other hand, was the kind of woman Vikings took captive. Striking features. Aloof and delicate. Tantalizingly gorgeous. Dale allowed the fantasy to play out in her mind. It was three o'clock in the morning on a lonely stretch of Illinois highway. Why not?

There she was, Dale of the North, dressed in a furry animal hide, a horned helmet on her head as she steered her ship up the fjord. On the dock, a buxom woman waiting with a basket of flowers, her golden hair twisted into a long braid. Below deck was Dale's booty, treasures plundered from battle. Chests of gold and jewels. Barrels of rum and exotic spices. And a woman tied to a pillar so she couldn't escape. She would be Dale's obedient slave, her maid. Never questioning Dale's authority. But that's where the fantasy went awry. As she eased her ship closer to the shore the fair maiden sprang from below deck. She seized Dale's sword and ran it through her, the wench's delicate bosom heaving as she stood over her, cackling victoriously. With her last dying breath Dale lifted her hand to Thor for salvation then sprawled on the deck, her fur skin garment covered in blood.

"That'll keep anyone awake," Dale muttered. She slurped the last of her coffee and shifted in her seat, trying to ignore the tingle throbbing between her thighs.

# CHAPTER NINE

Dale cupped her hand over Taren's knee, gently massaging her thumb against her jeans.

"Taren," she said softly. She hated to disturb the peaceful look on her face. "Taren, you need to wake up." When she didn't move Dale gave her leg a nudge. "Taren, time to wake up." She pulled the jacket from Taren's grip. "We're here."

"Where?" she mumbled, her eyes still closed. "What time is it?" She snuggled against the window.

"Come on, Sleeping Beauty. We're here. Wake up and smell the parking lot."

"Parking lot?" Taren's eyes snapped open. "Where are we?" She straightened herself in the seat, blinking her way to reality.

"According to your GPS and the sign on the building this is the Concord Place Retirement and Assisted Living Facility." Dale looked up at the aging glass-paneled building. "It looks like a hotel right out of the fifties."

"What time is it?" She snatched up her cell phone to check the time. "It's almost eight o'clock. Why didn't you wake me up?" she demanded, rubbing her eyes and running her fingers through her hair.

"I did. I pulled into the parking lot and said wake up."

"Why did you let me sleep all this way?" She turned to Dale with a plaintive look. "You did all that driving and all I did was sleep. You should have awakened me hours ago."

"So your nap is my fault?" Dale teased. She climbed out of the truck to stretch her legs.

"Yes. And you should be ashamed," Taren said as she tapped in a number on her cell phone. The conversation was short, leaving her frustrated. "Mr. Holburn isn't here yet."

"Does someone have a key to let us in your aunt's apartment?"

"You'd think so but no. We've got an hour or so to kill. Do you want to sit in the lobby or…" she said, raising her eyebrows suggestively.

"Breakfast?"

"You read my mind. I could use something to eat and a ladies' room with a mirror." Taren rebuckled her seat belt and tossed a grin at Dale. "And I know just the place. You'll love it. Great food, even by Chicago standards, and it's only five minutes away."

"I'm all for that. My butt is growing roots in this seat."

"I really feel bad about you doing all the driving while I just slept," Taren said apologetically. She rested her hand on Dale's arm as if pleading for absolution.

"But it's my fault since I didn't wake you up?"

"Yes," she said and nodded, turning her smile out the front window. "Turn right out of the parking lot."

Dale waited for an opening before zipping into the line of cars. "I had forgotten how congested big city traffic can be."

"The funny thing is, this isn't really all that bad. Rush hour through the week is twice this heavy. And downtown by the lakefront? I think the water attracts idiot drivers."

"That bad?" Dale's fantasy wench came skipping across her thoughts at the mention of water.

"Oh, yes. I hate to drive on Michigan Avenue or Lake Shore Drive. I don't miss it in Joplin."

"Then you're a small-town girl at heart." Dale wondered if Lee was what kept her in Joplin. "Surely there's something you miss about living here?"

"Oh, sure. There's always a few things a small town can't provide. Turn left at the light and then find a place to park."

"Egg Harbor? Looks busy."

"Yes. And this is one of the places I miss. We used to come here a lot."

"We?" Dale asked. She waited for a car to pull out then took its spot.

"Uh-huh." Taren fished in her tote bag for a small zipper pouch Dale assumed was a toothbrush and the like. Dale slipped her own toothbrush into her back pocket and followed Taren inside.

"Do you mind waiting for our table while I...?" Taren nodded toward the ladies' room.

"Sure. Do you want coffee?"

"Yes, thank you. Hot and black." Taren held Dale's arm, squeezing it gently as she slipped through the other patrons waiting for a table. "I'll be right back."

Dale expected it to be a long protracted bathroom event. But she was back within minutes. She looked clean and combed, the escaped tendrils of her hair once again contained in a ponytail.

"Your turn," she said happily, sliding into the booth.

Dale already felt dirty from a full day of work and the long hours on the road. Taren's fresh scent and gleaming complexion made her feel even grungier.

"That was quick."

"You think so? I was worried I was taking too long."

"Can you order me the blueberry pancakes and bacon, crisp?" Dale pointed to the picture on the menu as she slid out. "No butter, just syrup."

"Oh, those look good. But I have to have the veggie omelet. It is wonderful," she said with an exaggerated groan.

Taren was sipping coffee and staring out the window when Dale came out of the ladies' room. Whatever had her deep in thought faded when she noticed Dale striding toward the booth.

"You're pretty speedy yourself." Taren's eyes widened as the waitress set a plate in front of her.

Dale's plate of pancakes was just as enormous. "Could I have some peanut butter?" she asked.

"Sure. Anything else, ladies?" the waitress said. "Will these be together or separate checks?"

"Together," Taren replied quickly. "And it comes to me."

"Separate." Dale said flatly, setting her coffee cup at the edge of the table. "And a refill, please."

"Some people are just plain stubborn," Taren mumbled, exploring the contents of her omelet. She took a bite, closed her eyes and savored the flavor. "Oh, yes," she said with a contented moan. "Now that's an omelet."

"That good?" Dale watched as her enjoyment of the bite bordered on an orgasmic pleasure.

Taren took another bite, repeating the satisfied moan.

"You have to try this." She eagerly filled her fork with a bite and held it up for Dale to taste.

Somewhere in her excitement to share the experience Taren seemed to have forgotten their history of discontent. That surprised Dale. Had she forgotten the arguments over Dale's drinking? The pleading for sobriety for Sydney's sake? Had she forgotten the harsh words over Dale's alcoholic indifference? Taren had made it very clear she hated her for the way she behaved as Sydney battled colon cancer. Yes, Dale was ashamed of what she had done. She couldn't change the past but for whatever reason, Taren seemed to be oblivious to it.

"Here, taste this. It's straight from heaven."

Dale opened her mouth and accepted the bite. Onions and green peppers weren't Dale's favorite thing in an omelet but Taren presented them so exquisitely she didn't mind.

"Eh? I'm right, aren't I?"

"Yes. Very good."

"Their pancakes are good but you're going to wish you ordered an omelet."

"Nope," Dale said after trying a bite of her breakfast. "This is better. Fresh blueberries. Not canned." She cut a bite and placed it on the corner of Taren's plate. "When you're finished eating that try the good stuff." Dale placed a large blueberry on top of the bite. She added a piece of bacon. "Now this is food worthy of Joplin."

Taren stabbed a bite of fried potato and reached across to add it to Dale's plate but stopped when she noticed someone coming through the door. The playful excitement of sharing their breakfast instantly drained from her face.

"Oh, God," she gasped, a look of desperation on her face. "Please, be my girlfriend," she pleaded in a whisper. "Whatever I say, agree with me. Please. Just this once."

"Okay." Dale knew something was wrong but didn't look. She was still dealing with Taren's request. She and Taren Dorsey, girlfriends? The idea had a strange but satisfying appeal to it. She didn't have to wait long to know why.

A woman appeared at the table, smiling down at Taren, a tall woman in her late forties. Her hair was short, combed back on the sides and mostly white. Her rugged face suggested makeup had never graced her face. She wore jeans and a polo shirt over small breasts. Dale guessed they never saw a bra either. She had brown eyes that twinkled fondly at Taren.

"Hi," she said softly.

"Hello," Taren replied, her eyes darting back and forth between this woman and Dale.

"It's nice to see you again."

That sounded like an invitation to the bedroom, Dale thought. The look on Taren's face was unmistakable. These two women had a past together.

"What are you doing back in Chicago?" The woman seemed oblivious to Dale. She seemed consumed with Taren and the fit of her shirt.

"We came to pick up my aunt's things and empty her apartment. Dale, this is Menzi, an old friend of mine."

"Hello, Menzi," Dale said, thrusting a hand at the woman. "I'm Dale Kinsel. Nice to meet you."

"Hi." Menzi gave Dale a quick dismissive glance then turned her attention back to Taren. "How long will you be in town? Couple weeks? A week?" She sounded hopeful.

"No, we'll be in and out by tomorrow," Dale inserted before Taren could reply.

"You can't stay a couple days?" Menzi asked, her eyes burrowing down Taren's top.

"No." Dale slurped her coffee.

"Yes, we have to get back. Dale needs to be at work Monday morning."

"So, you're still a hilly billy?" Menzi joked as she slid into the booth next to Taren, forcing her to scoot over. "Where is it you live? Arkansas?"

Aren't you supposed to wait to be invited before you sit down, Dale thought. There's plenty of room on that bench. You don't have to sit right up against her. And it's hillbilly, you twit. Not hilly billy.

"We live in Joplin, Missouri," Taren said.

"That's right. You had the tornado last month." Menzi's frown suggested she was at least mildly concerned. "How close was it to you?"

"Dale's house was destroyed," Taren said, her gaze softening as she looked over at Dale. "But thank goodness she wasn't hurt."

"You were in your house when the tornado hit?" Menzi asked as a scowl creased her forehead. "Shit. Was it scary?"

"Yeah, a little bit." Dale took a sip of coffee as the memory went back into place.

"It was a lot scary." Taren noticed Dale's hand begin to tremble and covered it with both of hers. "A lot. I wish I had been there with her." Their eyes met. The tenderness of it took Dale's breath away.

*So this is what it would be like to be Taren Dorsey's girlfriend, a compassion so deep it was palpable.*

"I see you got the veggie omelet, just like always." Menzi picked a mushroom from Taren's plate and ate it. "And I bet you don't finish it, just like always." She smiled at Dale. "She never finishes it. I'd have to do that. Does she do that to you? Expect you to finish her meals so it doesn't look like she wastes food."

"All the time." Dale chuckled as if it were true.

"I'd buy her a hot fudge sundae and she'd only eat half. Then she'd hand it to me to finish." Menzi bumped Taren's shoulder playfully.

"Here. Knock yourself out," Taren said, sliding her plate in front of Menzi.

"Just like old times, babe." Menzi wasted no time in devouring the rest of Taren's breakfast, down to the chopped onions stuck to the plate.

Dale felt the need to defend. After all, she was supposed to be the girlfriend.

"We just get one sundae and share it. A bite for her. A bite for me. I let her have the cherry on top first. She eats it nice and slow, playing with it on her tongue. Very sexy. Isn't that right, sweetheart?"

"I don't play with it," Taren said, shifting in her seat. "And since when is eating an ice cream sundae sexy?" She raised a suspicious brow at Dale.

"Not as sexy as when you wear one of my T-shirts to bed."

"Don't you still sleep naked?" Menzi asked Taren.

"Oh, she sleeps naked," Dale quickly added. "But we start with a T-shirt so I can take it off. I love her perky boobs." She grinned, waiting for a reaction.

*Top that, you breakfast stealer.*

"I think we need to go," Taren interrupted as Menzi opened her mouth to reply. "Mr. Holburn will be waiting for us."

"I'll get this, honey," Dale said, snatching both receipts off the table. She knew Taren wouldn't argue if she was trying to sell the girlfriend scenario.

"Do you need help with anything?" Menzi asked, slurping the last of Taren's coffee then following them to the front. "If you're in a hurry to get this done I'll be glad to lend a hand lifting furniture or packing boxes."

"Do you have a couple hours you could spare?" Taren asked.

"Don't you think we can get it?" Dale glared at Taren. She didn't need her ex's help. And she didn't want to listen to her stories of their good old days.

"You bet." Menzi was obviously pleased to be asked.

They crossed the parking lot, Dale on one side of Taren, Menzi on the other, both posturing for dominance.

"Shit. What happened to your truck?" Menzi asked, ready to open the passenger door for Taren.

"Tornado had its way with it." Dale opened the driver's door and waited for Taren to slide in. "We didn't use that door anyway. She usually gets in my side." Dale beamed, proud of herself for thinking of it.

Dale pulled out of the parking lot and retraced the route back to the Concord. Menzi was visible in her rearview mirror the entire way.

"You don't have to try so hard, you know," Taren said.

"You wanted a girlfriend. I'm just obliging."

"Yes, I know what I said. But perky boobs? What was that?"

"I thought it was pretty good on the spur of the moment. I could have done better if you'd given me some warning I needed to play the girlfriend role. By the way, how long has this relationship of ours been going on? In case I'm asked."

"She's not going to ask."

"How about sex? How often do we do it? Every night? Twice a week?" Dale teased.

"She's definitely not going to ask that."

"You never know. She looks like she's still smitten with you. She might want to know if she still has a chance."

"Well, she doesn't."

"Then why did you ask her to help? I can do this."

"No, you can't. The furniture is heavy and I'm not that strong."

"Is that the only reason?"

"I have no idea what you mean." Taren turned her gaze out the window. "Yes. It's the only reason."

"Are you still in love with her? I'd understand if you are."

"No, not like you mean. I'll always love her but as a friend. It was never going to work out with us for many reasons. We wanted different things from the relationship."

A few minutes later Mr. Holburn was waiting in his office with a key to Taren's aunt's apartment.

"Anything you don't want can be donated to our thrift store. They'll take about anything," he said, following them as far as the lobby. "You'll be finished by this evening, won't you?"

"I don't know. I thought I had until Monday."

"Yeah." He shrugged. "But the cleaning crew is kind of anxious to get in there so if you can get things packed up today they could get a head start."

"We'll let you know," Taren said as the elevator doors closed. She turned to Dale. "I have no idea what this is going to look like. It could be a pig sty for all I know. It's been years since I've been up here."

"No apologies needed," Dale said, reading the nervous look on Taren's face.

"Did the old lady die in the apartment?" Menzi asked, leaning against the elevator wall as they rode to the twelfth floor.

"No. She had a stroke and died two days later at the hospital." Taren led the way down the hall. She fit the key in the lock then took a deep breath. "Remember, I make no promises on what's inside." She pushed the door open and looked in the darkened apartment before entering. A stale musty breeze flowed out to meet them. Taren snapped on the lights. Dale walked past her and opened the curtains, flooding the living room with light. A cloud of dust rose from the drapes as if they hadn't been pulled in years.

It was a small apartment. The living room flowed into the kitchen where a table and two chairs were covered with flowerpots of dead plants, newspapers, old catalogs and stacks of plastic food containers. The counter was similarly covered with dishes, canned goods, a collection of drinking glasses, none of them alike and a roasting pan full of packets of jelly, catsup and mustard. The kitchen smelled like fish. Dale sniffed at the sink then turned on the water and the garbage disposal. It made a ghastly grinding noise then settled to a peaceful hum.

"I think your aunt's last meal was still in the disposal." Dale checked the refrigerator. "And there are more goodies where that smell came from." She closed it, gasping for breath.

Taren checked the bathroom then went into the bedroom.

"Did you find it?" Dale called, following her.

Taren peeled back a crocheted afghan tossed over a dresser.

"Yes," she said, fanning away the cloud of dust she raised. The walnut dresser was larger than Dale imagined. And the matching mirror on the wall above it looked heavy.

"Are you taking this?" Menzi asked, opening one of the drawers.

"Yes. The dresser and mirror belonged to my great-grandmother."

"It looks like your aunt saved old wrapping paper."

"My aunt saved a lot of things and unfortunately most of it is trash."

"Hello?" a voice called from the open door to the hall. "Anyone here?"

"Yes, may I help you?" Taren said.

The woman was well into her sixties and rolling a canvas-sided storage bin. "Are you Ms. Dorsey? Mr. Holburn said you might have a few things for us." She shook Taren's hand eagerly. "I'm Molly Eberhouser. I run the thrift store. Anything you can't use or don't want, we'll take it. Anything but food. We can't sell food. Or booze. But most anything else. You never know what one of our residents might need. A pack of sponges. A cookie sheet. A blue sweater. Everybody needs something." She laughed. "We keep our prices cheap so everyone can afford them."

"I don't know what we'll have but I'll let you know." Taren looked back at Dale, as if acknowledging she had first choice.

"I'll leave you this." She rolled the bin to the corner of the room. "Feel free to fill it up."

"Molly, did you know my aunt?" Taren asked.

"I knew of her. I saw her around but she kept to herself. She used to come down for bingo or bridge but it's been several years since she did that. She wasn't very social. Let me know if you need another bin. We've got a Dumpster out back for trash, too." She pulled the door shut behind her.

"Thank you," Taren called after her. "Okay, girls." She scanned the living room. "Time to get our hands dirty."

"Donating what you don't want seems like a good idea," Dale said, glancing around at what she had to pick from.

"Your aunt liked these things, didn't she?" Menzi held up a yellowed crocheted doily that had been draped over the back of a recliner, covering a stain on the fabric. "I see why." The arms of the chair had doilies covering wear marks. A flowered bath towel covered a large stain on the seat of the chair. The sofa was worn and stained as well. The coffee table was nicked and scratched with a deep gouge across the top. One of the legs of the end table was broken, held together with Scotch tape and a Popsicle stick splint. The mattress in the bedroom, one of the things Dale hoped to use, was stained and smelled disgusting.

"Do you want any of the furniture?" Taren stared at the sofa.

"I think I'll pass." Dale tossed the towel from the recliner into the canvas bin.

"I'm really sorry. I know this isn't what you hoped to find."

"That's okay. At least the dresser and mirror you wanted are in good shape. They seem to be the only things she took care of."

"Surely we can find you something." Taren lifted the stack of newspapers off the chair in the corner of the living room. It had a broken seat. "Maybe in the kitchen."

"Taren, don't worry about it. I'll survive." Dale chuckled at the stack of Cool Whip containers wedged between the kitchen counter and the under cabinet. "I could take these and never have to buy another Tupperware container in my entire life." Dale looked closer then pried the stack free. "It looks like there's something in some of these."

"Finders keepers," Taren said, heading back to the bedroom. "It's probably something gross like a dead spider." She shuddered. "Please don't show me, if it is."

"It's not a spider." Dale unstacked the plastic tubs and arranged them across the counter. "You should come see this, Taren."

"What is it? Rotten food or disgusting body parts?" Taren spun on her heel and headed back.

"Money." Dale held out one of the tubs, swirling several dollars' worth of coins in the bottom.

"You're kidding. Well, like I said, finders keepers."

"They all have money in them." Dale picked up another one. "Some have dollar bills in them. It looks like your aunt was using these plastic containers as a bank. They all have something in them."

"Taren, look at this," Menzi called from the hall closet. She held out an open cigar box full of crinkled dollar bills. "Must be forty, fifty bucks in here. Maybe more."

"Before you donate any of this stuff you might want to look through it," Dale said, consolidating the money into one container.

"Didn't your aunt believe in banks?" Menzi asked.

"There can't be that much money hidden in here. She wasn't that crazy."

"Come on, Menzi," Dale called. "You and I can carry this big stuff down to the thrift store while Taren looks through the drawers and closets." Dale and Menzi picked up the sofa and headed for the door.

"Wait." Taren checked under the cushions. "Okay, you're good to go." She tossed Dale a be-careful-what-you-say look.

Dale wondered if Menzi would ask anything personal about their supposed relationship. She didn't have to wait long. As soon as the apartment door closed Menzi's curiosity got the best of her.

"How long have you two been together?"

"Depends on when you start counting." Dale bumped the elevator button with her elbow. The elevator door opened just as Dale's shoulder began to scream at her.

"Do you need to set it down?" Menzi said, not even breathing heavily.

"Yes, I think so." Dale's pride was overruled by her pain. "How long did you date her?"

"About four years. We lived together two of those. Where do you work?" The question sounded like a diversion.

"Home Depot. How about you?"

Menzi pointed to the V logo on her shirt and said, "Vulcan. Largest aggregate producer in the US. We mine crushed stone for ready-mix and asphalt companies. Our stone built the Sears Tower. I'm the buyer at the quarry."

"So the bags of rocks we get in the garden center could come from you?"

"Could be," she said proudly.

Menzi and Dale made several trips to the resale shop, laughing and chatting about cars, sports, vacation destinations, even which brand of jeans each one liked. But nothing else was said about Taren. It was as if they had mutually excluded that subject.

"How are you doing?" Taren asked, squatting next to Dale as she unbolted the bed frame. "You must be exhausted."

"I'm okay, so long as I don't sit down."

"Do you want to take a nap for a couple hours? We can do this."

"No, but thanks for offering. I'll survive."

"How are you and Menzi doing? I mean what are you two talking about?"

"We've talked about lots of things. She's thinking about a Subaru for her next car. We wear the same size jeans, but she likes Wranglers."

"Anything else?"

"Oh, yeah. There was something else. I told her you purr like a kitten when I let you be on top."

"You did not." Taren scowled at her. "Did you?"

"No," she chuckled.

"Are you sure?"

"Taren, I'd never say anything to embarrass you. Our history is our business."

"Thank you." Taren squeezed Dale's arm then went back to work.

A few minutes later, Menzi handed Taren a hinged picture frame she found in a drawer. "Do you know who these kids are on the pony?"

"Oh, wow. I haven't seen this in years. This is Sydney and I."

"Really?" Dale came to look over Taren's shoulder.

"Sydney was sure we could ride bareback together. Poor little pony."

"I'm really sorry about your sister," Menzi said. "I should have come down for her funeral."

"I understand why you didn't." Taren glanced up at Dale.

Dale knew this was hard for Taren but she didn't know just how hard until she saw a teardrop splash onto the picture glass. Then another. Dale draped her arms around her as tears continued to drip onto the picture. She felt Taren's body slump in her embrace.

"It's okay," Dale whispered as Taren sobbed quietly. "I've got you."

Taren finally took a replenishing breath. She slipped the picture frame in a box to keep and went back to work, picking through her aunt's closet. Menzi and Dale carried lamps, clothes, stacks of magazines, wall hangings and most of the furniture to the resale shop. When Menzi showed interest in two short bookcases Dale didn't want, Taren insisted she take them.

"Do you want any of this food?" Menzi asked, peering into the refrigerator.

"No," Taren said, barely considering it.

"How about mustard and mayo?" She held up two partially filled jars.

"No. I didn't bring a cooler and I don't want any of it. Dale, do you want any of it?"

"No," she said adamantly from the hall.

"You take them. Take the can goods, too," Taren insisted.

"Okay." Menzi pulled over a box and a trash bag and began sorting.

"Promise you'll throw out anything that's expired. I'm sure there's lots of that."

"Wow, your aunt had good taste." She pulled two bottles of wine from the bottom shelf. "You want these? They haven't been opened."

"I don't want them." Taren gave a quick look then went back to sorting.

"They don't have to be refrigerated. This is expensive stuff."

"I don't want them."

"Hey, you want to open one? There are glasses here on the counter." She grinned wickedly. "We could toast the old gal."

"No," Taren said firmly.

"Are you sure? This stuff is better cold than piss-warm."

"She said no," Dale said as she went out the door with an armload of coats. When she returned the wine bottles were in Menzi's box, still unopened and Menzi had a dejected look on her face.

The more they worked, the more Dale struggled with fatigue. The short nap she'd taken in a rest area just before dawn hadn't been enough. And her shoulder wasn't helping. She didn't have time to nurse a chronically sore shoulder. When she returned from a trip downstairs Taren was sitting cross-legged in the furniture-less living room, sorting through boxes of canceled checks, old receipts and newspaper clippings her aunt had saved. Occasionally she lingered over a photograph or bit of memorabilia then set it aside to keep. Dale sat down on the floor and pressed her back against the wall.

"You look whipped," Taren said sympathetically. "I'm starting to feel really bad about this."

"Don't." Dale propped her arms on her knees and closed her eyes. "I volunteered."

"I know but you did all the driving, carried all this stuff downstairs and all you're taking home is a box of kitchen doodads."

"To tell the truth, right now I'd trade it all for twenty minutes on a pillow." Dale knew her words sounded slurred.

"I bet you would, sweetie," Taren replied, her voice trailing off into a fog.

* * *

Dale opened her eyes to the sound of giggling. She didn't know how long she had been asleep or who put the folded towel under her head but she was curled up on the floor listening to strange noises coming from the bedroom. She stumbled to her feet, bracing herself against the wall as she fought to bring the room into focus.

"Anybody in here?" she said, opening the door.

"Hi," Taren said, looking up with a smile. "How was your nap?" She and Menzi were sitting against the wall, each holding a can of pop.

"Hey, woman. You snore," Menzi said. "You want a Coke?" She held an extra up for Dale.

"No, thanks." Dale wasn't sure what she expected to find behind the closed door but this wasn't it.

"Okay but don't say we didn't offer." Taren climbed to her feet and dusted off the knees of her jeans.

"How long did I sleep?"

"Not long enough." Taren patted Dale's belly as she slipped past. "You need a good night's sleep. And after dinner, we're checking into a hotel. I confirmed our reservation. It's not far from here. We'll come back in the morning to load the truck and head home."

"Don't you want to load the truck now?"

"Do you want your stuff stolen off the truck tonight?" Menzi asked.

"Oh, I hadn't thought of that."

"Here in Chicago anything left in the back of a truck is considered fair game. You could park it under a streetlight and they'll still steal it."

"That's all tomorrow. This evening I'm taking us all to dinner," Taren announced. She grinned and shook the cigar box. "Between the bedside table, the kitchen and the miscellaneous cigar boxes, Aunt Bess left three hundred and eighty-six dollars plus a bunch of change."

"You can leave your truck at the hotel. I'll drive," Menzi said, as if it was understood. Dale was too tired to argue.

They locked the apartment and let Mr. Holburn know they'd be back in the morning. He wasn't happy about it but Taren pointed out she had the entire weekend as per their agreement.

Taren and Menzi chatted like old school chums all through dinner, catching up on friends and neighborhood news. Dale didn't mind. She smiled and nodded but barely had the energy to chew her food. She was dragging by the time Menzi dropped them off back at the hotel. She promised to meet them at the apartment in the morning and help load the truck. Dale suspected she wanted one more day with Taren.

"Do you want to shower first?" Taren asked, stepping out of her shoes and snapping on the television. "I can wait."

"I'll wait until morning." Dale loosened her belt and flopped down on the bed closest to the window without turning back the covers. "Can I ask what's the deal with you and Menzi? Why was I your beard?"

"Like I told you, we each wanted different things from a relationship. I just didn't want to encourage anything today."

"What was it she wanted?" Dale folded her arms behind her head, allowing Taren all the time she needed to reply.

"Whatever it was, it wasn't me." Taren propped the pillows against the headboard and leaned against them as she flipped through the channels.

"I don't understand. She's in love with you, Taren. She'd take you back in a heartbeat, if you'd let her. I can see it in her eyes. Why did you break up with her?"

Taren was silent for a moment then said, "Have you ever been in love with someone but something just didn't feel right? The person was kind and funny and caring but you're just not happy. I can't explain it." She looked over at Dale. "I just couldn't do it. She wasn't what I wanted. I couldn't settle."

"If not Menzi, what is it you want?"

Taren smiled slightly but didn't answer.

"Is it Lee?"

"No," Taren replied and turned back to the TV. "Definitely not Lee."

Dale had more questions she wanted to ask but she was too tired to keep her eyes open. Sometime during the night she felt Taren pull the blanket over her and her hand brush against her forehead. Like many nights since the tornado, she wrestled with nightmares of her screaming for help. She didn't know if she had been dreaming or if she actually heard Taren's comforting whisper. "Shh, it's okay. You're not alone. I'm right here. Just sleep."

They ate breakfast at the hotel then met Menzi at the apartment. With her help they loaded the truck and headed back to Joplin.

It was after ten when Dale drove through the darkened streets of the tornado zone and into her driveway. She had only been gone two days but the reality of the disaster gave her cold chills. She unlocked the trailer and stood listening to the night sounds. In the distance she heard the faint hum of a generator. It was a reminder of what was out there in the darkness she couldn't see.

She stripped out of her clothes and climbed into bed. She knew she should be tired. They had driven back in ten hours, stopping only for restrooms and drive-through meals. Taren had arranged for her neighbor to help unload the heavy dresser. Dale knew they'd still be struggling up Taren's front steps without his help. Dale was almost asleep when she remembered she left her cell phone in the truck. She scurried out to get it, wearing only sneakers and carrying one of the solar yard lights Taren had given her. When she returned to the trailer she noticed a text message was waiting. It was from Taren. She crawled back into bed then opened it.

*Wanted to say thanks again. Couldn't sleep until I told you how much I appreciate your help.*

Dale tapped out a reply. She didn't know how long Taren's text had been waiting so didn't expect a reply from her.

*You're welcome. Glad I could help. Anytime.*

She plugged the phone into the charger and turned over, ready for sleep. A minute later the chime announced an incoming text.

*You should be asleep. You have work tomorrow and you must be pooped after all that driving.*

Dale chuckled and replied.

*You have work, too. Why aren't you asleep?*

There was a longer delay then Taren's reply.

*Good question!!!!! Nite!!*

Dale didn't reply. She needed sleep more than she needed to start a conversation with Taren although she was tempted. She wasn't sure what she would say anyway. She couldn't explain it but something about the trip to Chicago had Dale's brain twisting in the wind when it came to Taren Dorsey. Were the bad times all behind them? She had been sober for three years and Taren knew that. She no longer turned to alcohol, even now, through the tornado and heartbreak it brought, she clung to her sobriety. Three years was a long time to carry a grudge. Taren had seen her at her very worst, her most vulnerable. Was she now ready to forgive and forget? Could they be friends? True friends?

# CHAPTER TEN

On Dale's way to work Monday morning she was pleasantly surprised to receive a call from Janice apologizing for the misunderstanding about the weekend and a promise to make it up to her. They had been invited to a pool party at a friend of Janice's on Saturday at two. Dale would have preferred a quiet evening with just Janice, a steak dinner and a chance to catch up on rest. But she agreed. Janice called on Wednesday with a reminder and instructions to the friend's home.

Saturday morning Dale iced a case of pop and slid the cooler in the back of her truck. She also bought a veggie tray and a platter of cheesecake bites. She remembered Janice liked salsa with a kick so she bought a bag of chips and a jar of hot salsa. She tossed a pair of running shorts and a sports bra in the truck in case she needed something for swimming. She followed Janice's directions down a country road that wound through a thick stand of trees for nearly a mile before she saw a line of cars parked in front of a sprawling ranch-style home. As soon as she rang the bell a dog began to bark.

"Get back, Rosie," someone said. "Hush." The door opened to a stunningly beautiful blonde in a bikini top and floral Hawaiian skirt tied at her hip. She was tanned and trim and holding a glass of iced tea. "Hi."

"Hello. I'm Dale. And I hope I'm at the right house." She held up the food trays. "I brought goodies."

"Oh, yeah. Janice's friend. I'm Jill. Come on in. Everyone's out by the pool."

Dale followed her through the house to the kitchen. She added the food trays to the snacks already arranged across the counter. The party looked like it was well underway. Twenty or so women wearing everything from jeans to swimwear stood around the pool deck, holding drinks and visiting. Reggae music played in the background. Inflatable rafts and pool toys floated across the surface of the water. If they were meant to be an invitation to swim, no one seemed to notice.

"Hey, peaches," Janice called, waving from the far side of the pool.

She looked good. Her hair had an exotic ruffled look. Even from a distance her white tank top left very little to the imagination. She, too, was wearing a floral sarong, tied low on her hip and showing off her trim abs. She hurried over and gave Dale a big hug, wrapping herself around her and holding on.

"Hi there," Dale said, enjoying the feel of Janice's body against her.

"You're late. I was worried about you."

"You told me two o'clock." Dale checked the time on her cell phone. "It's five after."

"I told you noon, baby. You must have forgotten. But that's okay. You're here now."

Dale knew she had told her two o'clock. But there was no need to argue about it now. It was probably a simple mistake.

"Sorry I'm late. By the way, you look hot." She took Janice's hand and turned her, soaking in a full view.

"You really think so?" She batted her eyes dramatically.

"Absolutely."

"I'm not wearing a bra, just for you." She gave Dale a coy wink. "I'm so sorry we had the misunderstanding last weekend. It was all my fault. Forgive me."

"Already forgotten." That was the third time Janice had begged for forgiveness about last weekend.

"I'll make it up to you. I promise. Let's get you something to drink." Janice pulled Dale by the hand toward the outdoor bar.

"Iced tea?" Dale said, her cooler of pop still in the back of the truck.

"How about a Long Island iced tea?" Janice took a pitcher from the small refrigerator under the counter and poured a tall glass full. "This is really good. I love Lynn's recipe."

"No, thanks." Dale quickly scanned the bar for something non-alcoholic. "Any Coke or Pepsi back there?"

"There's ginger ale. What do you want in it?" She reached for a glass, ready to mix Dale's choice.

"That's okay. I'll run out to the truck. I brought Coke. Be right back."

The sound of ice cubes clinking in a glass and the haunting aroma of alcohol followed Dale out the front door. She opened the cooler and pulled out a can. Her hand in the stinging cold ice bath couldn't erase the memory of the first sweet taste of scotch on her tongue. Dale popped the top and took a drink, enjoying the coolness as it slid down her throat. She leaned against the side of the truck, swirling the Coke in the can then drinking until she had finished it.

"Shit," she muttered and threw the can in the back of the truck. Even fantasizing was wrong. She opened the cooler and pulled out three more cans to take inside. She dropped one and it rolled across the bed of the truck and lodged under a bag of trash she intended to drop in Zoe's Dumpster. She thought about ignoring it and getting another but she knew a can of pop left in the hot summer sun would soon explode. She climbed in to retrieve it. When she moved the bag, she noticed something else. Taren's sunglasses, the bejeweled ones she had worn during the softball game and on the way back from Chicago. She must have dropped them when they were unloading the truck. Luckily they weren't scratched. She smiled, remembering the way they perched on her nose as she wandered the outfield.

"You are SO not a softball player, Taren," she chuckled. Dale set the cans on the hood of the truck then tapped out a text.

*Found a pair of sunglasses in the truck and I KNOW they aren't mine. No self-respecting softball player would be caught wearing these. Wonder who they belong to. LOL*

She sent it, collected the cans and went back to the party. Janice was refilling her glass at the bar and visiting with a woman in a blue bikini.

"There you are." Janice looked up, surprised at seeing Dale. "Where did you go?"

"Pop," she replied, setting one can on the counter and putting the rest in the refrigerator.

"I was beginning to think you got lost." She gave Dale a kiss on the cheek then went back to her conversation with the woman in the bikini.

Dale opened her Coke. She perched on a barstool and scanned the women around the pool. A few looked vaguely familiar, probably customers from the store, but no one she could name. Janice hadn't bothered to introduce her to anyone but that didn't stop her from offering casual conversation to whoever stopped at the bar for a refill.

"Don't I know you?" a silver-haired stocky woman asked. She narrowed her eyes as if trying to identify Dale.

"I don't know. I'm Dale. And you are?"

"Francine. Do you live in Springfield?"

"Nope. Joplin. All my life. Born and bred Ozarkian."

The woman finally gasped and smiled. "Yes. I remember now. East side of the street, middle of the block. You've got a smashed hot water tank on your trash pile."

"Yes, I do." Dale still didn't recognize the woman.

Francine laughed out loud. "I have you at a disadvantage. When I was working in your neighborhood after the tornado you were still in shock. You probably don't remember names or faces."

"You were in my neighborhood?"

"Yes. Several times. I'm a Red Cross volunteer. We were handing out bottled water from the back of a golf cart. I was wearing a yellow vest and a Red Cross ball cap. I looked like a crossing guard. I asked if you needed anything and you said yes, you needed a trash bag the size of Rhode Island." She gave an endearing chuckle.

"I remember now. You came the next day with bottles of Gatorade."

"Yes. How are things going for you?"

"Okay. I work at Home Depot and they've reopened so that helps."

"Do you still have a lot of branches and debris in your yard? We can help with that. We've got volunteers working all over town with the cleanup."

"Thanks. But I'm doing okay. I've got most of the trees in the front yard piled up waiting for the city trucks to make the first pickup. I'm going through the house debris a little at a time, seeing what I can salvage. Lots of people are worse off than me. They need your help more than I do." She wasn't ready to have strangers come on her property and rake everything to the curb. She was still finding pieces of her life among the debris. A picture, a dish, a piece of jewelry that belonged to her mother or something of Sydney's.

"I saw you've got a trailer in your yard. Aren't you going to rebuild?"

"I hope so, eventually. I've got some details to work out."

"Well, if we can help, give us a call. Volunteers are coming in from all over the country. Busloads of them. You don't have to go through this alone." She gave Dale a hug.

"Thank you." Dale accepted the hug but steeled herself from the emotions talking about the tornado damage raised.

She hadn't eaten lunch and was hungry. She drifted inside and filled a paper plate with snacks. She made a plate for Janice and took it out to her but she barely touched it. The hot afternoon sun beat down on the pool deck, forcing many of the women to eventually take a dip to cool off. Janice refilled her glass and sat on the edge of the pool, dangling her feet in the water and swaying to the music.

"I love this kind of music," she said, her eyes closed as she swayed. "I am so going to Jamaica someday. I want to do that Bo Derek thing when she runs down the beach in slow motion."

"*Ten*," Dale slipped out of her shoes and took a seat next to her.

"Ten what?"

"The movie with Bo Derek running down the beach was called *Ten*. Dudley Moore and Julie Andrews were in it. And Bo played a cheater. She had sex with Dudley Moore while she was on her honeymoon."

"Who cares if she's cheating if she's sexy? I'd give anything to have skin like that."

"Julie Andrews was a hot woman when she was younger," a woman said, floating past on a raft. "What was that movie when she ripped her top off and showed her boobs?"

"Mary Poppins topless? Oh, gross," Janice scoffed.

"Julie Andrews was never topless in a movie," Francine said as she took a seat on the side of the pool.

"Yes, she was." The woman on the raft steered herself toward the conversation. "Hey, does anybody know the name of the movie where Julie Andrews flashed her boobs?" she shouted.

"*S-O-B*," someone yelled.

"You want to talk hot and naked, how about Jodie Foster in *Nell* when she comes up out of that water. Oh, my God. I thought I was going to cream myself." The woman splashed water across her lap. "Give me some of that. As a matter of fact, give me anything young and tan."

"I don't want some young, naive bimbo," Jill said, joining the conversation. "Give me a mature woman who knows what the hell she's doing. You want to talk great boobs, she's sitting right over there." She pointed at Janice. "Isn't that right, Dale?"

Dale felt a blush race up her face. She was uncomfortable talking about her girlfriend's breasts to strangers. She expected Janice to blush as well but she seemed proud of Jill's announcement.

"Well, are they, Dale?" the woman on the raft asked, positioning herself to see.

"Yeah, are they?" Francine giggled.

"They aren't bad." Dale felt awkward.

"What the hell do you mean they aren't bad?" Janice demanded. She set her glass down and pulled her tank top over her head, proudly exposing herself for all to see. "It hasn't been that long since we did it. How can you forget what they look like?" Every eye was on Janice's breasts. She arched her back and extended her ample C cups toward Dale, the raisin-size nipples plump and erect. "Now tell me these aren't the best pair you ever saw."

"Grab one of those puppies for me, Dale," someone said from across the pool and whistled.

"Well?" Janice insisted.

"Yes, they are great," Dale finally admitted, knowing she would be heckled until she did. She molded her hands over the plump breasts for modesty sake as much as for the sensuality of it.

"Dale's copping a feel, ladies," Jill announced. "You go girl."

Janice leaned into Dale, wobbling her breasts. She bumped her glass and spilled it across the deck.

"Oops." Dale grabbed the glass and swept the liquid away from the edge of the pool before it ran into the water.

"Hey, I thought I was getting some here," Janice whined, her words beginning to slur.

"Behave yourself or you aren't getting any later either," Dale teased.

"Get me another drink, babe."

"I'll get you a Coke." Dale hoped Janice would agree. She strongly suspected the Long Island iced tea was talking and she didn't like it.

"God, no. I'll get it myself."

Dale tossed Janice her tank top as she climbed to her feet.

"You better put this on before you sunburn those."

Janice shimmied then laughed and headed to the bar.

Dale went inside to wash the smell of booze from her hands. She had just finished when she felt her cell phone vibrate in her pocket. It was a text from Taren. Janice and her voluptuous taa-taas were waiting on the pool deck, begging to be fondled. But Taren's text seemed more inviting. She leaned against the kitchen counter to read it.

*I wondered where I left my sunglasses. Are you holding them hostage until I apologize?*

Dale had no idea what Taren had done that needed an apology. They hadn't argued since the wedding and that was a more of a disagreement about Janice than an argument. Dale tapped out a reply.

*I would if I knew what you did wrong. Clue me in.*

She stood at the counter, eating a celery stick as she waited for a reply. She didn't have to wait long.

*Chicago, of course. You drove me all the way up there to get my stuff and you came away with squadoosh. No wonder you're mad at me.*

Dale quickly tapped a reply.

*I'm not mad at you. I knew there was a possibility I wouldn't find anything I could use. It wasn't your fault.* She hesitated then smiled to herself and added, *I thought it was my fault. I'm the one who let you sleep.* She wondered if Taren still thought that joke was funny or was it just stupid. She waited several minutes but didn't get a reply.

"You can come out now," Francine said on her way to the freezer to refill the ice bucket. "She put her top back on."

"Good." Dale picked a handful of grapes from the bowl and headed outside, convinced Taren was finished texting. She hoped Janice was finished looking for attention. Sure she was drop-dead gorgeous but the newness had worn off and Dale found herself re-thinking what they had in common. What she once found cute and tantalizing now seemed immature, even occasionally annoying. Janice might be thirty but she sometimes seemed more like a teenager. They needed to talk about some things. But Dale doubted Janice was sober enough to have an adult conversation.

"Put your suit on and come swimming with me." Janice was sitting on the top step in the shallow end. Her tank top was wet and clung to her body like transparent tissue paper.

Dale was ready to join her when she felt her phone vibrate.

"Just a minute," she called and pulled it out. Taren had finally replied and Dale was anxious to read it.

*Sorry about that. I was sautéing mushrooms and they were starting to burn. Can I drop by this evening and pick up my sunglasses?*

Dale wished she were home.

*How about I bring them by tomorrow? I'm out of town right now.*

Dale really wished she were home. More than she ever thought she would, she wished she were sitting on the steps of the trailer, waiting for Taren's strawberry red hatchback to pull into the drive. She held up her hand, signaling Janice she would be right there. Taren replied almost immediately.

*Ah, yes. Dinner with Janice. Making up for lost time. We'll talk tomorrow.*

"What time tomorrow?" Dale muttered as she tapped in the letters. She stood staring at the screen, waiting for her answer. "What time?"

"Stop playing with that thing and come play with me," Janice demanded. She came up behind Dale and pushed her in the pool, clothes, phone and all. Dale came up, sputtering and coughing. Janice stood on the side, laughing hysterically. "That'll teach you to ignore me."

"Dammit, Janice. I had my phone in my hand."

"So, dry it off."

"I dropped it." Dale circled as she treaded water, looking for her phone.

Jill came to the edge and pointed. "Look down by the drain. Everything gets sucked down there."

Dale took a deep breath and swam down, searching the floor of the pool. She surfaced, gasping for breath then dove again. The phone was wedged in the grate. She wiggled it free then pushed off and rose to the surface. Dale swam to the side and climbed out without looking at Janice. She knew if she did she'd say things she'd regret.

"Open the case and take the battery out," Francine said, bringing her a towel.

Dale suspected the phone was ruined but opened it and removed the battery anyway. She poured the water out and set the parts in the sun to dry. She squeezed the water out of her wallet and left it next to the phone as well.

"Sorry, babe," Janice said, looking over her shoulder. "I didn't mean to get your phone wet."

"What did you think would happen when you pushed me in the pool with it in my hand?" She pressed her hands through her wet hair.

"I don't know." She shrugged. "I thought you'd drop it or something."

"And dropping my phone would have been a better idea?"

"Don't make such a big deal out of it. It's just a freakin' phone."

"A freakin' phone that cost two hundred bucks." Dale looked down at her wallet and gasped. "Sydney's picture." She opened her wallet and carefully pulled out a stack of receipts and photographs. She peeled them apart, one by one until she got to a photograph of Sydney. It was soaking wet. The glossy finish was sticky. "Shit," she said under her breath. Other than the framed picture Taren gave her, this was the only one she had of Sydney. The rest had been sucked out the roof of her house or trapped in her flooded laptop.

"Who's that?" Janice asked, barely interested.

"Sydney." Like a surgeon doing brain surgery, Dale carefully blotted at the photograph. She wanted Janice to just go away. She didn't want to talk to her and she certainly didn't want to explain who Sydney was. At this moment, Janice hadn't earned the right to know.

"Sydney who?" She picked up the picture and stared at it then smirked indifferently and dropped it back on the table.

"Careful." Dale grabbed for it but it fell to the floor. It landed upside down on the hot deck, instantly sticking to it.

"Oops," Janice said with a giggle and headed to the bar.

Dale carefully peeled the picture from the concrete. Bits of it remained like colored confetti. She placed it on the towel to dry then heaved a decisive breath. She was about to do something she might regret later but she headed to the bar. She took the drink from Janice's hand and poured it in a nearby flowerpot then gathered Janice in her arms and carried her onto the diving board.

"You want to play in the pool, here you go." Dale tossed her in the pool.

Dale's revenge brought cheers and laughter from the women around the pool. But Janice came to the surface mad. She glared up at Dale.

"You asshole. I didn't want to get my hair wet."

"I didn't want to get my phone wet either."

"Well, it's not funny." She paddled to the ladder and climbed out. Dale was waiting for her and picked her up. She carried her onto the diving board and dumped her in again.

"And that was for my wallet," Dale said as Janice came to the surface. The crowd laughed and cheered even louder. Janice was not amused. She had venom in her eyes as she climbed out.

"You better run, Dale. She does *not* look happy," Francine said.

"Damn right you better run," Janice said. She picked up a towel and cocked it as if she was going to snap Dale with it. But she couldn't catch her. Dale trotted around the pool to hoots and cheers, staying just ahead of the towel. "You owe me a drink."

"No, I don't." Dale slowed to let Janice catch up then took off running again.

"Yes, you do. You poured mine in the bushes."

"You've had enough." Dale ran backward, teasing Janice to keep up with her.

Janice stopped at the table and snatched up the picture of Sydney.

"You refill my glass and bring it to me or I tear up this picture." She held it up, her fingers poised to tear it.

Three years ago Dale chose sobriety over alcoholism. From that day forward she didn't handle liquor. She didn't make drinks for friends. She didn't buy booze for relatives. But she strongly suspected Janice had consumed enough that she'd rip Sydney's picture in half without a second thought. And she probably wouldn't remember it in the morning.

"Wait, Janice. Please, don't do that."

"Get my drink or I swear to God I'll do it," Janice said viciously, poised as if she had her fingers on the pin of a grenade.

"Don't tear up her stuff, Janice," Francine said. She seemed to know this was one of Dale's few surviving treasures.

"Janice, don't do that," Jill added. No one was laughing anymore.

"Shut up. She owes me a drink," Janice snapped.

"Okay. Okay. I'll get it." Dale kept her eyes on the picture as she moved to the bar. She dropped several ice cubes in a glass then took the pitcher of mixed drinks from the refrigerator. The smell of alcohol permeated the air. Dale took a deep breath, searching for fresh air but there was none. Just the smell of liquor. The sound of ice in the glass, the splash as she poured, the feel of the cool drink in her hand all conspired to challenge Dale's inhibitions. And she hated Janice for it.

"Here," she demanded, handing Janice the glass with one hand and reaching for the picture with the other.

Janice took a drink before relinquishing the picture as if testing what Dale poured.

"Here." She thrust the picture at Dale's chest, bending it in half.

Dale didn't say a word. She collected her phone and slipped the still damp receipts back in her wallet. She thanked Jill for the hospitality, waved goodbye to Francine and turned to leave.

"Where are you going?" Janice asked with surprise.

"Home. I've had all the party I can stand for one day."

"Aren't you going to at least kiss me goodbye?" Janice asked, grabbing her sleeve.

"No. I'm not kissing you." She pulled Janice's fingers off her shirt. "I told you I don't drink. And I'm sure you taste like alcohol."

"Ah, come on. We were just having fun. Don't go away all mad."

"That's not my kind of fun."

Dale strode through the house and out the front door, her wet shoes squishing with every step. She climbed in her truck and slammed the door, mad at the beckoning smell of alcohol still filling her nostrils.

She was still fuming when she turned north on highway 71. It would be easy to blame Janice. She was the one who had had too much to drink. She was the one who pushed her in the pool. Yet she only had herself to blame. She had gone to the pool party. She should have known what it would be like. She also knew Janice's behavior and personality were starting to wear on her. She had turned a blind eye to it long enough. Maybe too long. Had she been blinded by a pure physical attraction, too lazy to see the real Janice?

She needed to talk to someone. She reached for her cell phone to call her sponsor then remembered it didn't work. "Dammit!" She tossed it across the cab of the truck as a fresh round of anger bubbled to the surface. Anger at Janice, anger at the tornado, even anger at Sydney. She banged her fist against the steering wheel, fighting the urge to scream. She turned west on Thirty-Second Street. She wasn't in the mood to drive past Home Depot

Even though her clothes were still damp and were starting to itch, she wasn't in the mood to go home either. She didn't want to sit in that cracker box of a trailer and stew. For a brief moment she thought about stopping by Zoe's apartment. It was dinner time. She and Sasha would probably be home. But the thought of Zoe's meddling questions put a quick end to that idea. She meandered through Joplin without a destination in mind other than to avoid the tornado damage. She sat at a stop sign daydreaming when a car horn blasted her back to reality. She realized she was just two blocks from Taren's house. She turned the corner and pulled up to the curb. She finger combed her hair then trotted up the front steps and rang the doorbell. Taren's car was in the driveway but she didn't answer the door. Dale rang again and knocked.

"Just a minute," Taren called from somewhere inside. When the door finally opened Taren was holding her hand over her mouth as if hiding something. "Hello." Her eyes got big. "I thought you were out of town."

"I got back early." Dale held up Taren's sunglasses, an afterthought once she stopped at the curb. "I thought you'd need these."

"I could have waited. You didn't have to bring them all the way over here today." She kept her hand over her mouth and didn't invite Dale in either.

"That's okay. I was in the area. What's wrong with your mouth?"

"Nothing." She opened the screen door a few inches and stuck her hand out.

"Do you have food stuck in your teeth or something?"

"No. Now give me the sunglasses and go away. I'm busy." Taren didn't sound convincing.

"I've changed my mind." She drew the glasses back. "I think I *will* hold them hostage. You take your hand down or I keep the bling." She twirled the folded sunglasses around her finger as she pulled the door open and stepped inside. "I know what it is. You've got a huge zit on your chin and it needs to be popped."

"NO!" Taren cupped both hands over her mouth as her expression changed to dread. She hurried down the hall and into the bathroom, slamming the door. "Go away."

"I don't think so." Dale followed. She turned the knob and pushed the door open.

"Don't you dare come in here." Taren quickly clasped her hands over her mouth again.

"What are you hiding?"

"I'm not hiding anything. And it's none of your business." Taren backed into the corner as Dale stepped closer.

"Let me see the zit."

"It's not a blemish. If you must know, I'm waxing." She opened her hands for a brief moment to expose a thick smear of amber wax across her upper lip, then closed them again. "Now that you've seen it, you can leave so I can finish."

"Let me see." Dale pulled at her hands.

"No." She turned her head to hide. "I look silly with this goop on my lip."

"No, you don't." Dale cupped her hand under Taren's

chin and held it as she scrutinized the hardened wax. "Now I know what you'd look like as a Texas cowboy with a handlebar mustache."

"That's not funny." She pushed against Dale's chest.

"Can I peel it off?" Dale grinned.

"NO! You are *not* peeling my wax." She pushed harder but Dale didn't move.

"I promise to do it quick. It won't hurt." Dale reached for her lip but Taren grabbed her hand.

"Some things are private."

"Yeah, I know. Like going potty and changing your pad. But I just want to peel wax off your lip."

"Did you bother Sydney like this when she waxed?" Taren leaned her forehead into Dale's chest, unable to stifle a giggle.

"No. She didn't use this stuff. She plucked. So, can I yank it off?" The timer on the bathroom counter dinged. "Does that mean it's ready?"

"Yes, it's ready." Taren heaved a sigh and released her hold on Dale's hands. "Do you promise to be quick?"

Dale ripped it off before Taren had time to brace herself. "Yes, I promise."

"Ouch!"

Dale held up the strip of wax, studying the tiny shafts of hair. "Wow, hairy little beast, aren't you?"

"Give me that." She snatched it out of her hand. "Now you can go out so I can wash my face." She pushed Dale out the door and closed it.

"How often do you do that?" Dale asked, leaning on the doorjamb.

"Obviously not often enough." Taren opened the door, blotting her face with a towel. "Now if you're through ripping the hair from my upper lip, do you care to tell me how your date with Janice went? And by the way, I thought about what you said and I completely agree. Who you date is your business. And yes, it probably has a lot to do with Sydney. When you come through the door, I naturally expect to see my sister with you. I'm sorry. I shouldn't have said anything at the wedding. Janice is a gorgeous woman. I'm sure she has some wonderful qualities. So how did it go?" Taren hung the towel in the bathroom then headed to the kitchen.

"It was different." Dale followed, shoving her hands in her damp jeans pockets to loosen their grip on her crotch.

"Good different or bad different?"

"It started out okay. It was a pool party at her friend's house."

"And?"

"And it pretty much went downhill from there."

"Anything in particular that caused this southern migration?" Taren opened the refrigerator and took out a large glass jar with a spigot. "Do you want some iced tea? I made sun tea."

Dale burst out laughing.

"What's so funny about iced tea?"

"Iced tea played a very large part in today's fiasco. They were drinking pitchers of Long Island iced tea."

"Oh, my. With the booze in it?"

"Oh, yeah. Lots of booze."

Taren opened the refrigerator to put the jar back.

"No, no. Don't put it back. So long as it's just iced tea, I'd love some."

"Are you sure? I can find something else."

"Actually I've been thirsty for iced tea all day. They didn't have any that wasn't already doctored."

"I promise. This is plain old Lipton tea bags." She took two glasses from the cabinet and filled them with ice before adding tea. "Unsweetened," she said, handing one to Dale.

Dale took a long swig. "That's good." She clinked her glass against Taren's. "Here's to plain old Lipton."

"Are you saying Long Island iced tea was to blame for the demise of your afternoon?" Taren leaned against the counter and took a sip.

"There were other things but it was probably the underlying cause."

"Okay, I have to ask. Does this have anything to do with your wet clothes?"

Dale chuckled, looking down at her jeans stuck to her legs.

"I got pushed in the swimming pool."

"I can see how that would be a bummer." Taren smiled behind her glass.

"That wasn't the worst of it. My phone went in the pool with me."

"Your phone was in your pocket?" she gasped.

"My phone was in my hand. In fact, I think it's why I got pushed in the pool. I was texting."

"Janice did it, right? Who were you texting?"

"You."

"She was jealous you were texting me so she shoved you in the swimming pool?"

"She didn't know it was you."

"She just shoved you in because you were texting?"

"Probably. And before you ask, yes, she had been drinking." Dale looked out the kitchen window at the spot where the trailer once sat.

"I can't believe she is so rude and disrespectful to you. And I don't mean just the pool thing." She drew a quick breath. "There I go again. I'm sorry. None of my business."

"Taren, it's okay. Say whatever you want. We've known each other long enough to at least be honest."

"Okay, I will. I can't believe Janice can drink right in front of you. She should know what sobriety means to you."

Dale continued to stare out the window, wondering how to explain this. How did she tell Taren she was too chicken to tell Janice she was a recovering alcoholic? How did she admit her oversight backfired so badly?

"You did tell her, didn't you?" Taren asked. "She knows your history. She knows you are three years sober."

"She knows I don't drink. I told her that on our first date." Dale looked back at her. "I wasn't sure you'd remember exactly how long it has been."

"If you remember, I was there. It was just a few weeks after I moved to Joplin. I'm the one who picked you up and gave you the ride home that night."

"I remember." Dale vaguely remembered stumbling around the parking lot of a sleazy bar, unable to find her car. "God was watching out for me. He kept me off the roads that night. I'm very lucky I never had an accident." Dale groaned and shook her head. "I could have killed someone."

"Or yourself." Taren dropped a lemon wedge in Dale's glass. "That didn't answer my question. Why haven't you told Janice?"

"I don't know. I didn't want to scare her off I guess."

"Is she the first person you've dated since Sydney?" Taren asked carefully.

Dale nodded.

"You really should tell her. Be honest about who you are. Be proud of who you are. If it was me, I'd want to know how she was going to handle it."

"I know. But Janice and I aren't exactly seeing eye-to-eye right now. To be honest, I'm not sure we ever will." Dale felt a strange relief to admit it.

"Really? Then maybe you should…" Taren turned away.

"Should what?"

"Nothing. I hope things work out for you, Dale." She dumped the rest of her iced tea in the sink and put the glass in the dishwasher.

"Thanks for the iced tea. I guess I better head home and change out of these damp clothes."

"I appreciate your bringing over my sunglasses. And I'm sorry if they caused a problem for you."

"I don't see it that way. I think your sunglasses allowed me to see some things I needed to see. And they provided an excuse to knock on your door."

"You don't need an excuse to knock on my door. You are welcome here anytime." She followed Dale to the front door.

"Even when you're waxing?" Dale raised an eyebrow playfully.

"Don't remind me." Taren blushed.

"You weren't really embarrassed that I saw you like that, were you?"

"Yes, I was embarrassed."

"Why? It's just me."

"Because I care what you think."

"Me?"

"Sure. Why not? You're a friend. It's been three years. Things have changed. I hold no grudges, Dale." Taren reached up and kissed her on the cheek, her hand lingered between Dale's breasts. "You can never have too many friends."

"I hold no grudges either," Dale said softly as the warm touch of Taren's lips seared into her memory.

"Good." Taren opened the door and held it for Dale. "Good night." Taren stood on the porch watching as Dale started the truck and pulled away.

Later, Dale sat in her driveway and stared at the trailer without knowing how she got there. Her mind was on Taren's kiss and what it meant. She had never thought of Taren in that way before but there it was. A kiss. Dale leaned back against the headrest and stared at the ceiling. She didn't kiss her back. She wanted to. God knows, she wanted to. But it was just a kiss on the cheek. Maybe it didn't mean what Dale wanted it to mean.

# CHAPTER ELEVEN

Dale tinkered with her cell phone Sunday morning but it couldn't be saved. It was a good thing. She couldn't call Janice and demand an apology if not restitution. She didn't have to listen to Zoe's weekend rants either. But being cut off from work worried her. She spent the cooler morning hours stacking branches on the debris pile then collected her dirty laundry. She was ready to swallow her pride and head to Zoe's. They had an agreement. Zoe supplied the washer and dryer, actually provided by the landlord in each duplex, and Dale supplied the detergent and fabric softener sheets.

Zoe wasn't home. Dale used her key to let herself in and started a load. She used Zoe's landline to call the store and let them know she would be without a cell phone for a few days. She knew it might be longer depending on how many bills she had to pay out of her paycheck. When David informed her overtime was being cut back, she knew replacing the back window of the truck would have to be postponed. So did the purchase of a small air-conditioning unit for the trailer. She took a shower then poured herself a glass of apple juice and stepped out on the front porch to place a call.

"Hi, Kay. This is Dale."

"Dale? I wondered when I'd hear from you. I'm sorry I couldn't stay and visit with you after the meeting. How are things with you since the tornado, hon?"

"I'm okay. I just thought I'd check in. How are you?"

Kay gave a measured pause. "What's up, baby doll? I hear something in your voice."

Dale sat down on the step and took a deep breath. It had been several months since she visited with her sponsor. She had come to count on her guidance and wisdom as she worked the steps and came to grips with her addiction. Kay had eighteen years of sobriety herself, enough that Dale trusted her judgment.

"What's going on in your private life? Did you ever have a second date with that accountant in Neosho?" Kay asked. It was a friendly nudge, as if breaking the ice.

"Janice, yes. New relationships are hard."

"Yes, they are. Most certainly."

"We've got some issues and I'm not sure the best way to handle them. Things are different. Dating is different."

"Are things different or are you different?" Kay asked, patiently allowing Dale to fill the void.

"Maybe it's me. I'm not the same person I was eight or ten years ago."

"Absolutely, you are not the same person. So what kind of issues do you have with Janice?"

"Sometimes I question her loyalty and her maturity. But that's not the real problem I have. Should I have told her I'm a recovering alcoholic?"

"Why didn't you?"

"I didn't tell her because I was afraid a gorgeous woman like that wouldn't accept it. I told her I didn't drink but never told her why. I wanted to wait for the right moment. I wanted her to know the real me first before she judged me."

"And you don't think the real you is a recovering alcoholic?"

"Yes. It is. I know that now. I know I should have said something earlier. Now I have a situation I don't know how to solve." Dale heaved a frustrated sigh. "Janice drinks. Sometimes, a lot."

"I had a feeling that's what it was but I wanted to hear it from you."

"It didn't become apparent until recently. She didn't drink at all on our first date. I remember she was nervous all through dinner but I thought she was just stressed about our first meeting. Then it was a glass of wine at dinner. Or two. Slurred speech. Mood swings. She's been drunk more times than she hasn't."

"And how's that working for you?" Kay Timbers didn't mince words. She had a way of cutting to the heart of the matter.

"It's not." Dale groaned. "God, I'm so stupid."

"Dale, alcoholism is an equal opportunity destroyer. And you are not responsible for Janice's addiction or for curing it. That's her basket of worms. You are only responsible for Dale Kinsel."

"I know that. That's why I left the pool party yesterday. I couldn't stop her from drinking."

"Were you tempted?"

"No. Her behavior raised a lot of ugly memories but no, I wasn't tempted," Dale said.

"What is your truth about Janice?"

"I can't deal with her drinking or with her immaturity."

"But you're having trouble letting her go, right?" Kay asked, as if testing Dale's resolve.

"Yes and I don't understand why. But it gives me clammy hands and an upset stomach every time I think about it."

"I know why, hon."

"You do? Well, I don't."

"You've been through a lot, Dale. You've lost a lot. Sydney, your home, your friends, the security the tornado stole from you. Things you couldn't control. You don't want to lose anything else. You know if you break up with Janice you will have lost again."

"But I realize she isn't right for me," Dale argued. "I think on some level I've known for weeks."

"It doesn't matter. Good or bad, a loss is a loss. You've put up with Janice's shortcomings to protect yourself from the pain of losing something else."

Dale hadn't thought of it that way but Kay was right. It was easier to go along than confront Janice with their differences. "I know what you're thinking, Dale. You're thinking how the hell can she say that? She's never met Janice. And you're right. I haven't. But I know you and what you've been through. And baby doll, you've been through worse than this. Way worse. Taking care of you is number one. You'll know when it's time to bite the bullet and end things with Janice."

Dale knew she had a decision to make. She knew it yesterday when she left the pool party, desperate to put time and distance between her and that woman.

"Thanks for listening to me, Kay."

"That's what I'm here for, hon. Call me anytime."

Dale went inside to change the laundry. Kay was right. She hadn't confronted Janice for a reason. Doing it would add another layer to her already stressful life. But for her peace of mind, she didn't have a choice. She collected her clean laundry, scribbled a note to Zoe and headed home. She felt vulnerable and she didn't like the feeling. She needed to spend the rest of the day cleaning her yard and piling house debris at the curb. If she worked up a good sweat maybe she'd find the courage to call Janice and not vomit over the decision. She'd worry about that tomorrow.

It was after five o'clock and she was drenched in sweat when Zoe pulled into the driveway and honked. Sasha was the first to climb out and wave.

"Don't go far," Zoe called after her. "And be careful where you're walking. You're only wearing sandals."

"Hey," Dale said, wiping her sleeve across her brow. It would have been nice if Zoe was dressed to help but she had a just-stopped-for-a-minute look.

"Hey, yourself. Why don't you turn your damn phone on? I've been calling since yesterday."

"My cell phone's not working." Dale pulled off her work gloves and leaned against the side of Zoe's car to catch her breath.

"What's wrong with it?"

"It got wet. It probably needs a new battery."

"If you carry your phone in your pocket while you're sweating like a racehorse what do you expect?" Zoe quipped.

"Yep. I guess so."

"How was your pool party with Janice?"

"Okay." Dale wasn't opening that can of worms with Zoe. "Nice house."

"Sasha, don't climb on that. You're going to fall and need stitches," Zoe shouted.

"Give the kid a break. Let her play."

"Do you want to pay for a visit to the emergency room when she falls off that crap?"

It wasn't worth the argument. Zoe had been a sedentary child and thought her daughter should be the same.

"Did you need something, Zoe?"

"I was just checking on how you're doing. Have you heard from Taren? Oh, you probably haven't if your phone is toast."

"Actually, I have."

"Oh, great. What are you arguing about now?"

"We didn't argue. We get along pretty well."

"Pretty well?" That spiked Zoe's interest.

"Yep," Dale said, slipping on her gloves. "In fact, she kissed me." Dale knew that would stir her sister's curiosity.

"Really? I don't believe it. She kissed you?"

"Yep." Dale deliberately neglected to mention it was a kiss on the cheek. It was more fun to let Zoe think it was something passionate.

"Oh, she did not," she said bitterly. "Come on, Sasha. We're leaving. Your Aunt Dale is being a butt."

"Happy trails," Dale said with a chuckle as Zoe drove away. The thought of Taren's kiss was a pleasant diversion and lingered long after the taillights of Zoe's car rounded the corner and disappeared.

The hot summer day turned into a warm summer evening. Dale closed only the screen door, allowing the breeze to flow through the trailer as she went to take a shower. She had just squirted shampoo on her hair when she heard a knock at the door.

"Come in, Zoe," she called then went back to lathering. She heard the door slam. She presumed Zoe's curiosity was out of control and she was back to demand kiss details. "I'm in the shower. Sit down and take a load off. I'll be out in a minute."

"It's not Zoe. It's Taren."

Dale gasped, sucking in a mouthful of shampoo. She coughed and spit and said, "Oh, hi. I'll be right there."

"Okay but be aware time is not on your side. I think you'll want what I have sooner than later."

Something in her voice made Dale draw another gasp. She hurriedly rinsed, well aware she left the bathroom door open. Her clean clothes were on the bed and all she had to cover herself was a small bath towel.

"Could you toss me the shorts and T-shirt on the bed?" she asked, sticking her hand around the corner.

"The blue boxers?"

"Yes."

"No underwear?" Taren teased.

"No, just the shorts and shirt."

"Maybe I should hold them hostage like you did with my sunglasses."

"I didn't hold them hostage. I brought them back." Dale held the towel up to cover as much as she could and looked around the edge of the bathroom. Dale instantly noticed Taren had a new hairstyle. It was shorter, much shorter. It was no longer ponytail length but a bundle of soft curls and bangs.

"Yes, and you ripped the wax off my lip." Taren raised an eyebrow.

"You cut your hair."

"Yes, I did. I got tired of it being long. But back to the matter of my lip."

"I embarrassed you so you're going to embarrass me, right?"

"Don't you think it's only fair?"

"Not necessarily. And what is it I'll want from you sooner than later?" Dale continued to hide behind the edge of the bathroom.

"Ice cream sundaes." Taren held up two plastic cups with spoons protruding through the lids. "I had a two for one coupon at Braums. Which do you want? Hot fudge or strawberry?"

"How about blue boxers and white T-shirt first?"

"Fine with me." Taren looked at the clothes on the bed then back at Dale. "Help yourself." She sat down at the booth with a smug grin on her face. "You better hurry. The ice cream is melting."

Dale had no choice. She held the small towel up to her front, leaving her butt exposed as she crossed from the bathroom to the bed and back, hurrying past Taren's watchful eyes.

"Wow, you sure are a hairy little beast," Taren said with a giggle.

Dale clamped the towel tight against her crotch. Yes, she had a thick bush and no, she wasn't in the habit of exposing herself. She rushed back into the bathroom to dress.

"Are we even now?" Dale called, running a comb through her hair.

"Maybe. Hot fudge or strawberry?"

"I don't care. Which do you want?" Finally dressed, Dale slid into the booth across from Taren, hoping her blush had faded.

"You get strawberry."

Dale took a bite then sat studying Taren's new hairstyle.

"What are you staring at?" Taren tugged at the back of her hair.

"I don't think I've ever seen you with short hair. You and Sydney always wore your hair long."

"Don't you like it?" Taren had a momentary look of panic.

"Yes, I do. I like it." She returned to eating her sundae.

Taren nodded toward the window. "I see you're making good progress clearing the storm debris. May I ask how things are going with the insurance company? Where you able to get a more equitable settlement?"

"No. I'm hoping to work a deal with a builder to do some of the work myself. Painting. Plumbing. Anything to cut the cost of construction. It'll take longer to build but that's the only way I can see it happening. Worst-case scenario, I try and secure a second mortgage."

Taren pushed her cup back on the table as if Dale's news spoiled her appetite for ice cream.

"You didn't finish," Dale said.

"I'm full. Do you want it?"

"Sure. I didn't have dinner."

"Why not?"

"I got busy in the yard." She didn't mention that she often lost her appetite when she was working in the yard. Something about moving the storm debris gave her a nervous stomach.

"Dale, you've got to eat. You'll make yourself sick if you don't. Especially in this heat."

"I'm having ice cream." She grinned and took a big bite. "Thank you for thinking of me."

"I had another reason to come over. Ice cream was an afterthought." Taren pulled a baggie from her purse. "Did you replace your phone yet?"

"Not yet."

"Good. Because I noticed you and I have the same carrier. You don't have to take it if you don't want it but this is my old flip phone. It's not a smartphone but you're welcome to it. You can port your own number to it." She handed Dale the baggie. "There's a holster with a belt clip in there and a car charger as well as the wall charger."

"Are you sure you won't need it?" Dale asked eagerly, setting the sundae aside.

"I've got my iPhone. If you don't want it you don't have to take it."

"If you're sure you don't want it, I absolutely do. This is great." Dale grinned happily as she investigated the contents of the baggie. "A simple phone. No data fees. No apps to update. Just talk and text. You bet I want it. Thanks."

"It'll need a charge. I haven't used it in a couple years."

"Can I pay you for this?"

"Absolutely not. I was going to donate it to the tornado relief anyway. I'm glad you said something before I gave it away. Consider it my gift."

"Wow, ice cream and a new phone all in the same day. Thank you, Taren." Dale took the phone and the charger to the bedside table to plug it in but she couldn't get the plug to fit. "Are you sure this is the right charger?"

"I think so. It was all together in my desk." Taren sat down on the bed next to Dale to help. "Let me try."

Dale leaned back while Taren fiddled with the charger, enjoying the sweet aroma of her cologne and way the curls framed her face.

"There, I got it," Taren said, her eyes rolling up to Dale's. "What?"

"Nothing."

"You don't like my hair, do you?"

"Yes, I do. I like it. It's perfect. It's sophisticated. It's soft. It's you." Dale hooked her finger through one of the curls and twirled it. "I like your new look very much."

"Then why are you staring at me like I was someone else?"

"I'm not staring. I'm just admiring your hair. It's beautiful, just like you." Dale drew her finger down Taren's cheek, making her blush.

"Thank you," she said softly, their eyes swimming together.

Dale saw something in Taren's eyes, something unmistakable. A kiss. Not the kiss on the cheek from yesterday but a real kiss. One Dale wanted to experience. She laced her hand through the back of Taren's hair and pulled her close. In one breathless moment she placed a kiss on Taren's mouth.

"What?" Taren whispered but before she could say anything else Dale kissed her again. She plunged her tongue into Taren's mouth, the lingering flavor of strawberry and hot fudge swirling together. Taren slipped her arm around Dale's neck. She moaned as Dale leaned her back on the bed, their kisses passionate and demanding. Dale didn't plan it. She didn't feel it coming but she wanted Taren. She wanted all of her. She wanted to make love to her. She cupped her hand over Taren's breast and her hardened nipple.

"Wait," Taren gasped, pushing back on Dale. "Please, stop."

"Why?" Dale said as she placed little kisses down Taren's neck.

"Dale, please. I can't do this." Taren turned her face away, avoiding Dale's lips. "It's wrong."

"Why wrong?" Dale asked.

"I know why you're doing this."

"Me, too." Dale grinned. "You are a hot woman and I'm turned on."

"It's more than that." Taren pushed Dale aside and sat up. "You don't see me. You see someone else."

"Someone else? Who? Who is it I see?" Dale propped herself up on her elbow and chuckled, wondering what silliness Taren had in mind.

"Sydney. I think you see yourself kissing Sydney."

"What?" Dale laughed out loud. "No, I don't."

"I think you do. Can you honestly say she wasn't on your mind?"

"Sure, Sydney was on my mind. We talked about her hair. But I wasn't kissing her. I was kissing you."

"I blame myself. I shouldn't have allowed it to go this far."

"You kissed me back, Taren. I felt it. I saw it in your eyes. You wanted me to kiss you."

"I know. I know I did. But it was wrong." She diverted her eyes. "It's been a long time since…" Taren crawled off the bed and collected her purse. "I need to go."

"A long time since someone made love to you?" Dale asked, following her to the door.

"Dale, we can be friends but I can't become involved with you." Taren hurried down the steps of the trailer.

"Taren, wait a minute."

"You better go back inside. You're barefoot." She climbed in her car without looking back. "I hope the cell phone works for you."

"Can't we talk about this?"

"I really need to go."

Taren roared away, squealing her tires as she rounded the corner.

"Good grief, lady. You're a tough one to figure out. First you kiss me then you wish we hadn't." Dale stood staring down the empty street. She finally headed back inside, raking her fingers across her mouth where Taren's soft lips had been.

# CHAPTER TWELVE

Monday was a hectic day at work. And she couldn't get Taren out of her mind. Tuesday was no better. Wednesday's meeting with a builder to discuss construction costs was pushed back at least a week. Dale finally found time to activate the phone Taren had given her, but she wasn't able to salvage her contact list or photographs from her old phone. Maybe it was just as well. Simplifying her life was a good thing. She loaded a few numbers into the phone, the ones she could remember and knew she'd use.

Sitting in her truck in the parking lot, eating a drive-through hamburger for lunch, she loaded Janice's number into the phone. She thought about calling her but doing so with a greasy hamburger in her stomach didn't sound like a smart idea. Instead she tinkered with the phone, familiarizing herself with the features. It took some doing but she found a ringtone she liked. She also found the photo album and noticed Taren hadn't erased the images. She must have forgotten, Dale thought as she scanned the pictures. There were several group shots of students and a few of mountain scenery. Among the others was one of Dale taken at sunset. She didn't remember Taren taking it. She looked closer. It was at Bryant's house, the day Taren took the picture of Dale and Sydney on the dock. Why would Taren have a picture of Dale on her phone at a time when they seemed mortal enemies? She toyed with the idea of calling her but suspected she'd be on campus and busy. She returned to work, curious about the picture.

Dale knew the situation with Janice wasn't going to fix itself. They hadn't talked since the pool party and in her mind, their relationship was over. But it was a loose end she wanted cleared up, once and for all. She finally called and left a message.

"Call me, Janice. We need to talk."

It was sometime after midnight when her phone jingled on the nightstand.

"Hello," she mumbled, blinking herself awake.

"Well, hello yourself," Janice said, giggling like a teenager.

"What time is it?" Dale fumbled for the light switch.

"I don't know. One thirty. Two. You said to call."

"Yes, but during the day." She gave up on finding the light and lay back on the pillow.

"You'll never guess what happened. Jennifer came out to her boss and he already knew. He's gay too. Can you believe it?" She laughed hysterically.

"Janice, it's the middle of the night. I don't know who Jennifer is and I don't care."

"Sure you do. She was at the pool party. The one in the blue bikini."

"I don't remember." Dale yawned and wondered how many hours of sleep she would get before her alarm rang.

"Sure you do. You were talking to her. In fact, you had your eyes down her top all afternoon."

"Janice, this really isn't a good time for us to talk. I'm half asleep. You're probably half drunk. And I don't give a rat's ass about your friends or what happened at the pool party."

"I thought you had a good time at the party."

"I got pushed in the pool and my phone was ruined. No, I don't call that a good time."

"Oh, that." Janice chuckled indifferently. "But hey, the booze was free."

"Janice, I told you several months ago, I don't drink."

"So? Does that mean I can't?"

"I didn't say that. But that does seem to be the first thing on your mind wherever we go."

"Are you saying I drink too much?" Janice asked defensively.

"You're the only one who can decide that."

"Damn right, I am. And maybe you wouldn't be such a stick in the mud if you had a drink now and then."

"Janice," Dale said, pulling herself up on the headboard. "You're a nice girl. You've got a great body. But I'm afraid we just don't have a lot in common."

"What do you mean? Are you dumping me, you little turd?" she snapped. "I can't believe it. I get you invited to a great party and that's the thanks I get?"

Dale had worried breaking up with her would be difficult and painful. But Janice was making it easy.

"I'm sorry, Janice. I wish you well. I really do."

"Fuck you," Janice said and hung up.

Dale slid down in bed, wondering why she waited so long to end it. She slept well, not waking until the alarm sounded. That surprised her. What surprised her more was the strange sense of freedom she felt over divesting herself of Janice.

"Dale, there's a woman looking for you," one of the cashiers said as Dale returned from lunch the next afternoon. "I told her you'd be back shortly. She went that way." She pointed.

Dale assumed it was Zoe come to complain about something or to ask for an employee discount. Instead she found Taren reading the information on the garbage disposals.

"Hi. What brings you to my little corner of paradise?" Dale smiled. Taren brought a little sunshine into her life just by being in the store but Dale wasn't sure she should tell her that.

"Which is better? Continuous feed or batch feed?" she said without stopping for pleasantries.

"Depends. Do you need to grind tree stumps?"

"I beg your pardon?" Taren didn't seem in the mood for jokes.

"Batch feed disposals only run when you put the cover on so it's a safer but you can only run one batch at a time. If you need to shoot a lot of stuff down the drain it'll take you longer. Continuous feed runs as long as the switch is flipped. They're the most common since you can add more to it as it runs."

"So which is better?"

"They work about the same and the units are similar. It's really just a matter of preference and frequency of use. They cost about the same. We carry a larger selection of continuous feed disposals because that's what most people want." Dale couldn't keep her eyes off Taren's glowing complexion or the way her top hugged her figure. And what was that shade of lipstick? Sexy pink? "Are you in the market for a new one?"

"I think so. I either need a new disposal or a new drain hose. There's a leak under the sink. I've got a plumber coming over next week. I thought I'd take a look at replacements then see what he says."

"Can you see if the leak is coming from the hose clamp on the drain tubing or somewhere on the disposal's lower housing?"

Taren gave her a long blank stare.

"Where's the drip coming from?" Dale asked, grinning at Taren's puzzled look.

"I have no idea. All I know is I have to empty the pan under my kitchen sink twice a day if I use it or run the dishwasher."

"Why didn't you say something when I was over last week?"

"Because it wasn't dripping then. Well, it might have been but I didn't notice it until two days ago."

"If you need to replace it, I'd recommend this one." Dale patted a stack of boxes. "With my employee discount it'll be the best bargain. It has a three year no-questions-asked warranty and it's on sale. We sell a lot of these. It's a great unit."

"I won't need your employee discount. I think my plumber gets a contractor price."

"It won't be as good as mine," Dale said with a wink.

"That's okay. I'm just looking for now anyway." Taren moved down the aisle, scanning the shelves.

"Anything else you need? Dryer hose? Faucet handles?"

"Yes." Taren looked to see if anyone was listening. "Dale, may I ask you a favor?"

"Sure." Dale stepped closer. "Do you want me to put one of the disposals back for you?"

"No. It has nothing to do with the disposal. It's about the other night in your trailer. Pretend we never kissed."

Taren's request brought a lump to Dale's throat. How could she forget it? It was wonderful. At least it was for her. It wasn't planned. She never expected to feel that way about Taren. There was no way she could forget it. And the idea that she somehow envisioned herself kissing Sydney was just ludicrous.

"Please," Taren pleaded. "I'm Sydney's sister. I'm very uncomfortable with what we did."

A customer came down the aisle before Dale could ask why.

"Do you have submersible pumps?" he asked, scanning the shelves.

"Yes, sir. Aisle six. I'll be glad to show you." Dale turned to Taren and said, "I'll be right back, ma'am." She escorted the man down the aisle. She explained the features of the pumps and answered his questions. After he made a selection she returned to the disposals but Taren was gone. Dale felt her cell phone vibrate in her apron pocket. It was a text from Taren.

*Please, Dale. This is important to me.*

Dale quickly tapped out a reply.

*I don't understand. We didn't do anything wrong. Please come back and talk to me.*

Dale waited for Taren's reply. It never came. She waited all day, checking her phone every few minutes. Her imagination was running wild. Did Taren see her as a cheater? After all, Taren didn't know she had ended the relationship with Janice. Or was Taren dating someone else? Nothing else made any sense. When she didn't receive a reply the next day, she tried calling but Taren's voice mail picked up. Dale didn't leave a message.

Dale's curiosity was getting the best of her. She needed some answers. She stopped by Home Depot Saturday morning for a quick purchase and then headed across town to Taren's house. Her red hatchback was in the driveway but it took several rings and knocks before she answered the door.

"Hi." Dale carried a garbage disposal box under one arm and her toolbox in the other hand. "Kinsel Plumbing, at your service, ma'am."

"What are you doing?"

"I've come to look at your leak." Dale opened the door and walked inside without waiting for an invitation.

"I told you I've got a plumber coming next week to do that."

"Today was the last day of the sale and this was the last unit in stock."

"I really don't need you to do this." Taren followed Dale down the hall.

"Even if I can save you some money?" The cabinet under the sink was open and a large soup pan was half full of dirty water. Dale spread a drop cloth then crawled under the sink. She lay on her back and shined a flashlight up at the disposal.

"Turn on the water and flip the switch," she said. Taren did as she was told. "Okay. Turn it off. Come down here and look at this." She scooted over, making room as Taren joined her. "See the rust on the bottom of the disposal? That's where you're leaking." Dale caught the drip on her fingertips.

"Can that be fixed?"

"It's a sealed unit. You'll have to replace it. It's not uncommon for them to rust out like this."

"Okay. I'll tell Mr. Arnold when he comes. How much do I owe you for the new one?"

"Where's your breaker panel?" Dale crawled out and opened her toolbox.

"By the back door. Why?"

"Because I need to turn off the breaker for the disposal so I can wire in the new one. It's wired directly to the switch."

"Dale, I don't want you doing that. You'll get hurt. I don't want you electrocuted."

"Me either. That's why I'm turning off the breaker." Dale winked and headed to the back door. She opened the panel and tripped the breaker marked kitchen. "Try the disposal now."

Taren flipped the switch several times.

"It's dead but you don't need to do this. It's nasty under there. Who knows what kind of problems you'll find."

"Taren, I know how to do this." Dale moved her out of the way and slid back under the sink.

"Are you sure?"

"I'm sure. Can you hand me the Phillips screwdriver?"

"This one?" She passed a screwdriver under to Dale.

"That'll do."

"Do I need to hold something?" Taren turned her head sideways and looked under the sink.

"Not yet. When I get to the hard part you can take over."

"Oh, good. And why is it I'm letting you install my disposal?"

"Because hiring a professional would be way too easy." Dale slid out of the cabinet with the old disposal in her hands. She unpacked the new one, dropping some of the parts back in the box.

"Aren't you going to use those?"

"Don't need to." She retrieved a metal ring from the box and held it up. "You're replacing the same brand so you can use the same sink flange."

Taren looked at the new one in Dale's hand then at the one in the sink.

"But mine's all grotty."

"A little baking soda and vinegar will clean it right up. I'll show you later. I'd rather not break the seal on the flange. Yours is nice and tight. It doesn't leak so let's leave it alone. A plumber would probably change it just so he could charge you more." She handed Taren a black stopper. "Here. You get a shiny new one of these though."

Taren tried it in the drain.

"Look at that. It fits."

"You sound surprised." Dale chuckled as she slid back under the sink. "Yep, just as I thought." She heaved a disappointed sigh.

"What's wrong? Doesn't it fit?" Taren asked as Dale headed out to the truck.

"I need a different connector. I brought one with me just in case."

"You really do know what you're doing, don't you?" she said as Dale returned with a section of tubing and crawled back under the sink. She pulled the stopper out of the drain and looked down the open hole. "I'm impressed."

"Thank you, but maybe you should wait until it's installed and working before you pass judgment." Dale grinned up at her.

"Where did you learn how to install a garbage disposal?"

"I've done several. I worked for a plumbing contractor for a couple years."

"I didn't know that. When?"

"After college. My business degree was getting me nowhere fast. My roommate's father got me the job. The money was good but the hours were lousy. And I got stuck with all the nasty jobs. It seems some people don't want a woman handling their pipes. But they don't mind if we clean out clogged sewers."

"I didn't mean to doubt your abilities."

"That's okay. You didn't know. Can you hand me the pliers with the red handles?"

"What's the going rate for a plumber?" Taren asked as she passed her the pliers.

"I have no idea," she said with a grunt as she twisted the unit into place.

"Well, we need to find out because I want to pay you a fair price for the disposal and the installation."

"The receipt is in the box. You need to keep that for your warranty."

"That's all?" Taren said, retrieving the receipt. "That can't be right."

"On sale with my discount. Yep, that's it. And that's all you owe me. We'll call the rest an even exchange for the trailer."

"You already paid for that."

"Okay, we'll call it an even exchange for being a friend." She looked out to see Taren's reaction.

"Friends?"

"You said we can never have too many friends. I'm your friend and I'm installing your garbage disposal. Someday you can do something for me. That's what friends do."

Taren didn't reply. She leaned her elbows on the counter and watched as Dale finished the installation.

"Turn on the water and let's see if I have a tight seal," Dale said. Taren turned it on and waited.

"How's that?"

"Looks good. All dry." She climbed out and went to turn on the breaker. "Now the real test." She flipped the switch and listened to the quiet hum of the disposal.

"That's a lot quieter than my old one."

Dale squatted and looked under the sink for signs of a leak. Taren squatted next to her, admiring the disposal.

"I think you're back in business." Dale dropped her tools in the toolbox and wiped her hands on a rag.

"I'm impressed, Dale. I had no idea you knew how to do this kind of thing. I assumed you just knew what you sold at the store."

"Comes in handy when someone has a question about plumbing supplies. Like if their garbage disposal is leaking." She bumped her knee against Taren's playfully.

Taren went to her purse and wrote out a check. "I really appreciate your help," she said, handing it to Dale.

"Hey, this isn't what we agreed."

"Just take it. I'd have to pay a plumber a lot more but I want to give you something for your time."

"Thanks but that's not why I did it."

"I know but I need you to take it anyway."

"I'm doing okay, Taren. The store has reopened and I'm back to work."

"I know."

"I'll get my house rebuilt. It may take a while but I'll eventually move out of that trailer and back into a real home. Someday I'll even have trees again. They may not be big but they'll grow."

"I know you will and your house will be gorgeous. What is it they say? One day at a time and enjoy the simple pleasures along the way."

"Taren, we need to talk."

"Talk about what?"

"You know what. This kiss I'm supposed to forget."

"Dale, please. Let's not do this, okay?" Taren asked softly.

"I didn't mean to force you into something that made you uncomfortable. If I was wrong, I'm sorry."

"You didn't force me into anything."

"If it makes any difference, Janice and I are no longer seeing each other."

"I didn't ask you to do that."

"You had nothing to do with it. It was never going to work with her. It just took me a while to come to my senses and end it. She deserves someone different."

"And so do you," Taren said then added hesitantly, "Have you got a minute? I have something for you."

"Sure." Dale carried her toolbox to the front door while Taren pulled an envelope from the desk drawer.

"I have something I want to give you."

"More pictures?" Dale asked.

"No." She took Dale by the hand and led her to the couch. "I've been fighting with myself about this for days." She waited for Dale to get comfortable before continuing. "I want to help. I know we've had our differences in the past."

"Differences?" Dale chuckled. "You mean me soaking myself in scotch while Sydney battled colon cancer and you trying to get me to come to my senses."

"It was a difficult time for everyone. That's history and that's not what I want to discuss. I can't take back the terrible things I said and you can't erase what you did." Taren took a deep breath and then thrust the envelope at Dale. "Here. This is for you. Consider it from me and from Sydney."

"What is it?" Dale peeked inside, almost afraid of what she'd find.

"It's my half of her life insurance policy. The one her company took out on all their employees. I want you to have it. The check is all made out to you."

"No." Dale dropped the envelope in Taren's lap and headed for the door.

"Dale, wait."

"I am NOT taking that. Forget it." She picked up the toolbox but Taren blocked her exit.

"Why not? It was rightfully yours anyway. I know it's not a huge amount but add it to your half and maybe you'll have enough with your insurance settlement to rebuild."

"No." Dale tried to push Taren aside but she held her ground.

"Why are you being so stubborn? I want to do this. Sydney would want me to do this. I know she would."

"That is your money. Sydney wanted you to have it. Her boss said she was very adamant both our names be listed as beneficiaries on that policy."

"That was years ago. She should have changed it to just you when you moved in together. You were her partner. I felt funny accepting it."

"Taren, I'm not taking your money," Dale said flatly.

"I knew it. I knew you would take this all wrong. I'm not belittling you. I just want to help. It's one of those little things you do for friends. For those you care about." She took Dale's hand. "Please let me help a friend. It won't build your house but it will ease the burden. We're friends. Allow me this small act of kindness. You'd do it for me. I know you would."

Dale felt tears welling up in her eyes. Taren's words touched her deeply.

"I hadn't thought about it until now. I put my half in my IRA. I assumed I'd need it in twenty years when I retired. Maybe I need it now more."

"Use them both." Taren gently slipped the envelope in Dale's hand. "Rebuild your house, Dale. Rebuild it with Sydney's help."

# CHAPTER THIRTEEN

August was hot, even for the Ozarks. Day after day simmered in the upper nineties, drying out the few blades of grass the tornado hadn't blown away. The disaster zone was a treeless, barren, brown swath across the middle of Joplin, made worse by the blowing dust from the heavy equipment brought in to help with demolition. Street after street was lined with tree branches and house wreckage piled too high to see over, waiting to be hauled away. The delay in removing it became a constant reminder of how much had been lost. According to the For Sale signs, neither Patty nor Marvin planned to rebuild. Milo and his wife were undecided. Excavation work had been begun on the house next door but Dale seldom saw the owners. The brick house on the corner hadn't been touched since the tornado. Rumor was the owner had moved away, taking the insurance money and leaving the house to be sold as-is. Since it had been blown a few inches off its foundation it was worth only the land it sat on minus the cost to bulldoze it to the ground.

Dale's neighborhood had been forever changed by the storm. The towering shade trees, home to songbirds and scampering squirrels, were all gone. She couldn't wait to clear a spot and plant a tree, if only to prove she survived. But it would have to wait. Between the trailer, the debris piles and the construction equipment, there wasn't room to do anything.

The city was crawling with out-of-town builders come to Joplin to take advantage of the construction bonanza. Most were honest and reliable. Some, not so much. Dale decided to hire local. She wanted to support the local workforce and found someone she knew and trusted to rebuild her home. She occasionally sent Taren a text or left a voice mail with progress reports. Dale obeyed Taren's wishes and didn't mention the kiss, although it was hard not to. She also didn't mention her growing feelings with each and every text that flashed across the screen. For now she would send benign reports of footings being poured and plans being finalized. But she wasn't sure how long she could oblige Taren's request.

Dale stopped by the trailer during her lunch break to change her shoes, a convenient excuse to check on her house.

"That's new," she said, pointing to the concrete forms framing where the master bedroom closet would be.

"That'll be your storm shelter," a workman replied. "It'll be poured this afternoon."

Dale had contracted for a storm shelter to be included but she didn't remember it would be in the closet.

"I didn't think it would be right there in the middle of the house."

"Lots of folks are putting them in a closet. It makes it easier to get to. You won't even know it's there. It'll look just like any other wall once the Sheetrock goes up. It'll just have a heavier door."

It seemed like a sensible solution but that night Dale spent several hours staring at the ceiling of the trailer as she contemplated having to use a storm shelter. She snapped on the bedside light and tapped out a text to Taren. Dale suspected she wouldn't read it until the morning but she sent it anyway.

*House is coming along, slow but sure. Subfloor couldn't be reused. Storm twisted the sill plate. I'll txt you a couple pictures. The concrete box in the middle of the house is the storm shelter. Kind of strange to have it right there in my bedroom closet. Oh well. Take care.*

Dale turned off the light and closed her eyes. Within a minute her cell phone jingled an incoming text. She grabbed for the phone, knocking the alarm clock on the floor.

*Okay, I give up. What's a sill plate?*

Dale sat up and tapped out a reply.

*It's the horizontal board attached to the foundation. Walls sit on top of it. What are you doing up so late?*

She sent the text then lay grinning at her phone as she waited for Taren's reply.

*Was awakened by a plumber with a cell phone.*

Dale chuckled and sent, *Hate it when that happens. Sorry.*

*By the way, I appreciate Kim and Bryant's invitation to the barbecue but I'm not sure I can make it. Might be out of town.*

Dale wasn't surprised Taren had been invited. She also wasn't surprised how disappointed she felt at Taren's news she wouldn't be there.

*Are you sure you can't make it? It'll be fun. Bryant has a new pontoon boat and a new 2-person towable. The lake is up. I've got a gallon of sunblock and a bag of Twizzlers. What more could you ask for?*

Dale sent the text, hoping to change her mind. It was several minutes before Taren replied.

*I don't think I can but thanks. Time to get some sleep. Nite!!*

Reluctantly, Dale replied.

*Goodnight, Taren.*

She didn't sleep well and it had nothing to do with the storm shelter or the rebuild. Dale wished Taren were coming to the barbecue. She also wished she didn't have such strong feelings for her. But she did. Maybe spending Saturday with Zoe and Sasha would take her mind off Taren.

\* \* \*

"Hey," Dale called, bumping her elbow against Zoe's front door.

"Why are you carrying all your laundry at once? Why not make two trips?" Zoe stepped back as Dale fought her way through the doorway with an oversized armload.

"Because it's more fun this way," she said, dumping it on the floor outside the laundry room, then groaned and stretched. "I'll pay you twenty bucks to do it for me."

"God, no. I've got enough of my own." She stared Dale up and down then laughed. "Why are you wearing pink camouflage shorts and an orange polo shirt?"

"Because it's all I had clean." Dale began stuffing clothes in the washer. "It was this or a sports bra and pantyhose."

"You own pantyhose?" Zoe giggled.

"Sure. I wear them under my jeans when I shovel snow. And why are you giggling?"

"Dale Kinsel wears pantyhose. I should post that on Facebook but no one would believe it unless I have photographic evidence."

"Well, you aren't getting any." Dale poured in some detergent and closed the lid. "What do you have to feed a starving woman?" She opened the refrigerator and stared into the abyss.

"Leftover pizza unless Sasha got to it already."

Dale pulled out a pizza box. It contained one small piece minus the toppings. She ate it anyway.

"Bryant and Kim are having a barbecue the Sunday before Labor Day," Zoe announced.

"Yes, I know. I'm providing a case of bottled water, pickles, olives and two pounds of deli salad." Dale dropped the pizza crust into the trash and went to the sink for a drink.

"When did she tell you about it?" Zoe's desire to be Queen Bee was insulted when Dale knew about family gatherings first.

"A week or so ago when she came to the store to pick out Bryant's birthday present."

"Yeah, she's getting him new patio furniture."

"That's not what she bought him."

"She's going to," she said as she leafed through a sale flyer.

"She got him a stainless gas grill with a side burner and a warming tray. She gave me the money and I bought it for her with my discount."

"She said she wanted new patio furniture. We talked about it." Zoe tossed the flyer in the trash.

"But *he* wanted a new grill. I got them a set of cushions for their existing chairs. They'll be fine. They aren't rusted through or broken."

"I was going to do that when she picked out the new furniture."

"We've got a matching patio umbrella at the store that would fit in their table. Why don't you get that?"

"Why don't you give them the umbrella and I'll give them the chair cushions?" Zoe raised an expectant eyebrow.

"Why don't you give them the umbrella and I'll give them the chair cushions?" Dale repeated matter-of-factly.

"Oh, come on, Dale. A patio umbrella is a dumb gift. Let me give the chair cushions."

"If you'll pay me for them, sure."

"How much?"

"I don't remember. I'll have to look at the receipt." Dale knew she'd be paying for both the cushions and the umbrella.

"By the way, you are supposed to invite Taren to the barbecue. Kim said so. Tell her to bring a swimsuit. We're going out on the boat."

"Why do I have to invite her? I thought Kim already did that."

"She said you were friends now so you should invite her to their barbecue."

"Zoe, did you already invite her and she turned you down?" Dale leaned back against the doorjamb and stared at her skeptically.

"I only saw her for a second. I had students waiting to fill out paperwork and she was on her way out of the registrar's office. She said no. She said it would be better if she didn't come. That's all."

"Why better?"

"I don't know. I didn't have time to ask her."

"Why didn't you call her later and ask?" Dale demanded.

"Because I was busy. I did my part. Now you can ask her."

"Dammit, Zoe. What did you say to her?"

"All I said was would you like to come to Kim and Bryant's for a family barbecue on Labor Day weekend."

"Why did you say family barbecue? She probably thought she shouldn't come because she isn't family. You shouldn't have said that."

"That's not the reason."

"Then what is it?"

"She just said she thought it would be better for you if she didn't come. That's the sum total of what she said. What have you done? Are you two at each other again?"

"No."

"Well, Kim said whatever it is, you're to apologize and invite her again. They like Taren. And if you've screwed it up, you're supposed to fix it. So call her up and do it."

"I didn't screw anything up," Dale said, digging in her pocket for her cell phone.

"Mom, Haley invited me over. Can I go?" Sasha came out of her room applying a band to her ponytail. "They'll bring me back later if you can take me over."

"I'll take her," Dale said, heading for the door. The ride back would give her time to call Taren without Zoe eavesdropping.

It was a fifteen-minute ride to Haley's house but it wasn't long enough for Dale to decide what she would say to change Taren's mind. She pulled up in front of a brick house. A girl Sasha's age was waiting on the front steps. She waved and came to greet them.

"Have fun girls." The cheerful tune from an ice cream truck could be heard in the distance, and Dale pulled out her wallet and handed each girl some money. "Ask your mom first, okay?"

"Thanks, Aunt Dale. We will." They went running up the walk, calling for permission even before they were inside the house. Dale chuckled as she pulled away. She would have enjoyed an ice cream sandwich herself but she had other things to do. She rounded the corner and pulled into a vacant parking lot. She took a deep breath then called Taren's number.

"Hello, Dale," Taren said, picking up on the fourth ring.

"Hi. Did I interrupt something important? Waxing your lip maybe?"

Taren laughed. "No. I'm not waxing my lip."

"Good." Dale felt a knot form in her stomach. She wasn't usually nervous when she called women. She rolled her window down and hung her arm across it. "Taren, I called because Kim and Zoe said I was supposed to."

"Call about what?"

"Zoe said you declined the invitation to Kim and Bryant's barbecue because of me."

"Dale, I just said I thought it would be better for you if I didn't go. Under the circumstances, I thought things might be a little…"

"Uncomfortable?"

"Yes," Taren said softly.

"Things wouldn't be uncomfortable for me. We're friends. Remember? We can both be there without any problem."

Taren didn't reply.

"Taren, I promised I wouldn't bring up what happened between us. And I won't. I'd very much like you to be there."

"Dale…" she started, a hesitation in her voice.

"I can't lie to you. I have feelings for you. If that doesn't work for you, I'll understand. I just hope someday we can talk about it. That'll be up to you. But don't blame Kim and Bryant. They like you. And they very much want you to be there. They consider you part of the family."

"Can I think about it?" Taren finally asked.

"Sure. How about this? If you are comfortable being there with me and my crazy family, show up about ten Sunday morning and bring your bathing suit. If you'd rather not, they'll understand."

"And you?"

"I hope you come." Dale closed her eyes and listened to the sound of Taren's breathing.

"Thank you for the invitation."

"So?"

"So, we'll see."

Dale returned to Zoe's to collect her laundry. The conversation with Taren rolled over and over in her mind. Had she said too much? Was she wrong to confess her feelings? She'd have to wait a week to find out, a painfully long week second-guessing each and every word she'd said. And praying with every breath that Taren would come.

# CHAPTER FOURTEEN

Dale stood at the edge of her brother's yard, watching a Jet Ski zip across the lake like a water bug. The morning clouds had given way to a bright blue-skied Sunday. Bryant and Kim's home was a modest ranch set on a bluff overlooking Grand Lake of the Cherokees just outside Grove. It had been little more than a weekend cabin when they bought it. With hard work and much of the labor done themselves, it was now a comfortable home where they loved to entertain their family and friends. The wide backyard funneled to a dirt trail that led down to a quiet cove and a boathouse where Bryant kept his favorite toy, a twenty-six foot pontoon boat with a two-hundred horsepower motor capable of crossing the lake at breakneck speed. Kim had stocked two coolers with everything they'd need for a picnic lunch while enjoying an afternoon of fun on the water.

Dale couldn't wait to get to Bryant's, hoping Taren had decided to come. But it was now after ten and no Taren. If Taren wasn't comfortable being there, Dale would have to live with it, regardless of how much it hurt.

"Will you play catch with me, Aunt Dale?" Sasha asked as she came skipping across the yard. She tossed a softball in the air but missed it as it fell to the ground.

"Sure. I like your new glove, by the way." Dale moved out into the yard, away from the picture windows across the back of the house.

"I picked it out. Pink and purple are my favorite colors. Mom said it would just get dirty but I don't care. I like it." Sasha repeatedly smacked the ball into the pocket of the glove. "Don't you need a glove?"

"I'll be okay. You'll just have to take it easy on me." Dale grinned at her niece, wondering how much Zoe had taught her about the game.

Sasha's first throw was short and wide. Dale scooped it up and tossed it back, floating a high easy one to her. Sasha held out her glove as if it were Dale's job to hit it. She ran the ball down and heaved it back without taking much aim. Dale dug the ball out of a bush and threw it again. It didn't take long to realize Sasha was very new to softball.

"Okay, Sasha. Lesson number one," she said, walking toward her with the ball. "Don't throw like a girl." She chuckled, knowing that sounded silly.

"But I am a girl."

"I know but that doesn't mean you have to throw like one." Dale put the ball in Sasha's glove. "Don't leap into the throw." Dale demonstrated the technique, keeping the motion simple. "Step toward your target. Lesson number two. Try to keep the ball in front of you when you go to catch it. Don't just stick your glove out. Use two hands."

Dale trotted back across the yard, ready to try again.

"Lesson number three. Never play softball with a fresh manicure," Taren called from the back porch.

"Hey, you decided to come." Dale grinned as a rush of emotion overtook her. Her first impulse was to run to Taren, gather her in her arms and kiss her. But she'd promised. But she didn't promise not to spend the day thankful she came.

"Hi, Taren." Sasha waved. "Want to play catch with us?"

"Hi, Sasha. That's okay. I'll watch. That's a pretty new glove you've got there."

"I picked it out. Dale says I throw like a girl."

"Oh, really?" Taren sat on the end of the picnic table, swinging her legs.

"She does. But we're going to fix that." Dale retrieved the ball and tossed it back. But Taren's turquoise halter top completely captured her attention and she threw it wide.

"Hey!" Sasha whined as she watched it roll away.

"Nice throw." Taren pulled a crooked little grin.

"Sasha," Zoe called from the back door. "You come in here and hang up your wet clothes this instant. You're not leaving a mess on the bathroom floor for someone else to pick up. You weren't born in a barn."

Sasha groaned but obeyed, handing Taren her glove as she headed inside. Taren slipped it on, trying out the fit.

"Here you go. Catch." Dale tossed the ball underhand.

"No, no, wait." Taren was caught off guard by Dale's throw and dropped it. She climbed off the table and ran it down.

"You put on the glove, you're in the game," Dale said, holding out her hands for a return throw.

Taren made a lunging toss. It went way wide into the bushes.

"I'm terrible at this. I hate that I can't even throw a ball." Taren took off the glove and frowned at it.

"Now wait a minute. You're not that bad." Dale retrieved the ball and trotted over to show her.

"I can't do this. I look stupid playing softball." She shoved the glove into Dale's belly. "Sasha picked it up quicker than I do. Softball isn't one of my skills."

"Don't get your panties all in a twist. You can do this. I'll show you." Dale put the glove back on Taren's hand. She stood behind her, demonstrating the correct arm motion. "Bring the ball back like this, keeping your opposite shoulder toward the target. Step with your opposite foot, don't lunge. And when you release the ball, bring your arm across your body and down to your hip. Like this." Dale moved Taren's arm across her body then stepped back so she could try it.

"Like this?" Taren's exaggerated motion gave Dale a clear view down her halter top.

"Better." Dale adjusted Taren's arm but her eyes made a quick search for nipples before returning to the task at hand. "Keep this elbow up."

"I really don't think I'll ever be able to throw like you do."

"We can work on it. I'll be glad to teach you." Dale stood behind, enjoying her sweet scent.

"Do you think I can learn?"

"There are a lot of things you could learn."

"Are we still talking about softball here?" Taren asked, leaning into Dale.

"Taren, I'm willing to teach you anything you want to learn. Just ask me. I'm in no hurry at all." She slipped an arm around Taren.

A shrill whistle from the path made them both jump. Bryant walked up the hill, dressed in camouflage shorts and a Dallas Cowboys ball cap.

"Can he hear his whistle?" Taren asked.

"No. He said he can feel the vibration though. He waits for a reaction to know if he did it right." Dale tossed the softball high in the air in his direction. He moved under it and caught it behind his back. He grinned and tossed it back then signed to Taren.

*You're just in time. We're going out on the boat.*

*Thank you for asking me. I couldn't say no to Kim's cooking,* Taren signed and gave Bryant a hug.

*You don't have to wait for an invitation. You're always welcome.*

"Tell him everything is loaded," Kim called to Dale. She slid a box of picnic supplies into the back of an old pickup they used to transport stuff down to the boathouse. "You've got sandwiches, fruit, pop, water, chips. Towels are in the storage compartments under the front two benches of the boat. First-aid kit and life vests under the back two." She signed a stern warning to Bryant about sunburn and keeping hydrated. She then turned to Sasha and said, "And you keep your life jacket on all the time you're on that boat, missie. I don't care if you can swim."

"She will," Zoe said, setting a tote bag in the cab of the truck. "Judy decided not to go. Her morning sickness is back."

"We can wait a while. Maybe she'll feel better later," Dale offered, straddling the side of the truck bed.

"No." Kim was adamant. "I'd rather she didn't go bouncing across the lake when she's pregnant."

"Lots of women go boating when they're pregnant. And she's only two months along."

"I don't care. This is my grandchild we're talking about. You all go have fun but be careful. There'll be a lot of crazy drunk boaters out today."

"There's room up here, Taren," Zoe said as she climbed in the cab.

"Or you can ride back here with the rest of the peasants." Dale extended a hand and a smile.

"Thanks, Zoe, but you go ahead. I'll ride back here," Taren said and took Dale's hand.

Bryant drove the dirt trail down to the boathouse, creeping along over rocks and potholes. It didn't take long to transfer the picnic supplies onto the boat and prepare it for launch.

"Get your vest on," Zoe said, handing one to Sasha. She buckled one on herself as well then began applying liberal amounts of sunblock as Bryant backed out of the slip.

"Do you want to wear one?" Dale said to Taren, pointing to the vests and flotation belts stowed under the seat. "You don't have to wear it unless you're in the towable. Bryant gets all freaky if people don't wear one when he's towing them." Dale nodded toward the round orange raft bungeed to the back of the boat deck. "It'll hold two people sitting with their rears in the holes or one really brave person standing up."

"I heard about this new towable. I'm not too sure if I'm ready to ride that." Taren studied the jumbo tube, swallowing back her fear.

"It's fun. But we won't force you."

"It's really fun, Taren," Sasha said, grinning with anticipation. "You have to hold on when it hits a big wave. And then you get splashed and water goes up your nose and everything."

"And you're an expert, right?" Dale said, tightening the strap on Sasha's vest.

"Yep. One time Mom missed the tube and fell in the water."

"It was a different tube and it wasn't my fault," Zoe said with a frown. "SOMEONE moved it."

Dale was signing the conversation so Bryant wasn't excluded. He laughed and signed something to Zoe she didn't understand.

"She'd smack him if she knew what he meant," Dale whispered to Taren.

Taren applied sunscreen to her arms, legs and face, removing her sunglasses to do around her eyes. Dale took the bottle from the bench and squirted a blob into her hand.

"Turn around. I'll do your back."

"Thank you."

Dale couldn't wait to have her hands on Taren's delectably soft skin. Taren tilted her head down, an obvious invitation to do her neck. Dale squirted more on her hand and gently drew it around and down.

"All done?" Taren asked, slipping on her sunglasses.

"Wait a minute. I missed a spot." Dale wasn't finished touching her. She squirted and applied again, running long strokes down her back, tucking her fingertips inside the edges of her halter top. Taren sat drinking it all in, seemingly enjoying it as much as Dale. "We'll need to reapply after you get wet." Dale was already wet but she couldn't admit it.

"Thanks. I'd do you but you're wearing a T-shirt."

Dale quickly peeled out of her shirt, revealing a navy blue sports bra that matched her blue and red board shorts. She had a rich tan, the result of hours spent working over the storm debris.

"Have at it," she said and turned sideways on the bench.

Taren squirted a trail of lotion across Dale's back. It was cold and shot a shiver up her spine. But Taren's soft hands instantly raised a different feeling in Dale.

"Sorry, was that cold?"

"Feels good."

"How's your shoulder? I haven't heard you mention it." She massaged the sunblock into it.

"Better. I think it'll be okay with time. The doctor was exaggerating." Dale didn't mean to let that slip.

"What did he say?" Taren continued to massage it gently.

"Nothing."

Zoe had been eavesdropping and added, "The doctor said she needs surgery. She has a torn ligament."

"He said maybe." Dale tossed a disgusted look at her sister.

"He said it's not going to heal itself in your line of work. You keep re-aggravating it by lifting."

"Dale, is that true?" Taren asked sternly. "Do you need surgery?"

"Maybe. Eventually."

"Why not have it done now?"

"Because I don't have time to be off work right now."

"You've got good medical coverage. And this is tornado-related. They'll understand," Zoe said.

Bryant asked what they were discussing. When Dale hesitated, Taren signed for him. His only reply was that Dale was as stubborn as a mule.

"It's fine today. Can we just enjoy ourselves and not talk about my shoulder?"

"Yes, we can." Taren rubbed her hand across it and gave it a pat. "Not another word about it. We're here to have fun. Not pick on Dale."

Bryant cleared the cove. He turned his ball cap backward, slipped on a pair of sunglasses and started for the middle of the lake, waving a signal over his head for all to see.

"Chug, chug," Dale said, pulling Sasha down next to her on the bench. "That means sit down, he's throttling up."

The boat gained speed until they were skimming across the surface, the wind buffeting their faces and hair. Bryant waved Sasha onto his lap to help him drive. She nodded eagerly and held the steering wheel proudly.

*Can we go faster?* Sasha said, using her limited sign language knowledge.

"No," Zoe shouted, shaking her head and giving Bryant a stern look. He winked at Sasha and gave the throttle a nudge with his knee. "Dale, tell him that's fast enough."

"You tell him." Dale leaned back on the seat and draped her arm over the railing.

"Taren?" Zoe pleaded.

"Sorry. I'm not sure how to sign that." Taren smiled at Dale and leaned back next to her, enjoying the ride.

Bryant finally slowed the motor to a crawl.

*Let's try out the new tube*, he signed.

Sasha cheered, climbing off his lap and heading to the back.

"You want to ride with her?" Dale asked Taren.

"No, I think I'll wait. Someone else can go."

Zoe agreed to take the first ride with Sasha. Dale released the raft into the water, attached the tow rope and lowered the ladder.

"How the hell do I get on this thing?" Zoe asked, clumsily climbing down the ladder, her view obstructed by her bulky vest.

"Turn around. Go down backward." Dale stood on the back deck holding the slack in the tow rope while she steadied the tube with her foot. "Drop your butt in the hole."

"How am I supposed to lower my ass in that little hole?"

Dale grinned back at Sasha, knowing she was ready to make the announcement. As Zoe let go of the ladder and dropped into the tube with a squeal, Sasha and Dale yelled, "Bombs away." Sasha climbed down the ladder and did the same. "Bombs away," she shrieked.

"You hold on real tight, Sasha Daline. Do you hear me?" Zoe hooked her hands through the handles and wiggled herself in snug. "Are you holding on?"

"Yep." She giggled with excitement. "We're ready."

"Remember, thumbs-up means you're good to go. Thumbs-down means you need to stop." Dale raised the ladder and released the tow rope into the water. Bryant started the engine and eased forward, slowly taking up the slack.

"Not too fast, okay?" Zoe yelled nervously, tightening her grip until her knuckles were white.

Dale gave Bryant the signal for throttle up. The tube eased forward then snapped at the end of the rope as he revved the engine. Zoe and Sasha immediately began to scream and laugh as they gained speed. Dale kept her eyes on the towable, ready to signal a problem.

"They sure are having fun, aren't they?" Taren knelt on the back bench next to Dale, watching them bounce across the waves. A passing boat sent a wake across their path, making them hop and rock all the more. Zoe was laughing so hard she couldn't speak. Sasha grinned and squealed, trying to make it bounce even higher. Finally Zoe signaled she had enough and Bryant stopped.

"Wow, that is so much fun," Sasha said, rocking back and forth.

"My ass feels like I just had an enema." Zoe laughed, finally releasing her hold on the handles. "We must have been going sixty miles an hour."

"Only twenty, Zoe," Dale said, lowering the ladder and pulling the tube in by the rope.

"It had to be faster than that." She grabbed the handrails and hoisted herself out of the hole. Her butt made a sucking sound as she pulled herself free of the tube. Sasha climbed up the ladder, still giggling.

"Are you ready to try?" Dale asked Taren, holding up a life vest for her.

"You'll really like it," Sasha said with a grin. She stood on the deck looking like a drowned rat.

"Will you ride with me?" Taren looked up at Dale with trepidation in her eyes.

"Sure." She pulled another life vest from the storage compartment. "Wear this one. It's mesh instead of nylon so it's cooler." Taren slipped it on and buckled it snugly. She stepped out of her sandals and headed for the ladder.

"Wait a minute," Dale said, removing her sunglasses. "We've had enough problems with these. Let's leave them here."

"What exactly does this feel like?" Taren stared down at the raft.

"It's a cross between white-water rafting, a roller coaster and being squirted with a fire hose. You'll love it." Dale winked. She could tell Taren was nervous but she climbed down the ladder and bravely dropped her tush into the hole. Dale waited for her to get settled then followed.

"Bombs away," Sasha announced, kneeling on the back bench to watch.

"Okay, we're ready." Dale dipped her hand in the lake and wiped it across her face to cool off.

"Wait a minute." Taren wiggled and fidgeted. "I feel like I'm stuck in a rabbit hole, bottom first."

"You are." Zoe cackled as she raised the ladder and gave the tube a push.

Bryant started the motor and eased forward until the tube snapped forward. He hadn't even come up to speed when Taren screamed and grabbed for Dale's arm. Dale gave Zoe a thumbs-up sign.

"Hang on. Here we go." She had no sooner said it than the boat roared forward, the tube bouncing at the end of the rope. Taren began to squeal and giggle. Every time the tube hit a wave they were doused. Bryant steered a zig-zag course, forcing the tube to cross its own wake and bounce even higher. As Taren continued to squeal, Dale continued to laugh. She had ridden a towable before and knew what to expect. She suspected Taren hadn't. But she didn't surrender. She bounced and splashed and giggled her way across the lake in what seemed like an endless ride. Finally she released the handle and grabbed Dale's hand, squeezing it tightly. Dale gave Zoe the signal they had had enough. The boat slowed and settled into its wake. Taren looked over at Dale, breathless from the ride.

"You were right. White-water, roller coaster, fire hose."

"Did you like that?" Dale wiped her hand down Taren's dripping face.

"Yes. Talk about your adrenaline rush." She leaned her head back, gasping for breath.

"Want to go again?" Dale asked eagerly.

"Can I have a little break? I see what Zoe means about the water up the rear."

Zoe dropped the ladder and pulled the rope until Dale's feet cushioned them against the back of the boat. Dale waited for Taren to climb out then followed. They peeled out of the life vests, both of them soaked. Dale signed to Bryant that it was his turn. It took some convincing but he finally agreed to ride with Sasha. Dale drove the boat while Taren and Zoe were the spotters. Even though he couldn't hear he could laugh and he did, loud and long as they roared across the lake. Zoe and Taren were next, both of them kicking and giggling as Dale drove them in circles, hopping over wave after wave. Sometime after noon they steered into a cove and dropped anchor for lunch. Afterward Dale dove in for a swim. One by one they all followed. Bryant kept a tow line hooked to his shorts in case he needed to get back on board in a hurry.

"Are you having fun?" Dale said, swimming up to Taren who was relying on her life vest to support her as she lay back in the water.

"Yes, I am," she said, her eyes closed as she gently bobbed between the waves. "I'm very glad I came."

"Me, too. It wouldn't have been the same if you hadn't." Dale lazily tread water, keeping herself within reach.

"I'm glad you invited me."

"I didn't invite you. Kim and Bryant did."

"But I wasn't going to come." She rolled her head to the side and peeked out at Dale. "Thank you for making me see this was the right thing to do."

"Is there any chance we can talk later?"

Taren closed her eyes and turned her face to the sky, once again peacefully bobbing. "I think so."

Dale wanted to start now but Bryant's blast of the boat horn snapped their heads around. He stood at the side gate and signed to Dale, *I bought a new water ski. Do you want to try it out?* Dale looked at Taren, wishing they hadn't been interrupted. She loved to water ski but today she'd rather be with Taren, and only Taren.

"We'll talk later," Taren said and started her swim for the boat.

They raised the anchor and headed back into the middle of the lake. With the towable bungeed out of the way, Dale connected the tow rope and dropped it in the water.

"Do you want to try?" she asked Taren.

"No." She chuckled. "I don't know how to do that and I'm sure I'd kill myself if I tried."

"Zoe? How about you?"

"The last time you talked me into water skiing I lost my bathing suit and drank half the lake. No, thank you. Not my idea of fun. And no, Sasha doesn't want to either." Sasha groaned in disappointment.

"Maybe next year, kiddo," Dale said, strapping on a life belt.

"Is one ski better than two?" Taren asked Zoe as Dale descended the ladder and pushed off.

"I can't do either one but Dale says one ski is easier. You don't have to worry about crossing your tips."

"Be careful," Taren shouted.

Bryant waited for the signal she was ready before starting the motor. Dale hadn't water skied since last summer and was a little worried she couldn't remember how but it came roaring back as soon as Bryant increased the throttle and pulled her up into a standing position. With the wind in her face and Taren's smiling face watching her every move, Dale couldn't help but grin from ear to ear. Bryant steered a serpentine course, allowing her to jump the boat's wake. Dale zipped back and forth, skipping over the water and spraying a tall rooster tail behind the ski. She angled toward the wake of an oncoming boat. She flexed her knees and prepared to jump the wave. As she landed the tow rope jerked her arm, sending a sharp pain through her damaged shoulder. She couldn't hold the tow bar and let go, settling into the water as the boat pulled away. She straddled the ski for support as she waited to be picked up, cradling her arm against her chest and trying to rotate the pain away.

"Are you all right?" Taren shouted as they circled around.

"Misjudged that last wave." She forced a smile and handed the ski up the ladder. "I'm done." The pain was like a hot poker against her shoulder blade as the grabbed the handrails and hoisted herself up.

"Are you sure you're okay?" Taren handed her a towel.

"Yep. Good run though."

*Does your shoulder hurt?* Bryant frowned at her.

*Just a little. I'm fine.*

*No more skiing for you this year.* His cell phone was flashing a bright light from the cup holder. He read the text then handed it to Dale. She read the message then placed a call.

"Hi, Kim. What's going on? Bryant wants clarification cause we're having a hoot out here. I wish you had come with us."

"Good. I'm glad, but tell Bryant we're going to eat a little earlier. I want to be finished before the rain gets here."

"What time do you want to eat?" Dale asked, scanning the horizon to the west. Nothing looked like rain, just a few fluffy clouds.

"If you'll head back now we can eat about five."

Dale signed the message to Bryant.

"We're on our way," Dale said and ended the call.

"Aw, are we going in?" Sasha whined.

"Yes, but how about one more ride on the way back." Dale knew what it was like to be a kid having fun. She prepared the tube for one last run. "Who wants to ride with Sasha?" She bumped Bryant and pointed. He shook his head adamantly. He signed for Dale to drive the boat as he settled into one of the chairs mounted on the front deck with a cold can of pop in his hand. "Zoe, ride with your daughter."

"My shorts are already up my ass. No more lake enema for me."

Dale turned to Taren with a grin.

"That leaves you."

"Okay, but you just want to hear me squeal like a baby pig." She climbed down the ladder and lowered her rear into the towable.

They bounced along, skipping over the waves, giggling and squealing as Dale headed for the cove and Bryant's boathouse. Her shoulder still throbbing from the jolt. She stopped just inside the mouth of the cove to collect the towable. She signed to Bryant, asking if he wanted to drive it into the boathouse, knowing how particular he was with his toys. He waved for her to do it, reminding her to go slow into the cove, pointing at the No Wake signs. Dale sat on the back of the driver's seat and headed into the cove at a crawl. Zoe and Taren stowed the life vests and gear. Sasha's job was to collect the trash scattered around the deck.

"Your shoulder is killing you, isn't it?" Taren said as she came to stand behind Dale. She placed her hands on Dale's shoulders and gently massaged.

"It doesn't hurt when you do that." She reached up to touch Taren's hand.

Bryant stood on the bow with an aluminum pole as Dale eased into the slip. It was a tight fit and tricky on windy days but she maneuvered it in on the first try, getting a thumbs-up from Bryant. Dale tried to carry one of the coolers to the truck but couldn't hide the pain.

"I'll get that," Taren said, taking it from her.

"I can do it." Dale didn't like being helpless. She was a doer, not a watcher.

Taren seemed to know that and said, "You can carry the towels."

Kim had dinner almost ready by the time they pulled up to the back door and began unloading the truck.

"Put all that stuff in the mudroom. I'll deal with it later. Go wash up. There's a stack of dry shirts on my bed. Go pick yourself one."

Kim scurried back and forth from stove to sink to counter, loading trays to be taken outside. The picnic table was already set with a red checkered cloth. Taren and Zoe helped in the kitchen. Dale and Bryant collected the chicken from the grill. The clouds had thickened and a breeze stirred the edges of the tablecloth but it still didn't look like rain. Dinner was an array of salads, casseroles and relishes that all complemented Kim's famous barbecued chicken. Taren sat next to Dale and across from Sasha and Zoe.

"Let's use our Sunday manners," Kim said as she passed the relish tray. "No reaching and no elbows on the table." She signed every comment so Bryant could see.

*Why not? We're just family.* He laughed and tossed an olive into the yard to amuse Sasha.

Dale bumped her knee into Taren's, wondering if she picked up on his reference to everyone being family. Lucas and Judy were at the far end of the table, whispering something that brought a frown to Judy's face. Dale thought it strange. Judy knew better than to whisper in front of her father and not sign for him.

"Would you like macaroni salad?" Taren said, passing the bowl to Dale. She then whispered, "Lucas wants a beer with dinner and Judy said no."

"Thank you, yes." Dale took a spoonful and passed it on then stood up and headed inside. She returned a minute later with two cans of beer. She set one in front of Lucas, patted him on the shoulder then headed to the other end of the table. She suspected Bryant would be having a beer as well if she wasn't there. She didn't want her issues interfering with their lives. She set the other can in front of Bryant then took her seat.

"You didn't have to do that, Aunt Dale," Judy said. "He could have waited."

"I know. But I don't mind. I'm not drinking it." She picked up her glass of iced tea and saluted them. She listened for the pop and fizz as Lucas and Bryant opened their cans. She could smell and taste it even without holding the can. That would always be with her, trapped in her memory. But she didn't need a drink. And she didn't want one either.

"That was very sweet of you," Taren said, dropping a tong full of pickle slices on Dale's plate. "I'm impressed."

*Thank you, sis*, Bryant signed.

*That's the one and only time I do that*, Dale replied without speaking the words.

"What did they say?" Zoe asked, licking the barbecue sauce from her fingers.

*Why don't you learn to sign and you'd know.*

"Don't be an ass, Dale." Zoe scowled at her.

*How come you don't sign?* Judy spoke and signed. *Even Lucas is learning.*

*I can sign*, Sasha said, working her little fingers feverishly.

Zoe grumbled something inaudible and headed inside to refill the bread basket.

*We'll be glad to teach you, Zoe*, Kim said and signed when she returned.

"Just tell me what they said," she demanded, dropping the basket on the table. The bread bounced out but she didn't seem to care.

Taren started to tell her and sign it but Dale covered her hand and said, "No. If Zoe wants to be part of a conversation with Bryant she can learn to sign like everybody else."

"I don't know how. Are you happy? I don't know how to fucking sign," she shouted as her face turned bright red. Zoe's eyes narrowed and the veins popped out on her forehead. She looked like a teakettle ready to explode.

"He's been deaf your whole life. Why didn't you learn? Everybody else did." Dale replied, trying desperately not to scream at her sister.

"Because Mom laughed at me, that's why. She made fun of me when I tried to do it. She never laughed at you, Dale." Zoe rose to her feet. "I hated it. I hated that I couldn't do it as good as you. I hated being laughed at."

Everyone at the table fell silent. Kim had kept a running commentary for Bryant but even she sat motionless.

Zoe began to cry. She covered her face with her hands and turned, ready to run in the house but Dale stopped her. She pulled her into a hug.

"She didn't mean to laugh at you, Zoe. That was just her way. And yes, she laughed at me, too." Dale closed her eyes and swayed with Zoe in her arms, listening to her sobs. She had never heard Zoe's reason before. She'd thought she was too selfish to learn. "Mom wasn't making fun of you, Zoe. That was her way of hiding her guilt. She blamed herself for Bryant being deaf. No one could ever convince her it wasn't her fault."

"I wanted to learn. I really did. It was just so hard," Zoe said through her tears. "You are good at it. I'm never going to be that good."

"You don't have to be good at it. Just try. That's all he wants. Just try. He'll help you."

Dale felt a strong hand on her shoulder. It was Bryant. With tears in his eyes, he reached for Zoe. He held her until she stopped crying then walked her to her seat, smoothed her hair and kissed the top of her head. He signed *I love you*, slowly and simply. It was one of the few things Zoe understood.

"We'll teach you, honey," Kim said with a warm smile. "Just a little at a time."

Dale took her seat. She noticed a trail of tears down Taren's cheek.

"I'm not a member of this family but that was amazing," Taren said, rubbing Dale's leg under the table. "You are a wonderful sister. I wish I had been that good at it."

Zoe was still gathering her emotions when a gust of wind blew the stack of paper napkins off the table and scattered them across the yard. The white puffy clouds had darkened over the lake.

"Eat up, folks," Kim announced, restoring an air of happiness to the conversation. "We've got about ten minutes before we need to start carrying stuff inside. We'll have dessert in the dining room. I'm not eating ice cream in the rain."

Dale tried to concentrate on her dinner but her eyes kept returning to the sky and the gray clouds moving toward them. It wasn't raining. It wasn't that close. But she couldn't help but stare.

"Are you finished," Taren asked, stacking plates on a tray.

"Yes." She hadn't finished but her appetite was gone. The warm summer wind had dried her clothes but Dale's palms were moist. So was her upper lip. She could barely breathe and panted to catch her breath. Faint echoes of whistling wind and debris pelting her back swirled in her mind. She couldn't stop them. She closed her eyes and stiffened, waiting for the screaming wind to subside. She desperately wanted to reach for Taren but fear consumed her. She sat transfixed, unable to move.

# CHAPTER FIFTEEN

"Do you want to come inside? Everyone's having brownies and ice cream." Taren sat down on the picnic bench and placed her hand on Dale's knee.

Her voice gently brought Dale back to reality. She didn't know how long she had been on the bench. Long enough that the table had been cleared. Even the tablecloth had been taken away. "We're all inside."

"What?" Dale turned to her, pulling herself back from the darkened memories. "Inside?"

"Dale, everyone is inside." She brushed Dale's hair across her brow. "Would you like to come in and have some dessert? You don't have to if you don't want to." There was a gentleness in her voice that felt like a comforting hug.

"How long have I been out here?"

"Not that long." She pulled Dale's hand onto her lap and held it there. "I told everyone we needed to talk so you decided to stay outside. But I think we'll save that for another time."

A rumble of distant thunder echoed across the lake. The first gentle drops of rain began to fall but Taren didn't move. She seemed committed to whatever Dale wanted to do.

"Do you want to go inside?" Dale finally said, fighting some unknown inner turmoil.

"I thought you'd never ask." Taren held Dale's hand, easing her to her feet.

The rest of the family had finished their dessert and were watching television in the basement family room. Dale couldn't believe no one saw the looming danger. Or was she the only one? She stood at the patio door and watched as the rain clouds continued to boil and darken. She couldn't take her eyes off them.

"I don't like the looks of these." She nodded toward the blackening sky.

"According to my weather app, it's a small rain cell. It'll move out pretty quickly." Taren studied Dale's face a moment. "There's nothing to be worried about, Dale. It's just rain. There are no weather warnings. No hail. No tornadoes. Just rain."

Taren's words didn't calm her fear. Dale had never been afraid of thunderstorms or rain clouds before the tornado. As a child she couldn't wait to run barefoot down the gutter, splashing and kicking in the runoff. But all that had changed. And she didn't like living in fear. Taren slipped her hand in Dale's as they stood watching the sheets of rain move across the yard and splat against the window.

"This is hard for me," Dale admitted quietly.

"I know, sweetie. I'd be surprised if it wasn't. I'm here. We'll go through it together."

Dale expected Taren to try and coax her away from the window but she didn't.

"Rain sounds so gentle against the glass, doesn't it?" Taren kept a firm grip on Dale's hand.

"Uh-huh." Dale swallowed back a nervous lump in her throat as the first startling flash of lightning and snap of thunder shook the house.

"I wish I was there with you during the tornado. I'm sorry you had to go through that alone." Taren squeezed her hand.

"I'm glad you weren't there. I never want you to go through something like that." Dale returned the squeeze.

"They said it was a once in a lifetime tornado. Joplin may never see anything like that again. But I know that doesn't make it any easier for you. You have to work your way through the trauma but please remember I'm here for you, sweetheart."

Another snap of thunder sent a shockwave through Dale. She gasped and jumped back. Her eyes darted back and forth as the rain sheeted down the window.

"I hate this," she said, unable to keep her voice from cracking. "I hate being afraid." She had no sooner said it but another even louder crack of thunder sent Dale to her knees, her arms protecting her head. Taren knelt next to her as tears rolled down Dale's cheeks. "I'm sorry," Dale blubbered. "I can't help it."

"Come here to me," Taren said, pulling Dale's trembling body into her arms.

"I can't get the memory out of my mind. It won't go away," Dale said as tears streamed down her face.

"Tell me," she whispered, encouraging Dale to say whatever she needed to say.

"After the storm. Everything was gone. My house. My trees. Sydney's tree. All gone. I couldn't fix it." Dale swallowed, tasting the memory of that day. "I saw it. It was in the street. I found it in the street."

"What, sweetheart? What did you find in the street?"

Dale was silent a long moment as she came to grips with the bitter image. Taren sat beside her, waiting for an answer.

"An arm." Dale closed her eyes as it crystallized in her mind. "I found someone's arm in the street. It had been ripped off their body and was lying there. I couldn't fix it. I couldn't put it back." Dale melted into great sobs.

"Oh, my God," Taren gasped.

"I couldn't fix it, Taren. And B.J. and Phyllis. Why them? Why them and not me? Why wasn't I blown away too? And Sydney. Why Sydney and not me?"

"Because it wasn't your turn." Taren took Dale's face in her hands and looked into her eyes. "It's not your fault. It wasn't your time. We don't know why but God gave you more time. Be thankful for it." She dabbed her thumbs across Dale's tears. "I am."

Footsteps on the stairs and giggling brought their heads around.

"They don't need to know this. Please." Dale quickly wiped her eyes, forcing control over her emotions. She climbed to her feet as the basement door opened.

"Hey, you missed a great movie," Zoe said, setting an empty popcorn bowl in the sink. "What have you been doing?"

"We were calculating the distance between us and the lightning strikes," Taren said, graciously stepping between Dale's tear-swollen eyes and Zoe's line of sight. "They got pretty close."

"Math professors are always looking for something to calculate. Just nod and agree with her, Dale."

"I'll remember that," Dale said and headed outside. Thankfully the rain had moved on, leaving the grass covered with tiny droplets glistening in the evening sun.

"Smell that," Taren said, stepping through the door. "Doesn't it smell wonderful? So clean and fresh."

Dale took a deep breath, flooding her senses with fresh air to drown out the harsh memories that had had her cowering on the floor.

"Come walk with me," Taren said, taking Dale's hand and leading her off the patio. They wandered down the path toward the boathouse. "I understand now why you don't want to have the surgery."

"You do? Then tell me because I don't. The doctor said it probably won't heal on its own and the rehab could take months. I know I should have it done but every time I think about it I want to throw up."

"You're still dealing with what happened to you during the tornado. And your shoulder is a reminder." She added, "Your shoulder is a reminder of the arm you found. That's a shock you're not over yet."

Dale squinted at the horizon. Taren could be right. Every time her shoulder hurt, the memories of that day in May came racing back.

"It's called survivor's guilt. It's a form of PTSD," Taren said. "Lots of tornado survivors are dealing with it."

"How do you know so much about Post Traumatic Stress Disorder?"

Taren chuckled then pulled a reflective smile. "Because I had it. After Sydney passed away I was a mess. In fact, I was a mess from the moment she told me her diagnosis. But I'm sure you knew that." Taren looked over at Dale and the puzzled expression on her face. "Oh, come on. You knew. Didn't you? I was a complete bitch. I was mad at everyone. Myself, you, Sydney." She heaved a resolute sigh. "I wish we'd never argued but I didn't know how to stop."

"We argued because I was being an ass. I brought it on myself. I don't blame you. We both had heartache to deal with."

"We argued because that's the only way I knew how to deal with my pain. It wasn't until I agreed to therapy that I learned to cope with my loss." She looked over at Dale. "Sydney was very proud of you for putting a cork in the bottle, as she put it."

"It sounds selfish but I didn't do it for her. I did it for myself. I wanted to be the kind of person she deserved. I wish I had done it earlier." Dale looked down at their hands, her fingers laced through Taren's like they belonged there. "Tell me why I can't kiss you," she asked. "I really don't understand what I did wrong."

"I owe you an apology. I'm very sorry if I hurt your feelings. That certainly wasn't my intent. Sometimes I wish…"

"I need to know, Taren. Please. I need to know. My future depends on it."

"Okay, I'll tell you. I shouldn't but I will," Taren finally agreed. "Sydney did something she shouldn't have done and made me promise to never tell you about it. I wish she never did that because I don't know that I can keep that promise. And I don't want to hurt you, Dale. You mean too much to me."

Dale heaved a sigh and walked down the path, leaving Taren behind.

"Dale, wait."

Dale didn't stop. She had begged and pleaded all she was going to. It was up to Taren to decide if she wanted to tell her the rest of Sydney's truth.

"She wasn't perfect. She had a beautiful relationship with you and she almost threw it away."

Dale continued down the path. Taren hadn't given her a reason to stop.

"She cheated. She said she loved you but she cheated," Taren said, her voice trembling. "She didn't want you to ever know. She made me promise to never tell you. God, I wish she never did that."

Dale quickened her pace. She heard Taren's footsteps on the path behind her.

"I'm sorry," Taren called, trotting to catch up. "I shouldn't have said anything. I'm sorry, Dale." She grabbed Dale's arm. "I'm so so sorry. I should have taken that to my grave. I had no right to break Sydney's confidence."

"You didn't," Dale said, turning to meet her.

"Yes, I did. I'm a terrible sister. I knew I couldn't keep her secret."

"Is that why you were afraid to become involved with me? You wouldn't be able to keep her secret?"

"Yes."

"You didn't break your promise to Sydney, Taren. I already knew about her affair. I didn't know who the other woman was but I knew she did it. And I wasn't going to ask her, not when she was going through chemotherapy. But I knew she had an affair. What would that have accomplished if I had said anything?" Dale gazed off across the lake. "I'll always wonder who it was. What did she have that I didn't? What was so special about this other woman that Sydney would go to bed with her?"

"She doesn't have anything you don't have. She's just another woman. And believe me, she has nothing on you. I ought to know." Taren drew a breath. "You've met her."

"I have?"

Taren nodded, leaving Dale to consider the possibilities.

Dale couldn't imagine Sydney having an affair with any of their friends. Who had she met that Taren knew? Only one name came to mind.

"Menzi!" Dale proclaimed.

Taren nodded.

"When Sydney helped you move your stuff down here from Chicago?" Dale said as the pieces fell into place.

"I warned her not to but she wouldn't listen. Menzi can be very persuasive when she's on the prowl."

"I thought she was very quiet and easygoing. The kind of soft butch anybody could fall for. I guess I was right. And to be honest, I was a little jealous of her."

"What could you possibly be jealous of? What did she have you wanted?"

"You." Dale whispered as she ran her fingers through Taren's hair. "She had you and let you go. I couldn't believe anyone could do that."

"She wasn't the right person for me." Taren leaned into Dale's hand.

"No, she wasn't. Someone better will come along."

"I'm sure she will." Dale reached for Taren and kissed her. This is what she wanted. There in the last glimmers of sunset, she wanted Taren in her arms.

"Dale, are you down there?" Zoe called from up the path. "Dale? Where are you?"

"We're down here, Zoe," Dale said, her eyes melting into Taren's.

"Sasha and I are leaving. Bryant and Kim look exhausted. I think they're ready for bed. Are you coming?" Zoe hadn't walked down the path, settling instead to shout.

"You go ahead. We'll be right behind you."

"I'll talk with you tomorrow. Good night. And good night, Taren."

"Good night, Zoe," Taren called. "I better go," she said softly, smoothing a lock of hair over Dale's ear.

Dale walked her to the house where Taren said her thank-yous.

"Are you leaving now?" Taren asked as Dale held the car door for her.

"Shortly. You go ahead." She leaned in and kissed Taren on the lips. "Good night."

"Good night." Taren put her window down and reached for Dale's hand. "Promise me something."

"More promises?" Dale chuckled.

"Please, don't laugh at me but I need to figure out my feelings. It's been hard for you to get past the storm. You need time to adjust. Well, this is hard for me. You belonged to my sister. I need time to figure things out."

"I didn't mean to laugh at you. You can take all the time you need. I'm in no hurry. I'll be waiting when you're ready." She planted a kiss in Taren's palm. "I love you, Taren. You are the simple pleasure in my life I don't want to do without." Dale smiled then stepped back.

She stood in the driveway as the red hatchback disappeared into the darkness. She wasn't ready to go home. She knew she'd only toss and turn, thinking about Taren. Dale said her good nights to Kim and Bryant, insisting they go on to bed. They seemed to understand the turmoil that gripped her.

"Stay as long as you want. Sleep on the sofa if you like," Kim said, kissing her cheek and heading off to bed.

Dale wandered down the path, hoping the moonlit night could help her think. She had a lot to consider. Could she begin to put the chaos of the tornado and what happened behind her? Could she ever face the surgery to repair her shoulder? Most of all, would Taren ever come into her life and her arms? Or was she damaged goods, something Taren could never want?

Dale stood on the end of the dock with her hands in her pockets, staring at the moon's reflection in the water.

"Are you sure?" a sweet voice drifted toward her from the darkness.

"Taren?" Dale peered up the path at the figure silhouetted in the moonlight.

"Are you sure, Dale? I have to know. I can't do casual relationships. I have to know for sure." She stepped forward into a moonbeam that lit her face. "Are you sure you love me?"

"Yes, with all my heart."

Taren came to Dale, her footsteps soft on the dock.

"I have to know for sure." Taren looked into Dale's eyes as if searching her soul. "Because I love you, too."

"Am I sure? How about I love the way your sunglasses can't hide the twinkle in your eyes when you look at me. I love when you drive away and give me a little toot on your horn. I love that you care what I think about the way you look. I love that you know what is bothering me even before I do. I love the feel of you in my arms. And I love the feeling I get when I think about you." Dale took Taren in her arms. "Yes, I'd say I'm sure. I love you, Taren." She took a deep breath then shouted, "I love Taren Dorsey." The words echoed across the lake and back again, bringing a dimpled smile to Taren's face. "Taren, I understand this is hard for you. I've got some baggage, heavy baggage."

"Shh," Taren whispered, pressing her finger against Dale's lips. "That doesn't matter. I'm in love with you. I fell in love with you a long time ago. I fell in love with you when you were my sister's partner. I knew it was wrong. You belonged to her but I couldn't stop myself. How do I justify that?"

"You don't have to. It doesn't matter anymore. That's history. We did nothing wrong. We love each other. That's all that matters."

"I've never been this much in love with anyone in my life. I feel like we're in a race car, speeding down an unknown road. It scares me."

"Take a chance, Taren. Recline your seat. Lie back and close your eyes. Unfasten your seat belt and trust the driver." Dale swept a curl from Taren's forehead. "Let yourself enjoy the ride." She untied Taren's halter top and let it drop then brought Taren's lips to hers and kissed them. Taren draped her arms around Dale's neck and kissed her back, melting into her arms. A distant splash and rumble of an outboard motor cut the silence.

"Someone's out there," Taren whispered, huddling against Dale's side.

Dale held her in a protective embrace as she squinted out over the lake. A small boat with a single light suspended from a pole chugged back and forth across the mouth of the cove, moving toward them.

"They're coming this way. Probably setting jug lines." Dale looked up the path then remembered something Bryant had disclosed in case of emergency. She reached behind the Kinsel name plaque mounted over the door and pulled out a key. She unlocked the side door to the boathouse and led Taren inside, feeling her way through the darkness. "Watch your step."

"I can't see anything. It's dark." Taren grabbed onto Dale's arm.

"I've got you," Dale said, lifting her on to the boat.

"I still can't see anything."

"I can. I see a beautiful woman," she said, holding tight to her hand.

"A woman without her top on and feeling a little exposed."

Dale took off her shirt and sports bra and placed them in Taren's hand.

"Is that better?" Dale said, standing behind her. She pressed her breasts against Taren's back, her arms folded around her waist.

"Mmmm," Taren moaned, leaning back. "Yes. Much."

The voices and the chug of the outboard motor drew closer.

"Be right back," Dale whispered and went to lock the door.

"If you can see, you have me at a disadvantage."

"I don't want to turn on the light. They'd see it. And you don't need to see. I'm right here," Dale said, taking Taren's hands and leading her to the bench.

The voices grew louder; loud enough for Dale to hear the

men's every word as they passed right outside the boathouse. The turn of the propeller churned the water and rocked the pontoon back and forth, bumping the sides of the slip. Taren was thrown back on the bench and gasped, reaching for Dale.

"What the hell? Did you hear that?" one of the men said in a gravelly voice.

"I didn't hear nothing. Drop one of them big jugs next to the boathouse and tie it to the dock." Dale heard him hack and spit.

"Well, I did. I heard something inside this boathouse." Their boat stopped next to the overhead door. Someone rattled the handle, trying to lift it.

Dale could feel Taren's heart pounding and her breath quicken. She pulled her closer and braced them against the seat as the pontoon continued to rock.

"It's locked. There ain't nobody in there."

"I heard something." He kept rattling the handle.

"Come on, Jake. Drop the damn jug and let's get out of here."

Finally the handle fell silent and the boat headed back up the cove. Taren didn't move until the men's voices dissolved into the night.

"Are you okay?" Dale asked as the pontoon settled in the water.

"Yes, but I'm glad Jake and Bubba couldn't unlock that door."

"I wouldn't have let them hurt you, Taren. You know that."

"I know but I was a little scared anyway."

"I'm right here," Dale said reassuringly.

"I know and I'm glad." Taren's hands moved up Dale's arms and across her chest. "I love the feel of you next to me. I don't think I've ever felt so secure."

"Do you know how much I want to touch you and taste you?" Dale wasn't sure she could control herself another minute. "Do you know how much I want to make love to you?"

"Do you know how much I want you to?" Taren whispered, placing Dale's hand on her breast and holding it there. Dale leaned Taren back on the bench, kissing her so demandingly she was sure Taren would push her away but she didn't. She kissed her back, her arms locked around Dale's neck. Taren moaned eagerly, raising her hips as Dale removed her shorts and panties.

"You have the most incredible body," Dale stammered, licking and sucking at Taren's breasts, her nipples growing erect. Taren placed her arms over her head on the bench and released a long slow sigh as if giving herself to Dale completely.

"I'm yours. I'm all yours," she uttered.

Dale felt for Taren's sweetness. She wanted to please her and possess her. Taren opened herself to Dale's touch. Through the darkness, Dale heard the soft sighs of her lover, guiding her deeper. When Taren's warmth tightened around her fingers, Dale held her close, allowing her to ride the rapture.

"Oh, sweetheart," Taren sighed. "That was incredible. You're incredible." She smiled up at Dale, tracing her fingertip around Dale's mouth. Dale didn't want to spoil Taren's glow but she felt herself begin to tingle deep inside, an electric tingle. Taren hadn't touched her yet but she was about to have an orgasm. She braced herself against the back of the bench as it began to grow. Taren seemed to sense it and reached for Dale, tenderly massaging, caressing and encouraging her. Dale stiffened as the hot volcano continued to build until her climax burned through her. Taren kissed her softly and pulled her down next to her on the bench.

"Damn, woman," Dale said, gasping for breath. "All I have to do is look at you and I'm turned on."

"I think I like that," she said, cupping her hands over Dale's bottom. "I've never had anybody do that before."

"Oh, baby. I'm the one. You turn me on like you wouldn't believe." Dale settled next to Taren on the bench, a satisfied glow consuming her. Tomorrow would come soon enough. For now, they lay in each other's arms, listening to the sounds of the night and each other's heartbeat.

# CHAPTER SIXTEEN

Dale hurried home from work, making a mental list of what she needed to do and how much time she had to do it. The trailer was a mess and Taren was coming over. They had squeezed a few rendezvous into the first weeks following Labor Day but with Dale's long hours and Taren's busy schedule as the semester got underway, there wasn't time to tour her new home. Today was the day and Dale couldn't wait to show it. She considered herself a fairly tidy housekeeper but she had so much stuff stored in the trailer there was barely room to exist. She had no sooner changed out of her work clothes and stuffed them in the closet than she heard the toot of a car horn.

"She's early." Dale quickly slipped the dirty breakfast dishes in the oven and smoothed her hand over the bedding on her way out the door. "Hello," she called.

Taren waved then lifted a plastic bucket from the back of her car.

"What ya' got?" Dale asked, grinning on her way down the driveway. She peeked in the bucket. "Oh, boy. A stick."

"It's not a stick, silly. It's a tree."

"Oh, boy. A baby stick." Dale took the bucket and gave her a kiss. "Umm, you smell good." She hooked an arm around her waist. "And you look even better."

"Thank you." She kissed her back.

"Hello, Ms. Dorsey," Milo called from across the street. He was taking pictures of his newly poured foundation like a new father taking pictures through a nursery window.

"Hi, Milo. How's the house coming?"

"Very good. We will have a house in two months," he said, holding up two fingers. "Maybe three."

"That's wonderful. I can't wait to see it."

He seemed pleased with her interest and went back to picture taking.

"What am I supposed to do with the baby stick?" Dale asked.

"You are supposed to water it and as soon as the house is finished, we are going to plant it. I want it to be the first thing planted in your yard. I know you and Sydney planted a weeping willow that the storm destroyed. I chose a redbud tree. I wanted it to be different. Something special from me to you."

Dale drew Taren to her and whispered, "Thank you. I love it but you're something very special to me."

Taren looked back in Milo's direction then gave her a complete kiss.

"And how is Casa Kinsel coming along?" she asked, scanning the front of Dale's house. "I like the siding you picked. It complements the stonework nicely. Sydney would be pleased."

"Come inside and take a look." Dale unlocked the front door and used the bucket to prop it open as the smell of fresh paint and new carpeting swept out to meet them.

"Oh, wow, sweetheart. This is wonderful. Big living room. Great light from the windows."

"I really like your suggestion on light fixtures."

They wandered through the dining room and kitchen as Dale pointed out the features and what was left to be done.

"Appliances arrive next week. I wanted stainless steel but I couldn't justify the price when there was no increased efficiency value. I settled for good quality white."

Taren stood at the sink, looking out the window at the trailer.

"I like the height of the countertops. You don't have to stoop over. What are you going to do with the trailer? You aren't going to leave it there, are you?"

"No. I'm going to sell it. I've had a couple offers. I don't want it. I don't need it as a reminder of what I've been through. Do you want it back?"

"Heavens, no. Sell it. Give it away. If we decide to go camping we'll get a tent." Taren leaned into Dale's side. "Now show me more of your new house."

Dale took her by the hand and led her down the hall, opening and closing closets along the way. Taren liked everything. Wall colors. Window placement. Even the tile in the bathrooms.

"That's the guest bathroom. And this is the master bedroom." Dale opened the bedroom closet and stepped back for Taren to see. "This is the storm shelter."

"It looks like a regular closet. A big one."

"It's supposed to but there's steel reinforced fibered concrete a foot thick behind the sheetrock." Dale stepped inside and took a seat on the bench bolted to the wall. "It'll withstand an EF-five tornado, if Joplin ever has one again. It'll hold up to ten people."

Taren came in and sat down next to her.

"Does it bother you to be in here, sweetheart?" she asked.

"Not as much as it did the first time I saw it. It was a bad reminder. But I've had time to adjust to it. Actually it's reassuring to know it's here." Dale ran her hand down the polished wood of the bench. "I'm glad it's here. And I'm glad you have a basement. I won't have to worry where you would go to be safe."

"I'm very proud of you." Taren picked a Twizzler stick from Dale's shirt pocket and took a bite. "I'd be prouder if you were ready to consider surgery to repair your shoulder."

Dale leaned her head back against the wall and closed her eyes. How did Taren know that had been on her mind?

"I'm not saying you have to do it tomorrow. But consider it," she added.

"I have been." Dale gazed at Taren. "But it's hard." She stood up, ready to walk away from the conversation but Taren grabbed her arm and pulled her back down.

"Where do you think you're going?" Taren hooked an arm through Dale's as if securing her to the bench. "You're going to hear me out."

Dale nodded sheepishly.

"I know this is hard for you. You like to do things in your own sweet time and I understand that. But I want you to know you have options. I'm here for you, Dale. As long as it takes for you to heal, I'm right here. Three months. Six months. Six years. I'm here for you. Have the surgery then stay with me. Let me take care of you. You don't have to do this alone." Taren stepped out of her shoes and climbed on Dale's lap, hiking up her skirt as she straddled her with a mischievous smile. "You definitely don't have to go through this alone." She began unbuttoning Dale's shirt, slowly. Tantalizingly slow. "I'll cook for you. And clean for you. And help you get dressed." She opened the shirt and kissed across Dale's neck. "I'll take very good care of you," she whispered, nibbling at Dale's ear. "You won't have to do a thing." She raised an eyebrow seductively and then slipped her sweater over her head, giving Dale an unobstructed view of her lacy black bra.

Dale tried to listen to what she was saying but she couldn't ignore what Taren was doing. Normally modest and reserved, Taren flirting with her was a pleasant treat, one that had Dale quivering in her Levi's.

"I've gotten very good at undressing, too," Taren said then reached around and unhooked her bra.

"Yes, you are. Very good," Dale said, anxiously watching as the bra slid down Taren's sinewy arms. When Dale reached for one of her firm round breasts, Taren pushed her hand down. She placed the red licorice stick in her mouth, offering the other end to Dale. Slowly and methodically they chewed their way the center, their lips meeting in a kiss.

"I'm willing to do whatever it takes. Whatever you need," Taren whispered then peeled Dale's shirt back over her shoulders.

"I think you know exactly what I need."

Dale wanted her hands on Taren's soft skin but settled for holding her bottom. Taren was in the driver's seat and was doing a wonderful job. She pulled Dale's sports bra over her head and tossed it aside. She traced her fingernail down Dale's chest, slowly circling her breasts. Dale leaned her head back, panting as a tingle raced downward through her core. Taren unzipped Dale's jeans, teasingly folding them open. Dale couldn't wait any longer. She wrapped Taren in a hug and kissed her hungrily. Taren backed off her lap and lay down on the closet floor, pulling Dale down on top of her. Dale gently molded herself over Taren, feeling her heart race. Taren slipped her hand down inside Dale's jeans. She was ready. Taren softly guided and encouraged her to an exquisite climax, something she never thought could happen here, inside her storm shelter. Whatever fear she had, whatever memories the thought of it held, had melted away within Taren's sweet arms. Dale heard the muffled sound of meowing. Or was it her own soft purr of satisfaction.

"Was that you?" Taren asked, spooning within Dale's embrace.

"I don't think so." Dale listened intently. The sound grew louder. "There's a cat in the house," she said quietly. "I left the door open."

A cat appeared in the doorway to the closet. It was scrawny, malnourished and looked like it had been in a fight. Its orange fur was matted, tufts of it missing. It meowed at them, its body trembling as if it was cold.

"Butterscotch?" Dale exclaimed, sitting up.

"Do you know this cat?" Taren asked, sitting up and pulling on her sweater.

Dale held out her hand as if she had a treat in it.

"Butterscotch, is that you? Where have you been?" The cat came to her, rubbing its face against Dale's hand. "She belonged somewhere up the street. All the houses are gone now." Dale scooped up the cat. "Butterscotch, you old furball, you. I thought the tornado took you away."

"I think it did." Taren gently stroked the cat's frail body. "Poor little thing. She looks emaciated. She's got scabs along her side. And she looks like she hasn't eaten in days."

Dale snuggled her face into the cat as tears welled up in her eyes. "You came back to me."

"Yes, I think she did. She found her way back from wherever the storm took her. I think you have a kitty now. We need to find her something to eat."

Dale looked down at the floor and her clothes then up at Taren, knowing they had some pleasant albeit unfinished business.

"Do you mind, babe?"

"If you mean do I mind I didn't have my turn," Taren smiled softly, "No. And the evening isn't over." She kissed Dale then took the cat in her arms, stroking it lovingly as Dale dressed and then locked up the house. Dale followed Taren toward the trailer but stopped on the driveway as a searing shaft of pain shot through her shoulder nearly buckling her knees.

"What is it?" Taren asked.

Dale closed her eyes and held her breath as the pain moved through her.

"Dale? It's your shoulder, isn't it?"

"Yes." She looked at Taren, waiting for the pain to subside. "You said I'd know when the time was right. Well, it might be time to talk to a surgeon."

"Oh, sweetheart. Bad?" Taren frowned sympathetically. "That's okay. I'll be right here with you every moment."

* * *

"Trick or treat," Sasha said happily, knocking at the screen door.

Taren burst out laughing.

"That is so adorable. Come in," she said, holding the door for her.

Dale climbed off the couch and came to see. Sasha's face was covered with white sparkly makeup. Her clothes were covered with a mass of white balloons so only her head, hands and feet were visible.

"Hey, Sasha. I like it." Dale leaned against the newel post at the bottom of the stairs. "But what are you supposed to be, kiddo?"

"I'm a bubble bath," she declared proudly. She wiggled back and forth so the balloons bounced against each other.

"Of course, she is," Taren agreed, smiling at Dale as if to say I had no idea. She stood next to Dale, her arm around her waist. "I love it. It's very creative. And it isn't one of those plastic store-bought costumes. Good for you, Sasha."

"I'd say that's worth extra candy. Grab a couple handfuls from the bowl." Dale pointed to the hall table.

Zoe knocked then opened the door and stepped inside. "Whose truck is that in the driveway?" she asked.

"Mine," Dale said. "I had the dents taken out and the window replaced. Looks pretty good, huh?"

"Sasha, that's enough candy. You're going to end up with a mouthful of cavities. And remember what I told you. This is your last year. Halloween is for little kids." Zoe gave Taren a hug then glared at Dale. "Shouldn't you be in bed?"

"No." Dale took several deep breaths hoping to stop her head from spinning.

"The doctor said she can be up so long as she takes it easy." Taren adjusted the sling supporting Dale's arm and shoulder. "How are you doing, baby? You look tired."

"I'm okay." But she wasn't.

"Shit, Dale. You just had surgery yesterday. If it was me, I'd still be passed out in the hospital. I can't believe they let you come home already."

"Let's go sit down," Taren said, walking Dale to the couch. She arranged the pillows and helped her get situated.

"What did the doctor say? How bad was it?" Zoe followed at a safe distance.

"A torn tendon and a torn ligament. The doctor suspected she did it when she was holding on to the bathtub, fighting against being sucked out the roof. He said she's lucky she didn't pull it right out of the socket." Taren smoothed the hair over Dale's forehead. "She's my big strong tornado fighter." She smiled lovingly at her.

"I made you some zucchini bread," Zoe said, pulling a baggie from the jumbo purse slung over her shoulder.

"Thank you, honey. That was sweet of you."

"It's still warm so leave the bag open a crack." She set it on the coffee table then dropped into a chair.

"Mom," Sasha whined.

Zoe threw her head back and groaned. "All right. You may do this street. But only the houses with the porch light on and stay on the sidewalk and don't talk to strangers. And come right back." She waited for Sasha to trot down the front steps then said, "We never worried about trick or treating when we were kids."

"My neighborhood is fairly safe," Taren said, still fussing over Dale's sling and support for her shoulder.

Butterscotch wandered down the back of the couch, purring contentedly as she rubbed herself against the back of Dale's head. The cat looked plump and healthy, all of her scars hidden by her thick fur. Dale leaned back against her, acknowledging her presence as she meandered on down the couch.

"Your text said you needed to see me," Zoe said warily. "What did I do now?"

"I didn't say you did anything," Dale said, fidgeting to find a comfortable position.

"Do you need some ibuprofen?" Taren asked after checking her watch. "It's time."

"Ibuprofen?" Zoe chuckled. "Give the woman pain pills. Big ones."

"I don't take pain pills, Zoe." Dale closed her eyes as a shaft of pain burned through her shoulder.

"Why the hell not? Doctors always prescribe them after surgery. You don't even have to ask."

"She prefers not to take them." Taren placed pills in Dale's hand then handed her a glass of water.

"Alcoholics have addictive personalities." Dale swallowed. "Why would I take addictive pain meds?"

"Oh. I didn't think of that."

"We know it's a possibility but only as a very last resort. She's doing very well." Taren kissed Dale's cheek.

"The pain's not the worst of it, sis." Dale frowned painfully. "I can't have sex for a month. At least. I may not survive."

"Oh, yes, you will." Taren grinned. "Now if you'll stop undressing me with your eyes I'll go get the envelope."

"Envelope?" Zoe asked.

"I don't have the strength to make a big production out of this, Zoe. So here's the deal. Your apartment is too damn small." Taren returned and handed Dale a brown envelope. "Sasha needs her own bathroom." Dale shook out a key and tossed it to Zoe. "This is the extra key to my house. I want you and Sasha to live in it. It's a good neighborhood. At least it will be when the rest of the houses get rebuilt. I'll pay the taxes and insurance. You pay the utilities and mortgage." She handed Zoe a letter, explaining the terms.

"Are you shitting me?" Zoe gasped, reading the letter. "I pay more than this and have half the space."

Dale looked up at Taren. "We don't need two houses."

"No, we don't." Taren sat on the end of the sofa, softly stroking Dale's back.

"You're going to let me live in your new house?" Zoe seemed completely shocked.

"You have to take care of it. Keep the grass mowed. Water our new tree. We'll discuss the details next week when my brain isn't scrambled."

"You're going to let me live in your house even though we argue all the time?"

"We don't argue. We have intense conversations." Dale chuckled. "We're sisters. I love you, Zoe. I want what's best for you. If I can help, I will."

Zoe sat staring at the letter, her chin quivering.

"Oh, my God, Dale." She hurried to Dale's side, hugging her as she cried tears of joy. "Thank you. Thank you."

"You're welcome," Dale groaned, patting her back. "Easy."

"Oh, wow," Zoe leaped off the couch when she realized she was hugging Dale's injured shoulder. "I'm sorry. But this is so great." Zoe turned to Taren and hugged her. "Thank you."

"Hey, Zoe?" a voice called from the front porch.

"Hello?" Taren said, going to see who it was.

"I'm sorry but Zoe, are you about ready?" the woman at the door asked frantically. She was a middle-aged woman with long salt-and-pepper hair pulled back into a ponytail. One stray lock draped across her forehead. She wasn't wearing makeup and had a tanned albeit weathered complexion. She was dressed in a black turtleneck sweater and jeans, a scarf draped around her neck.

"Lily, come in." Zoe looked at the woman with a surprising affection. "The one on the couch in the flannel pants is my sister, Dale. And this is Taren."

"How do you do?" Lily said, offering a quick handshake. "I need to find a restroom, babe," she whispered.

"Bathroom is right down there." Dale pointed.

"Yes, help yourself," Taren said, snapping on the light for her.

As soon as the door closed both Dale and Taren turned to Zoe.

"Babe?" Dale chuckled. "Oh, my freakin'…"

"Zoe?" Taren stared at her in surprise. "Is there something we should know?"

"I didn't know how to tell you," Zoe said timidly as a blush raced up her face.

"How about hey sis, I'm gay too?"

"I wasn't sure." She shrugged then looked toward the bathroom door. "It crossed my mind when I was still married."

"Are you sure now?"

"Oh, yeah." Zoe grinned then giggled. "I'm sure."

Taren came to give her a hug. "I'm happy for you, honey. I truly am."

Dale sat back and smiled at her sister.

"Thank you so much," Lily said, reentering the room. "Whew. I really needed that."

Sasha came through the front door, still bouncing happily in her costume.

"Did you get lots of goodies?" Taren asked, dropping another piece of candy in her pillowcase.

"Yep. The lady next door gave me a jumbo Hershey bar. She said I was the best costume so far."

Dale was struggling to find a comfortable position and Taren seemed to know it.

"I think it's time for Dale to head upstairs to bed. She's had a long day. It was nice to meet you, Lily."

"Come on, Sasha. We're out of here," Zoe said, pointing to the door. She looked back at Dale with a glowing smile. "Thank you, Dale. You're my hero."

"Good night, sis."

Taren waited until they had driven down the street before turning out the porch light and locking the door.

"What about all the little ghosts and goblins?" Dale said, pulling herself to her feet. "We still have a bowl full of candy."

"They'll have to wait until next year." She turned out the living room lights and helped Dale up the stairs. "I have someone who needs me more."

Dale draped her good arm around Taren's shoulder as they walked the steps together.

"Maybe I could convince you to do a little trick or treat for me," Dale said with a sly grin.

"Are you propositioning me, Ms. Kinsel?"

"Damn right I am." Dale couldn't hide a groan as she took the top step.

Taren snapped on the bedroom light and helped Dale into bed.

"Remember the doctor's orders." Taren tucked and smoothed the covers. "No pressure on that arm or shoulder which means no sex."

"It's not my shoulder that needs pressure."

Taren gave her a deliberate smirk then turned out the light. Dale fidgeted, trying to get comfortable while Taren went into the bathroom to change into her pajamas.

"How are you doing? I hear moaning and groaning."

"I'm practicing."

Taren stood in the bathroom doorway, brushing her teeth. "Go to sleep."

"I can't."

"Why? Do you need more ibuprofen? I've got some here in the bathroom."

"Nope. Don't need pills. I need you here beside me." Dale patted the bed.

Taren snapped off the light. Dale heard rustling as she rounded the bed. She finally slipped under the covers and wiggled her way over, snuggling up to Dale's side.

"What happened to your pajamas?" Dale ran her hand down Taren's smooth skin. "I distinctly remember you wearing something blue when you came out of the bathroom."

"Trick or treat," Taren whispered, kissing Dale's cheek.

"Can I have both?" she asked, drawing Taren closer.

"Greedy little cuss, aren't you?" Taren giggled.

"When it comes to you, yes, I am. I love you and I always will."

"And I love you. With every breath I take, I love you."

Taren curled herself at Dale's side as they drifted off to sleep.

# Bella Books, Inc.

## *Women. Books. Even Better Together.*

P.O. Box 10543
Tallahassee, FL 32302
Phone: (800) 729-4992
**www.BellaBooks.com**

## *More Titles from Bella Books*

**Hunter's Revenge – Gerri Hill**
978-1-64247-447-3 | 276 pgs | paperback: $18.95 | eBook: $9.99
Tori Hunter is back! Don't miss this final chapter in the acclaimed Tori Hunter series.

**Integrity – E. J. Noyes**
978-1-64247-465-7 | 28 pgs | paperback: $19.95 | eBook: $9.99
It was supposed to be an ordinary workday...

**The Order – TJ O'Shea**
978-1-64247-378-0 | 396 pgs | paperback: $19.95 | eBook: $9.99
For two women the battle between new love and old loyalty may prove more dangerous than the war they're trying to survive.

**Under the Stars with You – Jaime Clevenger**
978-1-64247-439-8 | 302 pgs | paperback: $19.95 | eBook: $9.99
Sometimes believing in love is the first step. And sometimes it's all about trusting the stars.

**The Missing Piece – Kat Jackson**
978-1-64247-445-9 | 250 pgs | paperback: $18.95 | eBook: $9.99
Renee's world collides with possibility and the past, setting off a tidal wave of changes she could have never predicted.

**An Acquired Taste – Cheri Ritz**
978-1-64247-462-6 | 206 pgs | paperback: $17.95 | eBook: $9.99
Can Elle and Ashley stand the heat in the *Celebrity Cook Off* kitchen?

Printed in the USA
CPSIA information can be obtained
at www.ICGtesting.com
JSHW082202140824
68134JS00014B/379

9 781594 933707